FIC   Sayers, Valerie
SAY
        Due east

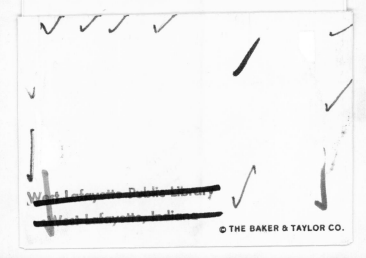

DUE EAST

Valerie Sayers

DUE EAST

A DOLPHIN BOOK
Doubleday & Company, Inc.
GARDEN CITY, NEW YORK
1987

In memory of my father

5-87   B&T   9.57

Library of Congress Cataloging-in-Publication Data

Sayers, Valerie.
Due East.

"A Dolphin book."
I. Title.
PS3569.A94D8   1987   813'.54   86-11554
ISBN 0-385-23673-5

Contents

A Pretty Girl

She walked down River Street every afternoon to buy the paper and her father's cigarettes. She was a pretty girl, tall and rangy, with slender hips and long graceful hands. But there was a vacant look in her gray eyes, a friendly, absent dreaminess, and her father's friends watched her with an awkward concern. There had been so much talk about sending her up to the state hospital when she was younger.

She had never been sent—it was only a rumor, only something her father had discussed with a handful of men—and no one had actually seen her do anything that could really be called crazy. She had jumped out of her aunt's car one night, and she would forget she'd been spoken to while she was buying her father's things at the drugstore; but she was only a teenager, and girls in Due East always got wild at that age.

1

A Virgin Birth

Since my mother died, I'd kept the same routine. In the afternoon I left the Point and walked down River Street to buy the paper and my father's cigarettes. If my father's friends were downtown, having coffee in Ralph's or fussing with their boats at the marina, they'd watch me down the street, all concerned and awkward. They were worried from the time my father told them he thought I was going crazy. All I'd said then was that I didn't want to wear choir robes anymore, that I thought Dr. Beady's version of Jesus made him sound like a right-wing dictator, and that I had my own little visions before I fell asleep. I had been complaining of dizziness, too, but I hadn't meant for my father or his friends to think I was on the *brink*. In all this time, though, they hadn't forgotten it, so someone's eyes always followed me through Due East. I didn't mind. It was like having a dog trailing after me, or a guardian angel.

I got back home at four-thirty. The house was still clean from the morning vacuuming, so I had two hours to make supper. I read the paper, and tried folding the napkins in different shapes. It never took two hours. Since I'd been pregnant I'd been waiting for my father to find out and the routine to change. But every night when he came in for supper he looked out past me, and I was beginning to think that he'd never see, that somehow I'd get through nine months and a delivery, and one night he'd say, "How did that baby get to the supper table?"

Then one night he came in more tired-looking than usual, and when he went to kiss me on the cheek he missed, and slid into his chair the way the saved slide into the baptism pool. Their eyes are half-closed.

I fetched him his tea, and we filled our plates, and he asked me if I had much homework, same as every night. Then all of a sudden he said: "Maybe you better not take any more of those potatoes, Mary Faith. Looks to me like you're getting a little pudgy."

So I stared at the bowl of new potatoes on the dinette table. I couldn't eat the tuna fish, and I couldn't eat the peas—they stuck in my throat like words that couldn't go up or down—and if I was going to get any food in my belly at all it was going to be those new potatoes.

"Daddy," I said, "I'll just take another. I'm not having any bread." He didn't answer, and when I looked up to see what was bothering him, I lost my appetite entirely. My father washes up for supper, but he never gets rid of the curls of oil around his fingernails, and he never changes his shirt, so the gas fumes settle into our food. He runs the Plaid King gas station on the Savannah Highway. I always liked the smell of gasoline, but the pregnancy had made me notice things I'd never seen before.

"You better take some that tuna fish," he said. He was spitting pea skins into the air. "How come you didn't put more mayonnaise? Tastes dried up."

"Mayonnaise makes me sick anymore."

"Everything makes you sick anymore," he said, and smiled a crooked smile. "What are you going through, one of those teenage rebellions? Mary Faith, you used to be a *good* cook. What's got into you? You act as bad as your momma did every time she was pregnant."

He hadn't mentioned my mother in a year. She'd been pregnant six times, my mother, but I was the only one that took; the others all ended in miscarriages, and then she had cancer. "Well, I could be pregnant too," I said, hardly knowing that the words were coming out of my mouth.

It didn't faze my father. He just kept pushing peas onto his knife, and spilling them down again on the brown shiny surface of our table. "Don't you fool that way," he said. "That's a crazy thing for a little girl to say."

We finished up the way we usually do, not saying much of anything, until he asked me what was for dessert. I told him we had butter pecan ice cream, and I thought he'd beam that we didn't have to eat canned peaches again, but he grunted instead, and held his head. "What'd you mean by that pregnant stuff?"

"Nothing," I said. I picked up the dinner plates and carried them to the sink.

"Mary Faith." He says it in a flat voice with a little edge of despair. He knows I hate my name, that I've asked him for three years to call me just Mary, but my mother changed her name to Faith one year when a tent preacher advised it, and he's always liked the sound of it. He's never once just called me Mary.

"It wasn't anything," I said.

"Uh huh. You tell your daddy you're pregnant and then say it wasn't nothing."

"Wasn't anything." That just slipped out, too.

"Don't you correct me," he said. "You are fifteen years old. You keep a civil tongue in your head."

"Yes sir."

That drives him crazy. There's something about the way I say *yes sir*—not with any mocking, and not with my voice raised, just flat, the way he says *Mary Faith*—that sets him off.

"You get back to this table," he said, and I did, but I couldn't keep my eyes on him.

"Are you pregnant?" he said. I had never expected that he would just ask, straight out like that, and in a way I was right, because he pulled back from the question and laughed his good relieved laugh and said, "What am I talking about? You don't even talk to the boys in your *Sun*day School class and I'm asking if you're pregnant. Mary Faith, don't talk loose about junk like that. Don't you even joke. Hear?"

"Okay," I said. I still couldn't look him straight in the face.

"You go get that ice cream." Out of the corner of my eye I saw him smile again, with the other half of his mouth.

"Okay." Maybe I should have looked him in the eye then, but I didn't, and when I brought the ice cream back to the table he'd figured it out; I could tell by the way he was chewing the inside of his cheek. It was what I'd been waiting for ever since I found out: one morning, when it was only ten days late but already I felt a heaviness in my ankles and wrists, I knew that there was no coming back from this baby. That morning I had fetched his breakfast, and felt heavy and fine, and kept thinking it *showed*, that my father would just look at me and know I was pregnant.

But it had taken all this time. Now he said, "No," and he couldn't look me in the eye either.

"No," he said again, with that same flat despair. When my mother was alive we sat at the same supper table, only she'd made roast pork and rice with gray gravy, and when we finished the whole heavy meal she said, "Jesse, Mary Faith, I've got something to tell you." She told us she would be going to the hospital in the morning, that she'd tried to stay away from the doctors but that the pain and the bleeding were too bad now. "They are going to take my womb," she said. "My sister says they do it all the time nowadays."

He said *no* then too, as if he already knew about the cancer, as if saying *no* would lift him up, out of the kitchen, and make her voice stop for a minute. "It's nothing to be frightened of," she said, and when he looked at her as if she'd betrayed him, she went to his chair and rubbed his back with her long knotty fingers.

Now I wanted to do the same for him, to rub his back the way he'd let me before she died, but he tensed his whole body. An oily curl fell from the top of his head, over his forehead, fell down and stared at me as hurt as the rest of him. "I don't believe it," he said.

"I'm sorry, Daddy." I meant I was sorry he didn't believe it.

"Who was it, Mary Faith?"

I couldn't answer that. "I don't know what you mean," I said. I wasn't going to tell anybody who the father was. He'd

been a senior at Due East High School until he took thirty
Quaaludes in front of the Breeze Theatre and went into a
coma. He died after a week. He'd been shy and guilty and I'd
let the whole town think it was a virgin birth before I'd let them
know it was him. He hadn't even known I was pregnant, and I
was glad he hadn't had *that* to be guilty over, too.

"What do you mean, you don't know?"

I tried not answering, but my father's stare bore down on
me. "I'm not sure," I whispered.

"Not sure!"

"Maybe it's kind of like a virgin birth?"

"A virgin birth!" Now my father's eyes lighted up in the
same alarm that fired him when he took me to the doctor to see
if I was really going crazy, but he held his voice low. "Mary
Faith, do you know what you're saying? Are you pregnant?"

"Yes sir."

"How far gone?"

"Five months."

"Five months," he said. "Five months. You know, if it's too
far gone, we can't have it taken from you."

"I don't want an abortion, Daddy."

"Mary Faith, you just quit that crazy talk. You tell your daddy
you're pregnant, you better let your daddy take over. Now, I
am going to try one more time. Do you know who's the father,
and wait a minute. Don't say you don't know and don't go
talking about virgin births. Virgin births! I know you know how
somebody gets pregnant, you're fifteen years old and you hear
from the other girls. Do you know who did it? Or have you
been—have you been sleeping with every boy in Due East? I'm
sorry, I don't mean that. I just mean. Mary Faith. You have to
talk normal now."

"Daddy," I said, trying to sound very sane, "I know how you
get pregnant but I don't know how this happened. I don't
know how this happened. Honest I don't."

And my poor father, who has raised me alone for three years
now and has put me in charge of his house, my poor father was
frightened by my answer and turned away from me. "You're
shielding some boy who took advantage of you," he said, in the

bitter voice of his heart breaking, in the voice that hurried me dressing for my mother's funeral. "Mary Faith, we're going to talk about this later. I've got to get out of here. I'm going to find that boy who did this to you."

And my father stood up with a jerk and opened the kitchen door, muttering, "Virgin birth." He'd left before, at night; he'd start up his truck and drive down a long, flat road, someplace where he could get some comfort. He'd go down to the water, to the trestle or the bridge or even out to the beach. I could hear him turning the key in the driveway, the pickup hesitating the same way he was hesitating, wondering whether he should come back and get me to tell him who made me pregnant.

Finally I heard him drive off, and I knew he'd be gone until late. It was April, and breezy in Due East at night. I'd picked the wrong month to tell him—he'd been pumping gas himself these past two months, taking in the spring in Due East, and every night when he came home it was lighter outside. We'd been talking about getting the barbecue out. We'd both been trying to be a family again. Next month we'd be eating shrimp every night, if he could get it cheap from Buddy Miles, and the school had invited him to come see me get the Latin award (that just killed him, the Latin award) because I'd won for South Carolina and nobody else from Due East had ever won the state before. But now none of his plans would fit into April or May or June anymore.

I don't know when it came into my head to tell my father it was a virgin birth. When I was little, I used to play in front of the statue of Mary the Catholics have in front of their church on Division Street. And then the baby's father had been a Catholic, until he found Quaaludes. Even if I didn't believe in God I was always fond of Mary, and I always thought the idea of a virgin birth was something fine. Fine and wicked, too, the way it made it seem as if Jesus Christ was too good for the love of a man and a woman.

How my baby was conceived was close to a virgin birth, anyway, and I decided to stick with my story. It would be easier for my father to explain a crazy daughter to his friends than it would be for him to explain a crazy dead father of his daughter's baby. It would be easier for my father if I kept making all the decisions. No abortion, no father, no telling his friends for another month. It would be easier if I just kept doing the housework and the homework and collecting awards and acting as if nothing unusual was happening on the Point. It was better to act crazy.

And my father's friends would be able to watch me walk down River Street, my belly growing bigger and bigger. They would say: "She's going right off her rocker and thinks it's a *virgin* birth. Jesus Christ! That's what happens to a little girl when her mother dies."

2

An Older Woman

The night his daughter told him she was pregnant, Jesse Rapple floated in a dull panic. He drove down to an old trestle he hadn't visited in years and sat like a boy, his legs dangling over the edge. There was no one he could tell, not if Mary Faith wouldn't even admit who the father was. He wasn't going to his sister-in-law for advice or money, and he couldn't even consider telling Buddy; he couldn't bear the pity. Not for a while. Buddy would try to give him fifty dollars again, and he'd have to refuse it, as if he had thousands in the bank. He didn't have a cent. He was still over his head with the hospital bills: Faith was dead three years, but he couldn't even pay off the Sears charge this month, and the prospect of filing for bankruptcy seemed more and more likely. The gas station was failing in the middle of a recession and his little girl—his *little* girl—was pregnant. Staring at the shallow water, he couldn't even think of her. He let his mind bring round figures and checkbooks and lawsuits and going out of business by the end of 1981, but he wouldn't let it bring round any picture of Mary Faith.

He drove around the county until he knew she would be asleep, and then he sneaked into his bedroom, where he slept until a dream of his daughter giving birth to a cancerous womb wakened him. It was five o'clock, two hours early, but he decided to leave the house before she was awake. He had an idea that looking at her pregnant would be like looking at her naked, and he couldn't face it yet.

The light was green-gray when he opened the station, and the smell of the salt marshes stung him. He was shaky without sleep, and he made a pot of coffee. He had two lube jobs that should have been done yesterday—Ricky Mahoney was pissy as a girl about leaving the car overnight—but he couldn't move from his seat, or move his eyes from the broken candy machine. A month ago he'd laid off the Marine who worked days, so he'd be alone at the station until Lee Mac from the tech school came in at noon.

Finally he made himself turn on the pumps, and then he walked across the islands to watch the traffic up the Savannah Highway. Three cars. "Mary Faith," he said idly. "Mary Faith." She said she hated the name, but he thought not; he thought she liked him to tease her with it. He thought she liked having her mother's name stuck onto her own. If there was anything she didn't like, it was probably just remembering the dying, a long death for a little girl to see.

He almost smiled at the thought of her saying she didn't know who got her pregnant, how it happened. It had given him a good scare the night before—who could tell when little girls were going to see too much, hear too much, go straight off their heads?—but by morning he'd realized it was just like her, just like the stubborn kid who said she didn't know how the library books got into her room without being checked out or why it took three hours to walk back from school. That had been going on since long before her mother died. She wasn't crazy, she was just covering for some boy, and she'd tell him who it was. Maybe.

The trouble was, she'd never brought a boy home. She'd never had a phone call from a boy. At church she smiled— more or less—at the ones she knew from school, but she'd never said more than a single sentence to one of them. She didn't have girlfriends, either; they'd started to slip away when her mother was so sick—he understood, it was too hard on little girls, but Lord, didn't any of them want to just stick by her?—and they hadn't come back. She didn't seem to mind.

She spent all that time walking through town, and she spoke so easily to the old biddies on River Street she didn't seem to need friends her own age; she didn't seem to belong to her age, or even the town. He'd always trusted in that smartness of hers getting her through. Aside from the real crazy silliness about not believing anymore, she'd been doing fine managing the house and just killing the schoolwork, just knocking them dead at the high school, leading her class and taking courses with the seniors and getting so close to the teachers.

The teachers. It hadn't occurred to him before that it might not have been a boy at all, that it might have been a man, and the sudden idea sickened him. *That* would make sense. She wouldn't be able to open her mouth about a married man, an older man who'd gotten her into trouble. He walked slowly back into the station and poured himself another cup of coffee without knowing he was doing it. *That* would make sense.

Two nights a week she'd been going to the high school to do some tutoring; he'd been angry about its being Monday and Wednesday nights because Wednesday night was service and she was slipping too far away from her religion as it was. But you couldn't hold a teenager that tight. He'd figured she was lonely and needed the outing, but maybe he should have smelled something fishy all along. She was only fifteen, and they had her tutoring high school dropouts, older kids coming back to take the GED exams. Half of them were girls who'd left school because they were pregnant: how could he have been so blind? The coffee slipped down his chin. Now she'd be one of the dropouts.

The teacher running the program was named Stephen Dugan. And he wasn't even a proper teacher—he had a day job reporting for the Due East *Courier.* He was taking home two salaries, and going out at night to tutor dropouts and offer fifteen-year-old girls rides home. The whole town knew the Dugans. They were crazy, all of them, especially since the father died. Stephen Dugan, years ago, had been a substitute at the junior high school until he showed up one day stinking of gin. What did they have to go and give him a night teaching job for? So he could lure Mary Faith to some seedy Marine motel? Hadn't she been late once or twice when he gave her a ride? Didn't she have that glow when she walked in the door? He was sure. Stephen Dugan—who must have been thirty years old, who had a wife and surely children—Stephen Dugan was the man Mary Faith had been seeing, and he must have been the man who got her pregnant. If that Dugan had taken advantage of her. Jesse Rapple put his coffee cup down slowly and deliberately. If that Dugan. He sloshed the rest of the coffee into the trash can and glared at the two lube jobs through the garage door.

The more he tried out the idea that day, the more it fit. Every gas tank he filled was divinely sent to remind him of Stephen Dugan's gas tank being filled as he drove Mary Faith to some hideaway with rumpled sheets. Every dirty windshield he wiped was Jesus's way of saying there was dirt in this life that had to be sponged away. He said a prayer of thanksgiving that her mother wasn't here to know about this, to have to imagine, as he was imagining, what a man like Stephen Dugan said and did to a little girl like Mary Faith. He considered storming straight over to the offices of the *Courier* and barging into Stephen Dugan's office, but as the day wore on, and Lee Mac showed up for work, he was less and less confident in the image of himself going over there in his work clothes. He thought of going over to the man's house directly after he left the station, but there would be a wife there, and he couldn't see accusing Dugan in front of an innocent wife.

As the afternoon wore on, and it came closer to the time when he'd have to go home to face Mary Faith, it came to him that he could go and see Stephen Dugan's mother. He knew Nell Dugan, vaguely, from fishing days, and if he looked her up casually he could ask for her son's address. And maybe the whole story might just spill out, and Dugan's mother might take over for him—she might call her son over to her house, and he'd ask Dugan for enough money to help Mary Faith out of this, to have the little one taken from her, and he would be firm and Dugan would come up with the money and they'd find *some*one who knew how you set up these abortion things, and when it was all over he'd like to take one long clean shot with his fist at Stephen Dugan's pinched face.

Or that was the plan at the gas station. By five o'clock, when he'd left Lee Mac at the station same as always, as if nothing had happened, it all seemed hazier. He pulled the pickup onto the highway and found himself engulfed in the same panic that had carried him the night before. He could not go home to Mary Faith.

Once he was headed toward Nell Dugan's, he settled down on the army blanket stretched across his front seat. He was taking charge. He would tell Stephen Dugan's mother the problem, and then it would be half over.

He wouldn't even have to go back into Due East—Nell Dugan was living now this side of town, and he only had to go as far as the shopping center and then off a side road to the big cluster of apartment houses. The Nell Dugan he had known on the river lived in a normal house, like everybody else in Due East, but the Nell Dugan he hadn't seen in a couple of years lived in one of the new apartments. Everybody knew her story; she had let her mortgage payments slide for over a year after her husband died, and then she'd waited for the sheriff to cart her out the front door. Now she was living like a queen in the new apartments. She'd had plenty of money all along, the pension and the insurance and God knows what else.

He hit the dashboard and then the windshield with his fist. This was a ridiculous idea. The Dugans were crazy. A woman who'd let her house go that way. Probably her son had nothing to do with Mary Faith getting pregnant. What could he *say* to her? He pulled into the shopping center, and rolled up in the no-parking alley by the drugstore. He sat for five minutes, thinking only about the people coming and going—Marines' wives, sharp-edged women in stretch pants—and at the end of his time sitting he had decided again that Stephen Dugan was the only one who could possibly have gotten Mary Faith into trouble. And the only thing to do was go to Stephen Dugan's mother's house and get his address.

He was shaky again when he turned off for the apartment

houses: Pinetowne, they called the development. Not a single pine shading the Charleston brick. When he pulled close to study the wooden directory sign his head felt light. N. Dugan, 246, it said, and he parked the pickup with a jamming of brakes. He barely knew Nell Dugan. Just somebody he'd see on the river every Saturday, before her old man died. Just somebody whose son had gotten his daughter pregnant.

The damp air slid over him as he hopped down from the truck, and he walked back to the sideview mirror to flick a comb through his short hair. It felt heavier in the evening; Mary Faith was always after him, cajoling him to wash his hair.

Apartment 246 was up a wide flight of stairs and down a long brick balcony. The flower boxes had poinsettias turned green —that was what your rent paid for—and the place reminded him of the Riverview Motel. Living in Pinetowne would be like living in a motel for the rest of your life. He half-expected a maid pushing a linen cart to surprise him, and he looked behind him as he came near Nell Dugan's door.

She didn't answer at first, but he heard the television and buzzed again. The image of Mary Faith, smiling blankly like that, saying she didn't know how she got pregnant, kept his finger at the button a third time, and a fourth, and after three minutes he was still standing there, pushing over the sound of "The Price Is Right."

Finally a huge cat, blue-black and complacent, came from around the corner of the balcony and stood beside him at the door. He heard the television buzz off and the flap of slippers progressing through the apartment, and anticipated Nell Dugan in the dark: he saw her coming from the shower, an old bathrobe over her leathery skin and a towel on her head. He wanted to jump over the railing.

"What is it?" he heard from behind the door. Her voice was deep and dry.

He looked down at the cat beside him. "It's Jesse Rapple," he said, "and your cat's here too." He heard her clearing her throat and slipping a chain off the door, and he looked over his shoulder again to see if anyone would witness this welcome.

He'd been wrong about the bathrobe. She was in one of her

husband's shirts, tail out and sleeves rolled up, and a pair of loose tan corduroys. The slippers were pink and fluffy over her dark feet, and her short gray hair was curled into an electric ball of fuzz as girlish as the slippers. He did not recognize her with the hair: in all the years her husband was alive, she had always wandered around Due East with her hair cropped dry and short and plain. She had always looked older.

Her voice was familiar, though: no inflection. "I don't answer the door at night," she said. "You never know."

He leaned a hand on the brick beside the door. "I got to talk to you."

"Uhm hum," she said, as if she'd been expecting him.

He blinked his eyes and wished she'd ask him in for a glass of tea. He could say he was calling for the ministry. He could pretend he'd been in Pinetowne anyway. "I think your boy Stephen got my little girl in trouble," he said quickly. It didn't sound crazy.

She stared hard and looked almost as if she were going to burst into a grin. He felt he'd taken away her breath. Finally she said, "Why are you bothering me with that filthy talk?" Her voice was still monotone, and she looked as if she'd like to sit. "And anyway," she said in a flat rush, "Stephen's not a boy, he's a thirty-year-old man. You must mean somebody else. I can't believe you come to my house that way. Come on, Puddin." The cat slipped in, and she closed the door softly.

Jesse Rapple stared at the door, turned, walked to the edge of the balcony, stared out at the parking lot. His truck looked old under the evening sun, dented. The paint was flaking away. "Lord," he muttered. He stood still for a second, turned to go back to her door, and watched it open again, quickly this time.

Her face was set hard. "You better come in, Mr. Rapple. I can't believe you've come here to tell me something like that."

He followed her in wordlessly. He had never known her or her family well enough to have been invited to their house, but he had known it just as he had known most of the houses in Due East: it was a pine-shaded little white frame house on Stearns Street, and it had always needed a paint job. He looked around now at the gold carpeting and the long sofa and the sea mural on the wall, and he couldn't imagine that she had ever lived on Stearns Street the way she was living here. When her husband was alive, their house had probably been as filled with junk as their boat had been filled with rags and gasoline cans. This room reminded him of a motel, too.

"Get you a beer," Nell Dugan said, and her slippers flapped behind her as she went to the kitchen. He didn't have time to protest.

She came back with two cans and set them down on the low coffee table. When she sat down on the sofa the plastic squealed.

"I don't drink," he said, still standing.

"You just give me a piece of news like *that*, you could take a beer." She laughed, low and mirthlessly. "Baptist? I was a Methodist, for forty-five years. Until Mike died, then I joined his church. Well, I've been drinking all along anyway."

He sat in the leather lounger and looked around the room to avoid her eyes. He could imagine her going on for hours about being a new Catholic—Catholics! It hadn't occurred to him before. If Dugan was a Catholic, was he going to put up a fuss about an abortion? He wanted to talk about how to get Mary Faith out of the trouble she was in.

"Look here," he said. "I don't know for sure."

She nodded, and he pulled a cigarette from the open pack in his shirt. The apartment didn't just look like a motel, it smelled like one, and it sounded like one, fans and ice machines and smoothness blocking out the night. He had seen himself punching Stephen Dugan in the face, but he didn't know what to say to Stephen Dugan's mother.

"You don't know for sure," she prompted him.

"That's right," he said. He didn't know whether to be nettled or grateful. "I don't know for sure. Your son's been teaching that night class for dropouts."

She nodded again.

He tapped the unlighted cigarette against his open palm and chose his words. "He got my Mary Faith to come help him out. She's one sharp little girl, and when they came asking for volunteers at the high school she put her hand up." He wished

Nell wouldn't stare at him so. Her eyes were pale and watery. "So look," he said hopelessly, "Mary Faith's not a girl who runs around. She doesn't have so many friends. But after she started going to these night classes she was always talking about your son. Stephen says this, Stephen says that." He could see Nell's eyes widening and brightening, and he lit the cigarette in desperation.

"I don't ever want you to repeat this," he started again, and then found he couldn't go on. He had already told her the trouble, but it seemed a sin to repeat Mary Faith's condition. Fifteen years old. Knocked up, the boys would say around town.

"Now she's in trouble," Nell Dugan said for him. She was losing the edge of harshness in her voice.

"That's right," he said, and then he found the words coming with no trouble. "That's right, last night Mary Faith told me she's in trouble, but she won't say who's responsible. And I don't know any other boys she sees, so I get to thinking, and I think maybe if I could just see this Stephen Dugan and talk to him—she's a pretty thing, Mary Faith. Looks older than she is. You got to tell me where I can find your son so I can talk to him. I think he's led Mary Faith down the wrong road."

He grabbed an ashtray off the coffee table without looking at Nell Dugan. He had been wrong to come. Her son didn't have anything to do with it. Or, if he did, they'd never admit it.

"Stephen wouldn't lay a hand on a young girl like that," said Nell Dugan, imperious. Then she sipped down a quarter of her can of beer. He looked at his watch: five-thirty. Mary Faith would have supper on the table in an hour. He didn't know where to go from here.

"I knew you had a little girl," she said suddenly. "But I never did know her name." Her voice was so expressionless it mesmerized him. It wasn't just that her hair looked different—her skin looked younger, not so taut from the sun. She couldn't have been out in the boat by herself lately. She must have been holed up in Pinetowne, watching television and drinking beer.

"You have this beer," she went on, and held it out to him. "I've seen you sipping one on the creek. Your little girl gives you news like that, you best drink at least one beer to get your mind off it." She waved the can at him, beckoning, and he stood up and reached for it. She was laughing at him, but he was almost tickled—relieved, anyway, that she was taking it better. He watched her watching him take the first sip, and almost choked on it. "It is a hard thing to come to terms with," he said, apologizing.

"My Stephen wouldn't have done a thing like that, Mr. Rapple," she answered. "It is a hard thing to come to terms with, but my Stephen wasn't the one. He's married. He's got a little girl four years old, and two good jobs, and a pretty wife—a little too pretty, you ask me. If anybody's running around in that family it's that wife of his."

He drank his beer down straight to the bottom of the can and felt the full chill that always followed his drinking. "I don't know who would do a thing like that," he said, "to a fifteen-year-old girl."

"I don't know," she said. "I don't know either."

"She's a good girl," he said.

"I bet she is," said Nell Dugan, and finally her voice rose to a higher, warmer pitch. "My Ruthie was a good girl, too, and don't tell me you didn't know she took up with a Marine when *she* was sixteen and had her own little baby."

He did know about her daughter; it wasn't that he had forgotten exactly, but more that Ruthie Dugan was just a page out of a catalog. Catholic Girls Who Got Pregnant and Kept the Babies but Lost the Babies' Fathers. The catalog was such a long one that the only reason he remembered her pregnancy at all was because Ruthie Dugan had been involved with a black Marine, and she hadn't married her Marine until her baby was three years old. She had been a real center of attention around Due East. Crazy Ruthie Dugan. Crazy Stephen Dugan.

Nell Dugan was watching him again with her light eyes and her wiry curls and he saw suddenly that she was tiny: a tiny woman engulfed in her dead husband's shirt, sitting on her big sofa in her new living room.

"I don't guess you want another beer," she said. She sounded almost wistful.

"I'll take one," he said. He couldn't go back to Mary Faith.

"You know," she said, on her way to the kitchen, "it might not be the worst thing in the world that you came over here tonight. I never did realize what a good-looking man you are." He didn't hear the words until she had slipped into the kitchen and then he looked around, panicked, to see if anyone else had heard.

3

As Far As My Family's Concerned

My father didn't show up for supper the next night. I'd heard
him sneaking in the night before, but I knew he wanted to be
alone. I figured there would be a few more days he'd want to
be alone, and I wasn't counting on him coming home for
supper, but I made black-eyed peas and rice in case he *did* show
up, and then I ate it by myself.

After dinner I went straight to the dishes. He didn't go out
much at night, but I knew from the times I'd been alone that it
was better to do housework than to concentrate on the solitude. When my mother was here he stayed out with Buddy
Miles, to go fishing on Goat Island, and she would clean the
whole house while he was gone.

So I did the dishes the way she did them, hard and fast, and I
tried to think of nothing while I washed them. By the time I got
to the rice pot I was thinking of my father out trying to raise
money for an abortion, so I started drying instead, and when I
found I was still thinking of my father then I hummed some
dippy song fifteen-year-olds are supposed to like.

My mother's cleaning always put her in a terrible humor.
She was easygoing and patient when her work was done, and
she never talked back to my father, but when she had an apron
on she could barely control herself. The only time in my life

she ever let go—when she said she was going crazy and wouldn't we please cart her away—she was cleaning under the sink and trying to smash palmetto bugs with a hammer.

When I finished drying I swept, and then I lifted up the electric burners to clean underneath and then (maybe thinking of my mother) I opened the lower cabinets and straightened the pots and pans and cleaned under the sink.

There was no more picking up to be done in the kitchen, and the rest of the house was just as clean. There was nothing to distract me while I waited for my father because, as the pregnancy had gone on, I had gotten stronger and more inclined to fuss, and I had gone over the floors and walls and window shades enough to make the house look as if it had been kept under plastic wrap for the last three years.

I knew from the books that I was supposed to keep my feet up, and I went to my father's lounge chair in the den and tipped it back. I wondered if he'd tell his friend Buddy; I wondered where he thought he'd raise abortion money, anyway. I wasn't sorry about being pregnant, but I was real sorry he'd be doing more worrying about money. I told myself that I was glad it was out, at last, that I could finally go see a doctor and stop treating myself out of books I stole from the Due East library. The books all told you to see a doctor first anyway, and they even tried to convince you you might *not* be pregnant, but they never convinced me. It would be a relief to see a doctor, a new doctor—I thought maybe my father would want to take me to see someone in Savannah.

I wandered around downstairs. It was seven-thirty by the wall clock my mother had ordered before she died, the one she meant for the bedroom. My father had hung it in the kitchen, not knowing it looked silly with the old plastic dinette. I stood in front of the clock and pictured my mother realizing I was pregnant, saw her closing her eyes and then cleaning. Smashing palmetto bugs with hammers.

The phone rang. I thought it might be my father saying, "You've got to tell me, Mary Faith. Who did it?" It was enough to make me not want to answer the ringing, but it kept on, to eight rings, nine, twelve, fourteen.

It wasn't my father; it was my Aunt Lizann. She is my mother's fraternal twin, and their parents named them with reversed names: my mother was Ann Elizabeth, called Annie until she called herself Faith, and my aunt was Elizabeth Ann. They looked as different as sisters possibly could; my mother, even before the cancer, was thin and pale. Aunt Lizann would be pale, too, except that she spends all spring and summer and fall at the beach on a beach lounger, and her freckles turn gold and then a hurtful red and finally brown and people tell her she better watch out for skin cancer. She is not so tall as my mother was, but she is more energetic. She teaches Sunday school and sings in the choir and keeps the books for Uncle Zack's used car business and still helps out with the school plays for the Due East Academy, even though my cousin Betsiann graduated there ten years ago. The Due East Academy is the segregation academy across the bridge.

"Mary Faith," my aunt said, "I saw your daddy speeding down the Savannah Highway like a poacher caught with a full bag and I been worrying all night what could be bothering him so much he didn't even look up when I tooted my horn." Aunt Lizann calls like that two or three times a day. She calls my father at work when she sees me walking down River Street "looking depressed, like a little old lost sheep dog" and she calls me when she sees my father looking angry, "like a coon at the garbage can when the lights go on." My father says Aunt Lizann should go to work for the FBI and report on people's innermost feelings from a block away.

"I don't know, Aunt Lizann," I said, "I think he had a hard day at the station."

"Oh, Mary Faith. You always put it down to a hard day at work. People have feelings and we got to watch out for them. Now, where was he going?"

"I think he was heading over to Mr. Miles's house."

"No, he wasn't," my aunt said. "Buddy Miles is down at the tech school giving his shrimp talk. There were signs all over town."

"Well, maybe he just went for a ride." I could hear myself trying to sound like my mother. My aunt would call her three or four times a day, and my mother would do all her mending while she was on the phone; she kept the basket handy just for her sister's calls. And she would answer everything her sister said, not just with a yes or no but with a real answer, only the answer would sound as if it were filtered through cheesecloth over the mouthpiece, as if my mother had decided to do her duty and have a conversation, but felt that her words and her sister's words should not be allowed to mingle.

"Mary Faith," my aunt said, "do you mean you are alone in that house again and don't even know where your daddy went? What if there was a fire? What if some escaped convict tried to break in the back door or the cellar window? Who would you call?"

"The police," I said.

"All right, Miss Smarty," my aunt said. "See if I take you to Savannah shopping for Easter clothes *this* year. Now, honey, do me a favor. When your daddy comes home you find out what's troubling him and then you give me a call in the morning. He looked a sight in that truck and I want to make sure everything's all right with both of you. Hear?"

"Yes, ma'am."

"Good, and Mary Faith, while I'm at it, if we are going to Savannah for Easter clothes I hope you can get ten of those pounds off. Just quit frying things. You have a lovely figure and I hate to see a tall girl like you getting heavy."

"Yes, ma'am."

"Because you know Betsiann has already had three little children and she still keeps her figure as good as the day she got married, so if a young momma with three children can do it I'm sure you can do it too."

"Yes, ma'am."

"And you could cut off that ponytail, friz your hair maybe."

"Yes ma'am. I could do that."

"Mary Faith, there's not something *wrong,* is there?"

She said it in a quiet, serious way that wasn't like her at all. I tried to think of how my mother would answer, chiding without any effort, the lack of feeling in her voice a reproach in itself. If my mother had been there to defend me, she would

have said, "Mary Faith's pregnant, Lizann, and what would you
like to do about it?" Then they would remember Betsiann's
reception at the country club and the trips to Paris and how
well Uncle Zack's business was doing and how the gas station
was making less every year, and how far we'd been left behind.
Way far behind.

"No, nothing's wrong, Aunt Lizann."

"I mean about you gaining so much weight, there's nothing
bothering you now, is there? Are they still trying to talk you
into that fancy go-away-to-school business? Carolina's been
good enough for everybody else in Due East but just because
the public school's finally got a smart little girl when all the
nigras are bringing down the test scores I don't think they have
to try to get you all upset about going away to Massachusetts
or somewhere when anybody can see you'd rather stay home
and take care of your daddy anyway."

"Well, that's not it," I said.

"Honey, I don't know what it is, but I hope you see fit to
unburden yourself real soon. Now, let me go, Uncle Zack's
hollering for me to fix the TV reception. You call tomorrow.
Bye-bye." She used to tell my mother to let her go, too, as if
Momma had been keeping her at gunpoint. My mother would
say my aunt had a list of calls three pages long to get through.

But when Aunt Lizann hung up, and I saw the clean, still
house, I wished she had gone on a little longer. I didn't think
she suspected I was pregnant—I didn't think any of them, even
Betsiann, would think that of me—but she had noticed that I
was heavier. That something was wrong.

I thought of getting out my bottle of wine, but my father had
to come home sometime, and tonight would be just the night
he would smell something on my breath. I wondered what my
mother would think of my drinking wine, how much cleaning
that would cause her. She never took even an aspirin up until
the very end, and it was way after the doctors said she was
dying that she started taking drugs to kill the pain. Before that
she had relied on Jesus Christ. Even Aunt Lizann and Betsiann
thought she should go ahead with treatments to save her life.
They were the ones who got her to agree to the hysterectomy

after she said it wasn't natural to give up your womb that way. It was way too late.

The wall clock said eight forty-five, and I could hardly stand it anymore. The only other times my father kept me waiting that way were when he was scared to come home, because he thought I was going crazy, because he couldn't bear my getting chest pains and then dizziness and then stomach pains and then saying the truth, that I wasn't believing in his choir and his Jesus Christ anymore. He couldn't listen to me talking about the little visions of my mother I had before I fell asleep.

I went back to the phone and dialed Aunt Lizann. I was so surprised it didn't ring busy I almost dropped the receiver.

"Aunt Lizann," I said, "did you hear about the nipples those kids painted on that statue of the Virgin Mary the Catholics have in front of their church?"

She giggled and then stopped herself short. "Mary Faith, is that you? You like to got me going. I tell you, it is the silliest-looking thing, but we shouldn't ought to laugh. What you calling over, sugar? You want to set up that Savannah trip? Or you figure out what's wrong with your daddy?"

"Uh huh. Aunt Lizann, Daddy's been worried about money. Do you think you could maybe lend me a little to go to Savannah?"

There was a ten-second pause. I know because I heard the Reverend Winbon Price on Uncle Zack's TV set, doing his thirty-second pitch.

"Of course I could, honey." She said it in a voice frosty enough to kill the first tomato crop. We had never asked them for money.

"I wouldn't have asked," I said, and started sponging the handle of the phone receiver, "but I think Momma would've wanted me to help Daddy out." It nearly made me throw up, saying that. I was still surprised I'd called her back.

"Well, I knew *some*thing was the matter, Mary Faith. I knew it was some little old thing."

"Yes, ma'am," I said, and hoped she'd keep on talking. By the time my father got back I wanted that baby financed and guaranteed, and Aunt Lizann was the one with the bankroll.

And then I heard the pickup pulling into the driveway. My father would be pushing open the back door in a minute, a fist in his pocket and his hair oily under the kitchen light. I would be saying again that I wasn't quite sure how I got pregnant.

"Mary Faith?" said Aunt Lizann.

I was going to have to tell her *some*day, maybe not that it was a crazy kid made me pregnant, but that I wasn't going to have an abortion and that I wouldn't be fitting in the choir robes much longer.

"Mary Faith!" said Aunt Lizann. I could hear my father slamming the pickup door. When he came back from the hospital after the hysterectomy, he'd stayed in the front yard for half an hour, pulling moss down from the trees. When I visited her that night there was a little cross by her bed, twisted out of Spanish moss. I wondered if my father would be able to see the moss tonight, in the dark.

"Mary Faith," said Aunt Lizann, "something is going on with you and I just know it. Are you going to confide in me or not? I am just about all the family you have got left, and if you don't tell me I don't know who you'll tell."

"I know it, Aunt Lizann," I said. "You and Daddy are just about my only family left except for Betsiann, and she's real busy keeping her figure."

My aunt sucked in her breath. My father was still out in the yard.

"Aunt Lizann," I said, "do you reckon you could give me about three hundred dollars?" It was a nice round figure.

"I got to know what kind of trouble you're in," she said.

"Honest," I said, "I just need some new Easter clothes." Now I could *hear* him pulling down the moss, scraping a long stick up in the pecan branches.

Aunt Lizann was quiet, scraping down her own moss. The silence stretched. She was getting the picture. Then she said, "Mary Faith?" in her slow, shocked voice. "Are you pregnant?" I hadn't had to tell her after all.

"Yes ma'am," I said. "I'm going to have a baby." And then, like my mother when she picked up her mending, I didn't have to listen to the rest of the conversation. I'd told the whole family now, and Aunt Lizann would be running over in Uncle Zack's Oldsmobile, and she and Daddy would sit around the kitchen table all night long with me. They'd badger and they'd bully, but they wouldn't get anything out of me, and I'd make them pots of coffee and say I was *too* going to have this baby, and my aunt would say this would have broken my mother's heart, and we'd all be a family again. In the morning I would find a little Spanish moss somewhere propped up against a tree.

"Yes ma'am," I said again. "I am having a baby."

4

Seduction

Driving home, Jesse Rapple couldn't believe what had happened to him. First, he couldn't believe he was drunk, because he didn't get drunk. But Nell Dugan had brought back a second beer, and a third, and a fourth, and he had drunk them all with long hard swallows and nothing on his stomach. He *was* drunk.

Then he couldn't believe that she had tried to seduce him—or he had tried to seduce her, or whichever way it had happened. Drunk, he wasn't inclined to fret over who had started it. Every time she brought back a beer she sat a little closer on the sofa, and it must have been after the third one that he said, "You're not bad-looking yourself," and then nearly fell back from the surprise of saying it. Ever since Faith died he had been dreaming of women with full white breasts and round hips and long legs and toenail polish, but he'd never thought he'd get closer to them than the magazines the 7-11 brought him; and he never dreamed that a little birdlike woman, sharp-tempered and tanned and graying and skinny, would sidle up to him on the sofa; and he never believed that after the fourth beer he would put his arm around the shoulder of the little bird-woman and then lean over and kiss her full on her thin lips; and he still couldn't imagine that, having kissed her, he had proceeded to put his right hand on her left breast until she squirmed underneath and pulled herself free and said, "Mr. Rapple!" He had not kissed another woman since Faith died.

Mostly he couldn't believe that he had put Mary Faith out of his mind that way. When Nell Dugan disappeared to get the second beer, he had been unable to summon up the picture of Mary Faith he thought he should be drawing; he not only couldn't imagine her in her ninth month, he couldn't imagine her now, in her fifth month—couldn't see the body thickening, didn't want to. Nell Dugan wasn't going to even allow the possibility that her son had anything to do with it, so he let himself erase Mary Faith and concentrated on the beer instead.

And the beer had been enough to make him kiss her. After she struggled up and chirped out "Mr. Rapple!" and stared at him with those pale eyes until he had to turn his face away, she had sat back down, and snuggled up, closer still, and he'd drawn in his breath until he was dizzy. She turned her face up to be kissed again, and he wondered how long it had been since *she'd* had another mouth on hers. He could see rings of powder on her wrinkled neck.

Finally she'd broken away to say, "You shouldn't try to seduce an old widow lady that way."

He didn't believe he'd ever heard the word *seduce* spoken that way, between a man and a woman. He didn't feel so dizzy anymore, and that picture of Mary Faith he'd been trying to draw was suddenly completed. "I better go," he said.

Nell Dugan looked down at her slippers. "You don't have to go," she said. "I know you're worried about your daughter, but she's still going to be pregnant whether you go home or not. There's not a thing in the world we can tell these children once they put their minds to ruining their reputations."

He stood up.

"I've been lonesome since Ruthie moved," she said. "Lonesome in this big apartment."

He hesitated. "Thank you for the beer."

"You might could say thank you for the kiss."

"Thanks for the kiss," he said, and smiled. She smiled back, suspicious.

"I don't guess you'd want another beer sometime," she said.

"I just might." He couldn't help himself grinning. "I'm sorry, I'm sorry about running off. I'm not used to my little girl being pregnant, and I can hardly remember where I parked my truck."

"I suppose you parked your truck in the parking lot," she said.

Then *some*how he'd driven home. He couldn't remember pulling out of Pinetowne, but he did remember his foot slipping off the clutch on the highway, and the truck jerking down the road while he tried to imagine what Nell Dugan would have done if he'd put his hand *in*side her shirt. He didn't think Faith would mind him fiddling with other women; three years was a good long mourning, and she probably would have minded Nell Dugan being a Catholic more than she would have minded her being a new woman in Jesse Rapple's life.

He drove through town wondering what a second trip to Nell Dugan's would be like, and he turned onto the Point wondering how many beers he'd drink the next time, and he pulled into his driveway wondering what Buddy would think of him getting it on with an old coot like Nell Dugan.

It wasn't until he stopped the truck that he remembered why he'd gone to Nell Dugan's in the first place. And she'd been cagey enough to turn it all around, to make him forget. He could see Mary Faith's profile through the kitchen window; she was talking on the phone and looking the image of her mother, all sharp angles to her face. He knew that if he could see her up close she'd be staring out the way her mother had always done.

Opening the truck made his muscles ache. He was moving through a heavy fog, and he felt old. He wondered how that woman had managed to make him forget that her son had to be talked to. He couldn't go in the house yet—not until Mary Faith was off the phone, anyway. He made his way over to the pecan tree on the side of the house and poked down some moss with a stick. There wasn't much there; Mary Faith was always dragging it down.

He was still drunk, but now it was just a weariness, a wonder that he'd ever kissed a wizened old lady, a fear of going into his house. How could he have *fallen* for that woman's tricks? The minute she'd said *seduce* he should have asked for her son's address. There was more than one seducer in *that* family.

Through the kitchen window he could see Mary Faith hanging up the phone. He could tell, from the way his daughter angled her head without actually looking out the window, that she'd heard him pulling the truck in. She'd be expecting her daddy to come in with a plan, a way to take *care* of this pregnancy, and the old widow lady had done him out of it.

Suddenly his weariness was gone, and he marched back to his truck. Nell Dugan wasn't going to outsmart him with kisses. She probably *knew* what her son had done. He started up the truck, and saw Mary Faith hesitate at the front window. She wouldn't run after him: she never did. "Sweet Jesus," he said, and backed the truck up.

He swung the truck down their block, and then out onto Oysterbed Road, until it curved into River Street. He was driving too fast. "Good Lord," he said, slowing the truck down. Look what these people had brought him to already, Sweet Jesusing and Good Lording, and he didn't even know them.

"Goddamn," he said. She'd tricked him out of getting that address. He didn't care how friendly she was underneath, he meant to get it. That was what he'd come for, and she'd driven it from his mind. She would have tried to tempt Jesus in the *desert.*

Now that he itched with how cleverly she'd kept it from him, the ride to Pinetowne was a fast one. Once you got past downtown, Due East was one blob of plastic and neon. You didn't even know who owned the strip of tire stores and boutiques and head shops (head shops!) and K-Marts. They were all chain stores, owned by somebody from out of town, managed by some beer-bellied twenty-five-year-old just passing through Due East. He saw Mary Faith standing by that window, waiting for him to come in and tell her what to do, and he almost let out a yowl. It was no wonder girls like Mary Faith got pregnant. All of Due East was turning into one big Pinetowne as far as he was concerned, and little girls had nothing to look forward to. What the hell was the matter with Nell Dugan anyway, letting

her mortgage slide and then moving into a condo*min*ium built
by more out-of-towners? That little frame house on Stearns
Street wasn't as good as *Pine*towne? At least the house had a
decent yard to keep the boat in, and some real pine trees
shedding needles through the winter so you knew what part of
the world you were in. At least it was near a creek that hadn't
been filled in for some garbage dump, like half the marshland
in the county. He passed Spanish Moss Square, the third new
shopping center in a year. Spanish Moss Square! They just
named it that for the newcomers who hid behind their tinted
glass windshields and didn't notice *what* was on the trees. And
there wouldn't be anything on the trees if they kept taking
down the oaks everywhere they wanted a wider road. The
whole country was going Pinetowne, condominiums here,
chain stores there, islands bought up by God Knows Who from
God Knows What Country. Arabs even. Arabs especially. And
he and Buddy Miles weren't going to be getting a crab or a
shrimp or even a catfish or a shark if those paint factories kept
up what they were doing to the water. Chemical companies
and Pinetownes and shopping centers and fifteen-year-old
girls who lost their mothers and were losing Due East and got
pregnant.

And Nell Dugan was willing to be part of it, willing to go
along with condos and apartments that looked like motel
rooms and then to lure him in with beer and cheap sexy talk
and send him back into the night without the address he came
for.

This time he didn't bother with the turn signal at the cutoff
for Pinetowne, and he screeched the truck into the parking lot
without so much as a glance at the white lines in the parking
spaces. There was no looking in the mirror to see how greasy
his hair was. She had tricked him.

He stormed across the balcony so she could *hear* him coming, and he kept his hand on the buzzer, half-expecting that
this time she'd come to the door with a pink nightie on and ask
him into the bedroom. He could hear her shuffling toward the
door, and the sound of her slippers excited him into pounding.

"You don't have to break the door down," he heard her call.

It was just too cute. Now he could see Mary Faith the way he had wanted to call up her image before, thick and in her ninth month, walking down River Street in the middle of the day, a sea of old ladies parting and muttering as she walked by.

"I got to have your boy's address," he said. He didn't yell it and he didn't mutter it, he said it firmly, the way he had meant to say it before. He could hear her idling up to the door, but the chain wasn't being pulled off and the latch wasn't coming undone. He could hear her just *standing* there.

"I forgot to get your son's address," he said, gentler. There was no sound on the other side of the door. He waited.

"Damn," he said finally. "Are you going to open up or not?"

"Not," she said, and laughed her gravelly laugh.

Well. *That* made sense for a family of seducers. She didn't think anything of making him wait out in the night, sweating for his daughter, while she teased from inside. "Are you going to give me that address?" he said.

"Mr. Rapple," she said through the door, "I am shocked that you could come back and talk to me that way after what happened to us tonight." Then she opened the door, and he took a step backward. She was batting her eyelashes, spindly gray lashes, and looking at his chest. Her voice was shaky and scheming and as gray as the lashes and the face and the hair. "Is it going to make you come back here to visit me?" she said. This was the very same woman who had called him—him, Jesse Rapple—a good-looking man.

"I don't see how getting your son's address and coming back here are connected," he said softly. He couldn't look at her. The whole of Pinetowne must be listening to this one. Not that he'd know anybody else who'd buy a condominium, but even if this was the new Due East, things had a way of getting around.

"You mean you might be back?"

He took another step backward. "I might," he said.

"Stephen's address is forty-seven Freedom Lane," she said. "Not that he has a thing to do with it. But if you're so bound and determined to talk to him, you'd best go over there and clear the air."

"That's right," he said. "I've just got to clear the air."

"Tomorrow night," Nell Dugan said. "Why don't you come back then? I could get us another six-pack."

"We'll see," he said shortly, and then—seeing her eyes close against the sound of his voice—"I might can call you from the station. You in the book?"

"In red letters," she whispered. "With stars by my name. You call. I'll be waiting."

He left her on that, without even saying good-bye or looking back to see her hanging off her front door. He wasn't ready for another woman. He'd rather stick to his dreams of full, fleshy magazine girls. He wasn't ready for Nell Dugan's beers or kissing or rings of powder and God knew, Sweet Jesus knew no matter how much Faith would be willing to forgive him, he wasn't willing to crawl into bed with another woman, to have to touch skinny brown breasts and a belly too old and oh my God while Mary Faith was alone at home, pregnant and not just slipping away from him, disappearing as if she'd never been his little girl, the way the shrimp were disappearing and the marsh was disappearing and his business was disappearing. He fumbled with his keys, and the engine wouldn't turn over. He didn't want to drive through the subdivision on his way to Freedom Lane and see everything turning on him, turning new and cheap and upside down. But the truck started with a jerk, and he was backing out of his parking space and leaving Pinetowne again.

A squirt of spring rain hit the windshield, and then another, and then it was really raining, and he was on the way to Dugan's house, Pinetowne behind him. He wished it would pour down until the creeks rose. They could take care of this thing. They could have the little one taken from Mary Faith, and Dugan could pay for it, and maybe it wouldn't hurt to get friendly with Nell Dugan as long as they were suffering through this thing together. Maybe it wouldn't be so hard to snuggle up with a skinny little beer-breathed woman who wasn't so sure of herself after all. Who knew what it would lead to? God knew, and had been telling him for some time, that Mary Faith needed an older woman to look after her and keep her out of just the kind of trouble she'd gone and gotten herself into.

5

Letters from the Dead

After I got off the phone with Aunt Lizann, I ran upstairs. I'd heard my father backing out of the driveway, but I had a feeling he'd be back, and I was sure my aunt would make an appearance.

Upstairs I had Michael Jagger's letters. I had decided to burn them four months before, but the deciding was easier than the burning. Someday this kicking baby was going to ask questions and I thought it might be nice, when a baby got to be twelve or fifteen, to say, "Look here, I've saved this pile of letters. They might tell you something about the father. Your daddy." I wasn't going to keep up the virgin birth business forever.

On the other hand, I didn't know what twelve-year-old was going to believe her father had gone and killed himself two weeks after she was conceived. It sounded even wilder than *I don't exactly know how it happened.* By then I would have thought up a real good father for her, a priest who couldn't leave his church or a married man who couldn't leave his six other children. And if I was going to come up with another father, I had to burn Michael Jagger's letters. Besides, if I burned them Aunt Lizann couldn't make a wild search through my bedroom for evidence. I'd let her in the house, but I wouldn't let her touch a finger to those letters.

Upstairs I unlocked the third drawer of the dresser, the only drawer that still shut. I hadn't looked at the letters in five or six weeks, but they were still there, in a brown envelope. When I saw them I got scared, and went to the bathroom, and then went downstairs, and then got out the wine from under the sink. I took the whole bottle out on the front porch to listen for the truck coming back. Nothing was coming. Just frogs croaking in the pond down the street, and a blue-black sky above. The rain would start soon.

It wasn't that I was angry at Michael Jagger for going off and taking thirty tranquilizers after he made me pregnant—he didn't know I was pregnant yet; *I* didn't even know I was pregnant yet. It was more that ever since he went and killed himself I had been trying not to think about what it was like to be chosen by Michael Jagger, more that I couldn't burn the letters in the upstairs bathroom without at least reading them. At least one or two. I went back to my room and sat on the floor and decided I would just read the first one.

Dear Mary,

I guess you will think it is pretty stupid of me to write you a note when I see you twice a week, but I am not the kind of person who can talk just like that. I would like to see you and discuss what is going on in these classes. If you would like to talk, you could write back. I will understand if you don't want to get together over something so serious. I think you are probably the kind of girl who goes to the movies or bowling or things like that. But if you are interested we could have a good talk.

Sincerely,
m. jagger

We tutored math to high school dropouts at GED classes on Monday and Wednesday nights, but Michael Jagger had never said a word to me. He'd barely said a word to Mr. Dugan, who ran the classes.

I found his note in my pocketbook one Wednesday night when I got home from tutoring, and when I saw the signature I laid the paper out on my bed to read it twice. Michael Jagger was tall and black-haired, with white skin and dark eyes, and his face was so thin that it might have been handsome, except that he walked around with a goofy grin all the time. I had tried to smile at him because he was the kind of boy you just want to smile at, in case nobody else ever does, but he had given me that same cockeyed look he always had on anyway. He wore a checkered shirt and striped pants to school, and his work shoes were worn thin all around. He was the kind of boy everybody at Due East High School called strange and weird, and whenever there was a standardized test he had the highest score in the school. He was at the bottom of the senior class. He ate lunch with two friends who were also tall and awkward, only one was blond-haired and had acne and one was black and limped, but when they sat together in the cafeteria or on the breezeway they dropped their goofy grins and talked hard. They looked happy together, almost serene. After school they would go out to the buses and hand out leaflets telling people to boycott the lunchroom or boycott the machine shop or protest Baby Rooney's suspension, and everyone would take the leaflets and grin and throw them in the dirt road. They would say, "Hey, it's Mick Jagger" or "Here comes the wizard"—he had worn a pointy hat and a cape on the day a reformed convict gave a talk in assembly—and they would make fun of him, or avoid him, or just look bewildered. Everybody knew him the way they knew the town idiot and the town drunk and the town whore, and he was the kind of boy cheerleaders and student council presidents were warm and friendly to, as another sign of their unbiased humanity and general sincerity.

So when I found a note in my pocketbook my first thought was that there was some kind of mistake, that somebody had put the note there as a mean trick. My second thought was that Michael Jagger had some kind of nerve thinking that I was the kind of girl who went bowling, for Christ's sake. I was surprised he thought I had dates. I wondered if he thought I blow-dried my hair and wore pantyhose and had a regular home life with a momma and a daddy and brothers and sisters and a Sunfish to sail in the bay on Saturdays. I wondered if I'd talk to him the next time I saw him, or whether he'd hover in the background, quiet. Mr. Dugan was crazy about him, but all the dropouts ran away from the table where he was teaching equations. He was just too strange.

I ended up writing a note back to him with my phone number. Then it got really silly—when I was getting into Mr. Dugan's car after class he slipped another note in my hand (and Mr. Dugan didn't say anything about it, but I always figured *he* knew why Michael Jagger had committed suicide, because he had seen the note, and my hand holding it). The new note said that he didn't like to talk on the phone and asked if I could meet him on Saturday at noon in the parking lot by the St. Jacques Marina. I was supposed to mail him a letter if I couldn't make it.

Well, if a boy like Michael Jagger has written you two notes already and you haven't completely rejected him yet, you don't write him letters telling him you can't make it. I was in the parking lot that Saturday and so was he, sitting on the bench nearest the Coke machine, holding a paperback copy of *The Idiot*. In the spring he had carried around *Crime and Punishment* for three months, with yellow scraps of paper sticking out to mark passages.

I smiled and he smiled, and I waited for him to say something, but he didn't. I had a feeling we should have brought a legal pad and pencil, and pushed it back and forth between us with messages. Finally I said, "So, how do you like tutoring?"

Up close I could see what made his smiles so goofy—his lips twitched at the end of his mouth, as if he wanted to say something in the middle of the smile. It took him forever to answer.

"I think it may be stupid. Trying to cram sums and grammar into the heads of those people. Just so they can get a diploma. But. It might help them get a job." He spoke softly. I had never heard him say so much at once before, so I had never known that his voice was smooth, or that he didn't have an accent. None. After all the nights of listening to nobody but my daddy and Baptist preachers talk, Michael Jagger's voice sounded like a foreigner's to me, and I didn't get it. He'd been in Due East all his life, probably. Maybe he hadn't gotten as much practice going on at the mouth as everybody else around here.

"I reckon that's so," I said. "It probably can't hurt them too much, anyway."

He shook his head sadly. "It might. They got to learn how to think before they can learn which tense you put the verb in."

I didn't know what I was supposed to say. Maybe he had in mind passing out leaflets protesting the tutoring. I asked him if he'd ever talked to Mr. Dugan about the way he felt.

He nodded.

"Mr. Dugan seems like a nice guy," I tried.

He didn't answer, and I sat next to him for five minutes memorizing the bottles lined up in the Coke machine, and the rows of fried pork rinds and peanut butter crackers in the next machine. The fall tourists were coming off their yachts in striped sailor shirts and blue caps. They looked at us as if we were chickens pecking at the side of the road.

Finally he got up and said, "Thank you for coming," in a deep voice, and walked away without turning back. I looked at the boats in the bay and then at his back—he had on a red T-shirt and black pants and a new pair of sneakers—and all of a sudden I wanted to cry, a good hard cry like the ones I had for missing my mother in the mornings. I'd felt that way when she walked into the hospital for her hysterectomy.

That afternoon there was a letter in my mailbox that said:

> Dear Mary Faith,
>
> Please forgive me for walking off that way. I didn't know what I was doing. You were good to come, and I wish you would come again, next Saturday, but I can see why you wouldn't want to.
>
> I had so much to say to you about those tutoring sessions, but when we were sitting next to each other I didn't know how to tell you how much they mean to me. They are the only thing I do connected with the school that is any way respectable, and I don't like being respectable. But I do it because of Mr. Dugan, because he asked me to, and I like most of the drop-outs even if they don't like me. They are, on the whole, much more intelligent than anyone at Due

East High School including the teachers. Especially the teachers. However, helping to continue a system that rewards people for not thinking sickens me. We don't teach philosophy or literature, only algebra and grammar. And it sickens me to think I am just helping people get a high school diploma so they can afford a better brand of color television.

I don't know if that kind of thinking interests you. For all I know, you are very respectable. I saw you win awards last year at Awards Day and you looked pretty respectable. But your dress was a little different from everyone else's. And I see you on the breezeway at lunch walking by yourself and not looking like it bothers you. All I really know about you is that you haven't run for class secretary, and that gives you three points, and you came today, and that gives you ten points. Even my best friends barely have thirteen points.

But I will understand if you don't want to talk again. Thanks anyway.

Sincerely,
michael jagger

He wasn't at the GED classes on Monday night or Wednesday night either, and when I saw him on the breezeway that Thursday he turned around and hurried off in the other direction. I didn't know if I'd lost my points or what.

I didn't think about him again until the next Saturday morning. While I was scrubbing the refrigerator I remembered the note and got it out of my drawer and went over the first paragraph. I wasn't sure whether he meant that he would be at the marina again, or whether he was already giving it up for lost. I remembered his face, white and guilty, when he saw me on the breezeway. I decided I needed to go downtown anyway, to buy some more floor wax, and I got the bike out of the garage.

It was September, warm. No need for a jacket, but I wore one anyway and zipped it all the way up my chest. I had a feeling Michael Jagger judged everything severely, that if he were at the marina he wouldn't like seeing my nipples through my shirt, that he wouldn't like the shirt anyway, that it would be too conventional or respectable, too navy blue. The jacket was red.

He was there, on the same bench, with the same copy of *The Idiot*—more yellow strips of paper—and this time he stood up when he saw me and said, "I like that jacket. I like that red." His voice was quicker and harder.

I told him I was going shopping (I didn't mention the floor wax) but that I had come down to the marina to see if he was there. He grinned.

"I'm glad you came," he said. "I wanted to show you something."

I sat down on the same bench as the last time, looking at the same pork rinds in the machine, and waited. After a few minutes he managed to pull some papers out of his backpack, and he held one of them to his chest, as if he couldn't make up his mind to give it to me. Finally he said, "I drew this a long time ago," and pushed the paper over to me. Then he walked over to the Coke machine and pressed all the buttons.

The paper was a mimeographed sheet with a hand-printed headline: "STOP BEING THIS STUDENT." Underneath, covering half the page, was a picture of a tall, skinny girl with hair tied back in a ponytail and long earrings dangling. Her face was jagged and angular—the chin came to a sharp point—and her eyes looked big and light and stupid. She was holding a scroll in her hand that said "Obedient Student Award." It was a very funny caricature. It was me.

Beneath the picture was a paragraph about the dull minds of students who study what they are told to study. I stared at the paragraph and then at the picture and then at the paragraph again. I tried convincing myself that it was only coincidence that the picture looked so much like me, but it was inescapable. I had big gold hoop earrings, just like those, and I wore them every day.

"I'm sorry," said Michael Jagger. He didn't even turn around from the Coke machine.

I walked to him, handed the paper back, and headed toward my bike.

"No, look," he said, "this thing's six months old. I did it six months ago, and then I never handed it out. Leroi and Hardy wanted me to, but I couldn't. I wasn't sure you were like that. Now I know you're not. Please wait." He could speak plenty quickly when he wanted to, plenty loud.

I didn't wait. I ran back to the bike and pushed it out into the River Street traffic. Hardy and Leroi had wanted him to. I could see the three of them, grinning goofy grins, laughing over the pictures, making the chin more pointed. They hadn't even known me. They'd seen me pick up a few awards in an assembly when I hadn't even known there were going to be awards. I could see them chortling on the breezeway. Miss Obedient Student. I pedaled the bike faster and faster, away from the marina, past the Breeze Cinema, past the drugstore, past the Lowcountry Yachting Club, until I came to the end of River Street. I pushed the bike up against an oak tree and walked down the bluff and sat on the seawall and hoped the oyster shells would rip my pants. I took my red jacket off and rolled up the sleeves of my navy blue shirt and watched the bridge open up and close for the Saturday shrimp boats. I waited three hours; then I pedaled home.

I guessed there would be another note from Michael Jagger in the mailbox, and there was. This time my daddy was home, drinking beer and watching television, so I had to hide the letter. When I got it upstairs, I tried to think of all the ways he could apologize—I figured he would say the flyer was all for a good cause. But when I opened the letter I had to read it three times to make sure I got it right.

Dear Mary Faith,

I don't know how I can ask you to forgive me. I thought once I explained how old the picture was you'd understand. Now I know how much I hurt you by showing you that stupid drawing. The reason I drew it was because I'd seen you up on the stage getting the chemistry award and I thought you looked

wonderful, very shy, and I couldn't stand it. Hardy
and Leroi pointed you out and I could tell they were
crazy about you too, only they made fun of anybody
who would go and win the government award. They
called you the Good Citizen. We used to watch you at
lunchtime, I always thought you must have noticed
us. Sometimes you were with that short girl but
mostly you were alone, carrying a library book but
never reading it. You could sit on the bench for the
whole half hour without looking bored or lonely.
Didn't you ever see us there? We used to all pretend
we despised you because you won those awards but
every day we'd be out there looking for you and if you
were with the short girl we'd make fun of you both. I
could hardly stand the summer, when we didn't see
you. Don't you see, we just wanted to make fun of you
because we were frightened of you? —Hardy said you
reminded him of his mother, walking on a different
plane of the universe.

And then you showed up at tutoring. I told Hardy
and Leroi I would be talking to you, and now they
don't see as much of me. They've stopped working on
the flyers, they say I'm afraid to offend anyone. I'm
not afraid to offend anyone, just you right now. I
didn't show you that picture to tell you how much I
hated you, I showed it to you to tell you everything's
different now. I'll understand if you never forgive me
but I hope you see that it was only out of wanting to
know you that any of this happened. Thank you for
coming today anyway, you looked like Natasha in that
red jacket. Sincerely, m.j.

I didn't know who Natasha was. They didn't teach Russian
novels in the South Carolina public schools; they taught American government and how to be a good citizen. I didn't think
he was right, that Hardy and Leroi were crazy about me; I
thought they probably despised me and talked about my

pointy chin. Didn't they know how strange everyone thought *they* were?

At the tutoring session Monday I didn't say a word, but Wednesday I handed him a note that said I would be there on Saturday. And then it was started.

He was never with his friends at school anymore—Leroi passed out flyers alone—but he was never with me either. If he saw me on the breezeway he smiled a little smile and hurried away. I found out he was hiding his lunch hours away in the library when I went to hide there myself, and then I had to go back out on the breezeway.

If Hardy and Leroi saw me they stared the other way, but they didn't point and gape. Sometimes I talked to Reba McFee when her best friend had a meeting but otherwise I was mostly alone. I had gotten by alone for a long time without its unsettling me, but suddenly I could sense his friends despising me and suddenly I could picture him in the library, hiding from me, and I felt my bench under the Buses sign had a big flashing light over it, that boys in groups of two or three were sketching cartoons of me.

I didn't try to tell him that when we met on Saturdays because we didn't do much talking. Once he tried to hold my hand, but it wasn't right—we both felt it.

My father was working most Saturdays at the Plaid King, so I started having Michael over to the house. He wanted to play war games, but I told him that was worse than bowling, for Christ's sake. I wanted him to hold me, but there wasn't even a kiss.

I'd been thinking about getting pregnant for a long time, since I was thirteen at least. I didn't mind getting those awards, even if I didn't study, and I didn't mind singing in the Baptist choir, even if I didn't believe in God, as long as everybody didn't think that was the type of person I really was. But that was exactly the type of person they thought I was. They didn't know I was the type of girl who spent trig class thinking about seducing the boys who didn't understand the math, the shy slow ones. Until he wrote me that note it had never occurred to

me to seduce Michael Jagger, but once he was in love with me
it seemed like a real nice thing to do. When I saw his face turn
white and his lips twitch in the middle of his sentences and his
hands shake when he went to touch me, I felt like protecting
him and showing him how to get started, even if I didn't know
anything about it, and mothering him and some little one and
running away from Due East and having a reputation with a
capital R, like all the Catholic girls.

But it wasn't so easy to seduce Michael Jagger. I didn't want
to hurt him—not after he'd given up Hardy and Leroi—and I
decided I'd better fall in love with him just a little. I didn't want
to have the fear for him that my daddy had for me: that he was
a crazy sad lonely case.

So every Saturday I got a little closer, until finally he was in
the bedroom to look at my new paperback copy of *The Idiot*, to
tell me if I had a good translation. We hadn't said a lot to each
other, but we were getting to understand each other's ways.

We sat on the bed together and he picked up the book the
way you would pick up a baby, carefully and gently and
sweetly. But he didn't open it up, or even read the cover—he
tried holding my hand again, and said: "You didn't really want
me to tell you if you had a good translation, did you?"

I shook my head no. We sat quiet. We were real practiced at
it.

Finally I turned my head to his, so close he had to kiss me,
and he did. His face and lips were as soft as a baby's bottom. I
had thought boys' lips were hard, their faces scratchy.

When he'd stopped and looked away I said, "I want to make
love to you." He didn't turn to look at me or breathe a word. It
came to me that I'd only known him two months, and that he
was shyer than any of the shy boys in trig class. It came to me
that he might be the only person in Due East who didn't think I
was the choir-singing obedient-student type. "I love you," I
said, so he wouldn't think it was all the other way, either.

He got up and put the book on the dresser. His shoulders
sagged.

"I'm sorry," I said to his back.

He spun around. "No," he said, "don't be sorry." He

sounded frenzied, and I was frightened. "Don't be sorry," he went on. "What do you think I've been thinking of? I want to take you away out of this stinking rich people's town and marry you. Not with a license, not with a priest or preacher, just marry you, just take you away and take care of you."

I didn't say anything. I didn't want to be married. I was fifteen.

He had turned around again and was tugging at his hair. "It's not right," he said. "It's like any other cheap high school romance, with your father out of the house on a Saturday afternoon. I don't want that with you." He turned around again and tugged at his hair.

"I'm sorry," I said again. I'll never know how he took that—whether he thought it meant I wouldn't marry him, or whether he thought I was sorry I'd brought anything up—but he came back to the bed and pushed me down and said: "This isn't right. You could get pregnant."

"I'd *like* to have a baby," I said.

He looked as if he'd cry. "We can't do this," he said.

"Yes we can," I said. So it *was* like a virgin conceiving; he really wanted to do right by me, and if his body was there, his heart was taking me away and marrying me. He gritted his teeth like a hunting dog, and when we had our clothes off we hid under the sheets and couldn't look each other in the eye. He was still in the frenzy, and he kissed me too hard. I thought his eyes flashed red, and afterward he put his head on my chest, as if I were the momma, and could comfort him for what he'd done wrong. He was crying.

I spent the next day waiting for another letter, waiting to hear him sneak up to the front porch and slip it in the box. I'd decided I loved him all right—I just had to make it less like a mother's love, less like I was taking care of him. He'd still been crying when he left the house, crying hard, and saying he couldn't tell me why he cried. Up close I had seen where he was trying to start a black mustache and how thick his eyebrows were. Crying, his face had looked twisted.

But no letter came Sunday or Monday or Tuesday or

Wednesday. I hadn't seen him at school, not even skulking around the halls, not at the GED classes. On Thursday it finally came.

Dear M.F.:
    I am sorry. I should never have taken advantage of you that way. I wanted to take you away and instead I went and used you. I can't tell you the things that go through a man's mind, but they don't have anything to do with you. I was crying because I couldn't see you, only some cheap picture out of the kind of magazines they sell behind the counter at the 7-11. I twisted you around and used you and now I can't see you again. I've done a terrible wrong.

He didn't sign that one. I knew what he'd thought when he'd held his teeth like that—he'd been imagining he was beating me, hurting me. Something like that. My daddy brought home dirty magazines and *I* didn't mind dreams swirling through his mind, but it disgusted him.

He dropped out of school. Mr. Dugan told me Wednesday night: he said Michael had come to him and told him he was running away, off to North Carolina to live in the hills. Mr. Dugan told him that was a crazy notion and Michael said all right, he'd run off to Atlanta, then, and live with the motorcycle gangs. I'd see him down by the marina and he'd fly off like one of the ducks my father was after scaring that fall. Or I'd see him walking home from downtown and he'd stare the other way, as if there were no girl in a red jacket pedaling a big white bike directly at him. I didn't have the courage to stop him. I didn't have the nerve to call, either, because from the minute it happened I'd known it was me taking advantage, me using him. I figured in a couple of weeks the guilt would lessen, and he'd come back to school and make it up with his friends. The way I hoped it would happen, he'd come back gradually to tutoring, and then in another couple of months there would be another letter in my mailbox.

There *was* one more letter. I found it the night before he killed himself. It said *Dear Mary Faith Rapple,* and then across half the page was a cartoon of me, sitting at a bar, with my long earrings dangling. I was swigging from a big bottle marked XXX, and tears were running down my cheeks. Below the cartoon, Michael had typed in a letter:

No seriously, Mary Faith, I'm sorry about what happened. I don't really think you're drowning your sorrows, I think you've probably forgotten already what happened. I wanted to say that you shouldn't feel bad. Thank you for being so nice.

I don't guess most guys would feel this way. The lesson I remember best from catechism is the one about the immaculate conception. I know it was just Mary who was supposed to be conceived without sin, not all women, but some of you have always looked that innocent. I remember seeing you on the breezeway or riding your bike, all shy and proud, and then I think about how I saw you that afternoon, and I might as well have been one of those jerks on the football team, telling all my friends, only I was worse, pretending it was noble and good and unconventional. I sicken myself sometimes.

Do you remember those black nipples on the statue of the Virgin Mary on Division Street? Everybody thought it was the catechism kids who did it, but it wasn't, it was me who painted them on. First I quit the church and then I quit the Virgin Mary. Now look what I've gone and done.

I'm sorry. I wanted to tell you to forget about it, and thank you, and now I'm telling you what a sinner I am. I've just been up so long, I need some sleep, I think I may go to Atlanta, nobody but you will speak to me in this town, but it takes more courage maybe than I have, and I wanted to leave with a thank-you. There was a minute when my head left my body and

that's what peace is, anyway. Sometimes I feel like an
old man.

Your friend always,
MICHAEL AMOS JAGGER

So the next night at supper, when my father said, "I reckon
you heard about that crazy boy at the high school," I knew just
what he'd gone and done, and I didn't have to listen to Daddy
droning on about how he took thirty tranquilizers downtown
and weaved around in front of the Breeze and how everybody
thought he was just drunk, since that is how high school kids
are always amusing themselves, and that when he passed out in
the alley nobody noticed, that it was his own momma who
found him, that she went downtown looking because he'd
been acting so crazy. Somehow I'd never thought of Michael
Jagger having an actual mother. So he'd had two of us spending all our time the last month fretting over him.

I didn't go to the funeral. I didn't want to see his mother or
him or count how few people showed up. The next week they
held a big assembly on drug abuse. A middle-aged housewife
got up and told how she'd popped pills, but how faith in her
family and Jesus got her through. She looked a lot like the ex-
convict they'd had to talk to us: they both had a way of darting
their eyes around the bleachers, and talking louder when they
heard a giggle in the back.

In another three weeks I knew I was pregnant, and I stopped
going by the marina and the Breeze. I avoided all of downtown
as much as I could, but I told myself that maybe it wasn't so
bad, that a boy like that would be tortured worse if he knew
there was a baby, that maybe crumbling down in the alley
behind the Breeze—while he was high and the winter wind was
whipping off the water—maybe that wasn't such a bad way for
Michael Jagger to go. I did wonder about that last cartoon,
about how he knew I drank, and then I remembered one
Saturday when he'd gone under the sink to get a rag. He must
have seen the wine bottles hidden way in the back and known
they were mine.

And anyway, it wasn't just one little incident that made Michael Jagger go kill himself. Everybody in Due East said they'd seen it coming, and we had another assembly on adolescent isolation and the Baptist church opened a phone hot line and asked if I'd take calls on Wednesday night after service. I said I was already busy.

6

Mr. Rapple
Takes Charge

Forty-seven Freedom Lane was a one-story version of Jesse Rapple's own place: by his headlights he could see a frame house with a big front porch and green metal swings on chains. Its paint job was chipped away by sun and wet air. He had driven through ten blocks of subdivision to get to Freedom Lane, and now it looked like home, one of the few blocks in Due East that had been left alone. The yards were big, and dogs ran in them, and azaleas and camellias and dogwoods bloomed in them, and every yard had a boat on a hitch, because Freedom Lane was on Chessy Creek and—even if you couldn't eat the crabs you brought up this year—it was still deep and meandering and clotted with marsh grass. Jesse Rapple loved Chessy Creek. He wished he could find something to disapprove of in Stephen Dugan's little house, but it was on the creek, set way back from the road in a corner, one side bordered by a thin row of pines. Real pines. It was a good Due East house.

The rain had stopped. Rapple followed the long semicircle of a driveway up to the front door and prayed the wife wouldn't be home to hear the accusation. "Please, Jesus," he said under his breath, switching the motor off. "Please, Jesus."

But when he rang the doorbell, it was the wife who answered. He took her in hopelessly. She was skinny and tall and had her long brown hair frizzed the way the girls were doing it nowadays. Only the Lord knew why. Looking at Stephen Dugan's wife, he could see what Nell Dugan meant by "a little too pretty"—she had painted her eyelids almost black, and her bare legs had been oiled. And he could tell she came from money: she showed a complete lack of interest in who he was or why he was calling on her husband, and she showed him into her husband's study without ever taking in his face. He was sure she thought he was a carpenter or a salesman come to talk business, and for a crazy second he could see why a man would prefer Mary Faith to *that.*

He was alone for a minute in the study and surveyed it. He felt like a Bible salesman, and tried standing straighter, like a father. No friends of his had rooms like this: Stephen Dugan evidently thought of himself as Mister Intel*lec*tual, and had littered his room with books and papers and magazines and, posed among them like models at a car show, his child's plastic dolls with blond bouffant hairdos. Jesse Rapple found himself especially annoyed at the desk—a square of wood balanced on two filing cabinets—because he was sure that Stephen Dugan could afford a real desk, that the makeshift desk was one of his affectations. He'd always suspected Dugan of putting on a show: those nights he'd peered out the front window to see Mary Faith coming in from tutoring, he'd felt Dugan drove that shuddering little Metropolitan just to impress people, and he'd felt the same thing about Dugan's hair, which was always just a touch too long over the edge of his collar, as if he'd for*got*ten to get a haircut, and he'd felt the same thing about Dugan's beard. All of them affectations, little signs that the man thought he was smarter and more sophisticated than the rest of Due East. And wouldn't getting a fifteen-year-old pregnant really make him feel smart?

Rapple smiled politely, though, when Stephen Dugan came into the room, holding a paper napkin in one hand and stretching out the other for a handshake. There was no proof yet. He wasn't com*plete*ly sure Mary Faith could fall for a man like that. When he saw that Dugan's beard was damp around the mouth, he felt more flustered than ever. He never thought people with a child would eat supper after nightfall.

"I'm sorry to disturb your evening meal," he said, and Dugan smiled and shrugged. Shrugged! He wouldn't be shrugging in a minute. "I guess you're puzzled as to why I'm here," he said, hoping against hope that he didn't sound like someone selling religion door to door.

"Well, actually, no," Dugan said. "My mother called me about five minutes ago to tell me you were on your way." He said it so clearly, so confidently, so matter-of-factly that Jesse Rapple knew his guess had been all wrong. Dugan wasn't the father of Mary Faith's baby. Not the father; probably didn't know anything about it. Dugan stood there wiping his mouth with his paper napkin, discreetly looking down at the old braided rug, and Rapple could have cried. If Dugan wasn't the father, he had to start all over. If Dugan wasn't the father, he'd made an ass of himself going over to Nell Dugan's and he was making an ass of himself in her son's house, and the skinny wife with the frizzed hair, inside at the supper table, probably knew the whole story and thought it very amusing. Now Rapple didn't feel like a Bible salesman, he felt like a fool. Stephen Dugan had known he'd be coming over here in agony, and still he'd sat down to his supper.

But having started, he didn't know how to get out of it. He had to see it through. He still had to ask. "Do you know anything—"

Dugan shook his head. Sympathetically again. "I'm sorry, Mr. Rapple," he said. "I'm sorry for your sake, I'm sorry for hers. I think very highly of Mary Faith."

Everything about Stephen Dugan drove Rapple crazy: his voice was deep, his accent was light. He wasn't a handsome man—he was too skinny, like his wife, and his brown hair was starting to thin at the temples—but he was sure of himself. That he could be Nell Dugan's son was a mystery. That he could be so polite and sympathetic was enraging.

"I hope you'll let me know if there's anything I can do," said Dugan, and Rapple found himself wishing Dugan would let him take a swing at him anyway. It almost made him grin.

When he looked up, he saw that now Dugan's eyes were embarrassed, maybe embarrassed for his wife and maybe embarrassed for his study and maybe embarrassed for teaching a
little girl who was pretty enough but not pretty enough to
seduce. "You've got no idea," he persisted, but Dugan shook
his head.

Now he really had to get back home. Ears burning with
shame, he pulled down Freedom Lane. To get involved with
crazy people like that, to have them know your worst secrets:
he remembered kissing Nell Dugan and went dizzy with embarrassment. He wondered if she'd told her son *that*, too, on
the phone. He tried to imagine them speaking to each other,
one with a gravel voice, the other with bored sympathy. He
tried to imagine how Stephen and Nell Dugan had ever been
connected, physically. He was pretty sure that her son's ways
probably drove Nell crazy, too, that she scoffed at the makeshift desk and all the magazines. He heard Nell Dugan's voice
berating her son, and then he saw her bony shoulders, and
then he remembered her asking him to call her and then he
was back to kissing her. Her mouth opening. That was it—that
was the way they were connected, with those thin lips that
barely fit over their gums. It was the same mouth on the
momma and the son, only Stephen had grown a beard to hide
his. Stephen had grown a beard, and his mother had taken to
kissing men to draw them past those stingy lips.
Faith had had full lips. Full lips that looked painted on, that
were painted on, with the same deep red year after year, long
after other women showed up to Sunday services wearing pink
and even tan on their lips. Faith had always stuck to her red lips
and her stockings, no matter how hot the summer got, and
once a week she had her hair waved off her plain face at Myrt's
Beauty Shop. He had grown so used to that red on her face and
those waves off it that he had barely been able to recognize her
lying in the hospital, and once or twice he had even wanted to
ask *How could you let yourself, how could you let yourself go like that?*
even though he knew it was craziness to think such a thought
about a woman dying in pain. He had composed a hundred

bitter lines like that, and when they popped into his head—*Do you have to keep up the moaning?* and *Do you think you maybe could think of the people around you once in a while?*—he could not believe the thought had originated with him, not about Faith. He figured the devil was tempting him, that only the devil could think up such cruel questions to put to a woman who curled up in her hospital bed and panted so heavily that she could not hear a question put to her. She'd had five miscarriages before her womb swelled up with cancer, and her death was like the labors she never went through. In the weeks after she died, he woke from nightmares of his wife, lying in her mossy hospital bed, deep in her grave. He stood above her throwing down questions: *Why couldn't you give us a son?* he taunted in the dream, and from below she screeched back (though she had never raised her voice to him, never) *Why weren't you ever home? You must have been in love with Buddy Miles, not me.* He had wakened from those dreams desperate to ask her what she meant about him and Buddy Miles. She'd never in her life said a word against their friendship, or against their fishing and hunting. She'd been a little sharp when he got home from those weekends, but cleaning always put her in a bad temper, and she'd never said anything like that to him. Not even the time he and Buddy had taken off for the afternoon without telling anybody, just shut the station down, and she'd had the last miscarriage, the fifth one, the baby they hadn't even hoped for anymore. She'd finally got her sister Lizann to drive her to the hospital, and Lizann had carried along a stack of newspapers for her to sit on, so she wouldn't bleed all over the front seat of Zack's car. He'd always thought it was Lizann she resented, not him. To hear that phrase floating up from the grave: in love with Buddy Miles!

He wondered if he'd go back to having more nightmares now that Mary Faith was in this trouble. They'd already started. He wondered if he would dream of Faith in her grave, accusing him of being in love with Nell Dugan. Probably not. There wouldn't be any chance for him to be in love with Nell Dugan, because Stephen wasn't the one who did it to Mary

Faith, and now there was no more connection and the whole night had just been too much for him. Just too much.

He told himself there was no call to think of any of them, not Nell or Stephen or even Faith. The only one to think about was Mary Faith, *her* mouth, lips full and deep like her mother's. That mouth, in her sharp face, had made him think she would be a little girl forever, grinning and sassing him, pouting and twisting her lips. Somebody had seen that mouth differently.

He circled the town three times before he turned down River Street, then Oysterbed, then down his own short block, O'Connor Street. All the way from the turn he could see his brother-in-law's red car hogging the driveway, shining under his headlights. The night wasn't over yet, not if Zack had come to call. Zack was the only car dealer in Due East, the only car dealer in South Carolina, Lord, the only car dealer in America who wasn't going broke in the recession. He had seen the worst coming back in '73, when gas prices shot up, and he'd started pushing used cars and standard transmissions and sub-sub-sub-compacts, cars that couldn't fit a family of *rabbits* in them, all the while keeping the biggest, reddest Oldsmobile— a new one every year—for himself. He hired kids to hand out flyers to enlisted men coming off duty at the air station, and then he fixed up financing for them with his own small-time credit company, long-term financing at close to twenty percent interest. He was sitting pretty. Now the newest red Oldsmobile was sitting in Jesse Rapple's driveway.

And if the red car was sitting in his driveway, it meant that Faith's sister had found out somehow about Mary Faith. Lizann and Zack would never drop over for a casual chat; they never dropped over at all, not since Faith died. Lizann called, and Mary Faith said she stopped by once or twice a week in the afternoon, but she never came over at night, when she knew Jesse would be there. She didn't even fill up her tank at his gas station.

It took him five minutes to get from the truck to the back door. He didn't care if they'd heard him pulling up, if they were wondering what he was doing outside. He took the little

clump of moss he'd dragged down before and put it by the side
of the road for the garbage men.

When he walked in the back door, they all looked up in
relief. The whole kitchen smelled of Mary Faith's coffee—she
always made it too strong, strong enough to give any man the
jitters—and she got up to fetch him a cup without meeting his
eyes. She was wearing one of his old fishing shirts, blue-checkered cotton, and he imagined that underneath it her breasts
were monstrous. His daughter was a tall girl, so tall and
straight that he could barely see the bulge of her belly, but his
eyes darted back to it the whole time she was moving.

"Zack. Lizann." He stretched out a hand to his brother-in-
law, across the kitchen table, and Zack rose to greet him.

"We know all about it, Jesse," Lizann said, and pulled out a
chair for him.

Jesse sat down, resigned. He could feel the imprint of Nell
Dugan's mouth on his lips; he was sure they could all smell the
beer. The way Mary Faith avoided his eyes!

"Listen, Jesse," said Zack. "I know you're a proud man." He
forced himself to look his brother-in-law in the eye, when what
he really wanted to do was follow Mary Faith around the room.
She had set out supper for him, black-eyed peas and rice, and
left it wrapped in plastic on the dinette. Zack was picking at the
edges of the plastic as he spoke.

"This is no time for pride," Zack went on, and it was all Jesse
could do to follow the deep pitch of his voice. Zack weighed
two hundred and fifty pounds. Sometimes he looked like two-
eighty or two-ninety because of the florid pants he wore, deep
greens and rose-reds and pastel stripes. Tonight he was wearing mustard-yellow pants and a navy alligator shirt. His hair
was sparse, and the rosy top of his head bled down into his rosy
cheeks and rosy chin. His eyes were as pale as creek water, as
pale as Nell Dugan's eyes. "Lizann can take Mary Faith up to
New York," Zack said, "and have it all fixed up without a soul in
Due East being the wiser. And if you want to pay me back when
you're on your feet again, that's fine. But it's not necessary.
They can make a little vacation of it."

Jesse sighed. "Thank you, Zack. But we don't need the money."

"I've been trying to tell them," Mary Faith said. She'd let her hair down, out of the ponytail, and she was standing just as easy as a shy person could be, hiding a hand behind the coffee pot. Just as if he'd been home for supper and they'd talked the whole thing out. Just as if she'd told him who the father was. "I told them I didn't want an abortion," she said. She wasn't looking *at* him, exactly, more past him.

"Well, that's not what I mean, Mary Faith," he said, and he looked past her, too. "What I mean is that we can take care of the money end of the thing by ourselves."

"Now, Jesse," said Lizann.

"Now, Mary Faith," said Zack. "You can't go around like a nigger having a passel of brats the time you're nineteen. Your daddy's not going to let you go on welfare."

"Don't say *nigger*," said Mary Faith.

"Well you know what I mean. *Negro*. Honey, the point of what I'm saying is that you don't have to have this baby. This is the nineteen-eighties. You can have an abortion."

"Let's don't dwell on that," said Lizann. "I don't think Dr. Beady would like us to dwell on that."

"Well, Lizzieann, that's what we're *talking* about. I mean, I'm not going to put you on a plane to New York and have you come back without taking care of the thing."

"Well, we don't have to dwell on it," said Lizann. "You can see it's upsetting Mary Faith. It's not a very nice word."

"Lizann. Zack," said Jesse. He stopped.

"Jesse, listen to me. Just you sit back a minute," said Zack, and he leaned forward with a selling look in his eye. "This happened to my Betsiann, I would have thrown her out of town. I'm not kidding you. I wouldn't have let her sleep under my roof. But Betsiann grew up a few years earlier than Mary Faith, and she had a good school to go to, not that crazy high school with the blacks running wild in the halls. Now, what I'm saying is this. We've all been worried about Mary Faith, about her acting a little strange since her mother died, and I'm not saying what she did wasn't wrong—we *all* know it was wrong,

Mary Faith knows it was wrong. But what I'm saying is that we have the resources to take care of this thing and that is what we are going to do. We are going to take care of this thing. You let your pride say no to the money I can give you tonight and it means the whole town knows in a matter of weeks. Look at your little girl, Jesse. She's starting to show. You know how these old biddies talk. It's going to be all over Due East by next Thursday."

Jesse took a deep breath.

"We're your family, Jesse," said Lizann. She smiled at him with her lips pressed tight together. Faith's lips. Faith had *never* smiled with her lips pressed together that way.

"Thanks for coming by," he said. "Thanks, Zack. Lizann. You're good family to show up. But Mary Faith and I can handle this."

Mary Faith reached across the table and squeezed his hand. She hadn't touched him like that in a year. Poor little girl—she probably thought he was going to let her keep the baby.

Jesse stood up, and Lizann and Zack glared at each other across the table. Zack said: "You're making a big mistake, Jesse. We know people we can call. We can write out a check."

"Thank you, Zack. I can take care of it."

His sister-in-law rose then, shaking her head delicately. "You look like a little lost boy, Jesse," she said. "Like a little boy who lost his momma. You ought to let us help."

Jesse shook his head just as delicately. "Thank you, Lizann," he said, "but no thanks."

"My sister—"

"Your sister would have *died* she heard you say the word *abortion* and you know it," Jesse said. "She would have died if she knew I was thinking it as easy as I am."

Lizann turned away without looking at him, without kissing Mary Faith good-bye, and Zack followed. Jesse turned the lock on the kitchen door and turned to face his daughter.

She was standing at the counter, stirring her coffee round and round, and now the breasts he had imagined being monstrous really were monstrous. It was silly to talk about people knowing soon: people must know now.

"Thank you, Daddy," she said, without looking up. He thought she knew everything he'd done that night. How he'd lain on the couch with Nell Dugan.

"Honey." Funny how *that* word spilled out, how the beer loosed it for him. "I hope you know what you're saying when you say thank you, Mary Faith. I can't let you ruin your life when you're fifteen years old. I never thought I'd say it, but Uncle Zack's right. We should have the thing taken care of. I'm working on it. I'm going to figure out where we can have it done, and then it'll all be over."

She smiled up at him with her full mouth, as if she hadn't heard what he was saying. As if she were still planning on being a mother. He knew that mother-look: she was glowing, her mother's glow through all those dead pregnancies, a deep glistening, her mother's mouth, her mother's full lips. He saw Faith coming out of the beauty parlor with her lipstick just painted on, and he saw Nell Dugan pulling him down on the sofa and pressing her thin lips against his. Stephen Dugan's wife, her hair frizzed, her lips pursed. Lizann smiling with her lips pressed together.

"Mary Faith," he said sharply. "Don't scare me that way with that goofy smile."

She stopped smiling.

"Don't worry, honey," he said. "We'll figure something out." And then, still light-headed from the beer, he brushed past her to go upstairs, to try for sleep. No more dreams, he prayed. Sweet Jesus. No more moss, no more wombs alive with disease. No more mouths full of that damp, deep red.

At the top of the stairs he could hear the stillness in the kitchen; he could sense her standing below, tugging on the tail of the blue-checkered fishing shirt. "You come on up to bed," he called.

"Okay, Daddy," she said.

"You're not going to tell me who got you pregnant?"

There was no answer.

"Come on up, Mary Faith. We'll figure something out. We will." Heading for his bed, he almost believed it.

7

Home Life

It was quiet the week after my aunt and uncle came to the house. My father came in late so he wouldn't have to talk to me, and the top floor smelled up of beer. I figured he was out on his own, probably at the Rebel Tavern: Momma would've died.

My aunt had quit calling me, too. Probably she and Uncle Zack had talked it over and decided to give it a ten-days rest. Then they would come over with cash and an airplane ticket.

Between them, they'd have me pinned, and I figured I'd better start making plans for running away. This idea of a holy abortion was stuck deep in all their heads. My father wouldn't tie me down to have the baby taken from me, but he'd probably drive me to doctors and airports and even psychiatrists again, and I wasn't sticking around for any of it. Daddy would be fine once I *had* the baby—he wouldn't kick me out or anything—so all I had to do was find a place to hide for another month, until no doctor would take it from me. Then I could come back and answer an ad in the back of the *Due East Courier* for addressing envelopes at home. I could pay for my baby, and my daddy could pay for me. I *was* only fifteen.

The trouble was, I didn't know where to run away and be pregnant. I didn't even have the money for a bus ticket out of town. Unlike Michael Jagger, I wasn't thinking of the hills of North Carolina or a motorcycle gang in Atlanta; I would settle for some nuns in Charleston or Savannah who would take me in and never breathe the word *abortion*.

But now that Michael Jagger was dead, I didn't know any Catholics to ask about homes for unwed mothers. I thought about an anonymous call to the priest, but I had seen Father Berkeley around town, shuffling and bowing, and I didn't want to talk to him. He was plump, and balding, and he wore blue seersucker priest suits. Everybody in Due East said he was an alcoholic. He had kind, light eyes, and I knew if I called him asking where I could go he'd call me *sweetheart* or *sugar* and try to find out who I was. Next thing I knew, he'd be talking to my father and driving me to the home himself. He'd feel sorry for me and ask me to address the Due East Right to Life Committee and his heart would break if I told him I didn't believe in God and didn't mind who else had an abortion.

No, what I needed was nuns, some tough cookies with a maternity center for girls who weren't praying when they said *Jesus Christ*. The sisters would talk to me about religion, but they'd know beforehand I wasn't going to buy it, and they'd see I had good books to read and they'd make all the mothers-to-be turn out the lights at ten o'clock.

So it occurred to me that the best place to look for a Catholic who could tell me where to find these tough nuns was in the Catholic church, and that was where I planned to go.

On Monday afternoon after school I walked from the elementary school, where the bus left me off, over to Division Street. Division Street still has a few old houses, a couple of which they are fixing up to be condominiums, but mostly it has turned into a strip of chain stores. The Catholic church does not even have a steeple. It is wooden and white, about a quarter the size of the Baptist church, with a little green cemetery out back. It is neat and tidy and looks completely out of place on Division Street. On one side of the church is the stone statue of the Virgin Mary that Michael Jagger spray-painted the nipples on. Now that the Catholics have cleaned up his statue, Mary's breasts are round white points on a browning body. Next to her is a sign that says: Our Lady of Perpetual

Help Catholic Church, Due East, South Carolina, Founded 1801 by Ignatius McGarrigle.

The mass schedule was taped on the front door. There were none in the afternoon, so I thought my chances of avoiding Father Berkeley were good. I'd already figured what I could say if he *did* walk in—I'd tell him I needed to sit down in the cool. But I thought it more likely that I'd get a pious Catholic coming in to pray in the afternoon.

I sat in the back pew to take in Our Lady of Perpetual Help. Next to First Baptist of Due East, it looked like a play church. There were only twenty narrow rows on each side, and the poor Catholics didn't even have a choir loft, just a sad little organ in the back corner. There was another statue of Mary facing the left-hand row of pews, but this one was not stone, just painted plaster. She was wearing blue and white, and her cheeks were a high bright pink. Jesus, on the other side of the altar, had reddish hair and a sparse beard, and his skin was as pale as Michael Jagger's had been.

Between the statues was the recess for the altar. The Catholics had two: against the back wall was an ornate one, with the Last Supper painted in relief. In front of it they had put a sleek modern one, with a long, narrow cloth. I liked the old one myself. I was willing to bet that any McGarrigles left in Due East were put out when the old altar was cast aside.

I stayed in the back pew for an hour, but no one came in to pray.

On Tuesday afternoon, I walked up and down to see the wall plaques dragging out every tortuous step of the crucifixion. In the Baptist church, there is one plain wooden cross, and Jesus has stepped down from it. He is *gone.*

After I looked at all the pictures, I read a pamphlet in the back rack called *Father Neumiller Talks to Teenagers.* Father Neumiller advised that we not do what I'd gone and done, but I didn't mind his saying it. He wrote lines like: "You have a beautiful soul." He probably read those lines aloud, and he probably drank as much as Father Berkeley did, and he probably wanted a woman until he ached. I put the pamphlet back in the rack before I'd actually finished it; if a Catholic did walk in, I didn't want him getting any ideas from my reading material.

I stayed for an hour again. No one came.

On Wednesday afternoon, I brought my trig homework, but I was finished in twenty minutes. No Catholics were streaming in to pray. I knew they had to come in *some*time—there were fresh roses at Mary's feet, and two candles were flickering under Jesus. They just weren't coming in for me.

I was sure by now that I had the church to myself for the afternoon, so I made my way up to the altar. If I was going to be spending all my afternoons in Our Lady of Perpetual Help instead of making my daddy's supper, I deserved a tour at least.

There was nothing on the modern altar but the clean white cloth and a Bible bound in red. On the back altar, though, was a golden tabernacle, signed with a cross, with a door on a hinge. I had never seen a tabernacle. I wondered if Father Berkeley kept his whiskey inside, and decided to sneak a look, but the moment I moved to open it, the big wooden church door creaked open, too.

For a second I stood still, facing the altar. Then I took a tissue out of my pocket and began dusting the golden door the way I dusted my father's house, polishing it in smaller and smaller circles, so that I would not have to turn around. I could say I was cleaning—paying my respects by cleaning. I hoped Father Berkeley was drunk.

It was not Father Berkeley. When I turned around I saw Mr. Dugan, Stephen Dugan, standing at the back door of Our Lady of Perpetual Help with his eyes cast down, paying not the least attention to me at the altar. He started to move into my back pew, but when he saw the school books he finally looked up. By now the tissue was a mashed ball in my fist, and I believe I was still holding my breath.

But Mr. Dugan did not look in the least surprised. He smiled and nodded, and then moved to the other side of the church, and chose *that* back pew. He kneeled down and hunched his shoulders forward.

I sprinted to the back of the church like a cornered rabbit, gathered up my books, and shoved open the back door. The sight of Mr. Dugan had almost cured me of wanting to find a Catholic, and I began to walk up Division Street with my mind wiped blank of any plans for running away. I would just go home, and make deviled crabs for supper, and make my escape routes later.

I had gone two blocks—up to the Mr. Tire Store—when a car horn tooted beside me. I knew it was Mr. Dugan's: there is only one Metropolitan in Due East, and even its toot sounds foreign and genteel. Up to three weeks before, when the spring tutoring sessions ended, Mr. Dugan had been giving me a ride home in that old yellow Metropolitan every Monday and Wednesday night, with Michael Jagger's space in the back empty.

I kept on walking. Mr. Dugan had seen me in the Catholic church, defiling a golden tabernacle.

But Mr. Dugan rolled down his passenger window and coasted up behind me until he could say, "Let me give you a lift, Mary Faith." His voice reminded me of Father Neumiller's, gentle and firm. Mr. Dugan had introduced me to Michael Jagger. Mr. Dugan had seen Michael Jagger hand me notes. Mr. Dugan could see my belly growing bigger. If anyone in the whole town besides my father and my aunt and my uncle knew I was pregnant, it was Mr. Dugan. And as far as I could tell, he was the only one in town who could figure out that Michael Jagger was the father. I slid into his front seat, but I could feel my jumper pulling too tight around me, and my hair too heavy and dank against the back of my neck. I was sure I was in for another interrogation, and I didn't so much as glance at Mr. Dugan. He was modern—he would probably vote for an abortion, too. He was the swell young reporter for the *Courier* who wore a beard and corduroy pants, even in the summertime, and he drove all Due East crazy with his columns. They called him liberal, except for my daddy, who said, "You watch out for that *radical* stuff." I knew he ran the tutoring sessions for money, but all the dropouts giggled and swooned at him; they liked him because he was distant, because they thought his

mysterious smiles meant he was lusting after them. He wasn't
even handsome: he was going bald, and he was so skinny his
pants almost dropped off. If you looked closely, you could see
he had grown the beard to hide a thin mouth, but he had a
deep clear voice and when you talked to him he raised both his
eyebrows, as if you were about to say something real important. Sometimes you did say something important, just to keep
his eyebrows arched at you that way.

"Where to?" he said—not *what were you doing in there?* or *are
you pregnant?* I hardly knew how to answer such a simple question. I didn't want to go home, so I didn't say anything, just
held on to my armrest, and looked at my knees poking through
the jumper. Mr. Dugan kept on driving. He didn't act surprised that I didn't answer him, and he didn't turn off for the
Point, to take me home, either. Instead he went up to River
Street and then all the way across town, back to where Chessy
Creek cuts into the subdivisions. Finally he turned off on Freedom Lane, a short block that ended on the creek. (Mr. Redleg,
the coroner, named all the streets in Due East up until 1969.
Back here, under the pines, he called the blocks Constitution
Street, Independence Road, and States Rights Alley.) I hardly
ever came to this part of town, and didn't know who owned
which house, so when Mr. Dugan pulled into the last house on
Freedom Lane, number 47, I thought he was turning me over
to the family court judge, or taking me to meet the Jagger
family. I froze against my door. I was calculating how far it was
up Freedom Lane to States Rights Alley and that big, empty
railroad warehouse.

But Mr. Dugan said: "We're home," and came over to open
my door as if he brought home schoolgirls every afternoon.
When he held out his hand to help me up, he raised both
eyebrows.

He took me by the elbow and guided me inside, through the
living room. When he called out: "Marygail? Maureen?" no
one answered, and then he propelled me straight into a dark
hall. *I* wanted to stay and look at the furniture. The Dugans
had big flowered couches with rolled arms, the kind of luxury
my mother would have killed for. The night courses must have

been paying for his wife's taste in furniture. Parrots and blue camellias, for Christ's sake.

He pushed me along into a little study, with worn furniture and windows looking out on pecan trees and crape myrtle in the front yard. I sank into a big stuffed armchair with fluff coming out of its seat, and Mr. Dugan left the room as soon as he saw me settled in it.

I didn't know why Mr. Dugan had brought me to Freedom Lane or his house or his study, and I struggled out of my soft chair to take stock of his room before he got back. The room was just what I'd expected from him: neat little piles of paper on his desk, an old Royal typewriter, books on the floor lined up just so. Over the light switch was a mimeographed flyer matted on a black board, and I knew before I went to look at it that it was one of Michael Jagger's. He had drawn it when Baby Rooney was suspended from school for getting caught behind the breezeway with her jeans down around her knees. They didn't throw out the football player she was with, because he'd kept all his clothes on. Michael's sign said: Don't Let Them Kick Out Baby! and the cartoon showed a football player kicking a baby in a bunting over the Due East goalpost. It got Michael suspended for three days himself. I hadn't counted on seeing it decorating anybody's walls.

Mr. Dugan came back with two beers and handed me one without so much as flicking the pop top back. I sipped my beer and looked out at the pine trees over his shoulder, and he sipped his beer and looked at Michael Jagger's flyer over my shoulder. We hadn't talked much on the rides home, either.

Finally, he said: "Would you like to talk about it?"

I shook my head no. It sounded to me as if he'd been listening to the kind of talk the local hot line people had been shoveling out ever since Michael took the Quaaludes: how teenagers had to talk, and parents had to listen.

"Your father came to see me," he said.

"What?"

"Your father came to see me," he said. "He wanted to know if I had any idea who the baby's father was. I told him I didn't know, but I've got some suspicions, Mary Faith. You don't have to be *that* brave." He raised one eyebrow, the right one.

"I'm not being brave," I said, and then I stood up again so I could face the Baby Rooney flyer instead of him. I had never noticed before that Michael had drawn little curves for breasts on the baby being kicked. "So I guess you know I'm pregnant," I said. "I'm sorry about my father coming over here."

"I was glad he came," said Mr. Dugan. He lit a cigarette and put his right eyebrow down. "Would you like to talk about what we were both doing in that church?"

"I've got to go, Mr. Dugan. I've got to get home and start fixing my daddy's supper."

He leaned forward with the cigarette. "Fine," he said. "Fine. But I want you to know that if you need me I'm here. Let me give you a lift."

"Thanks," I said. "No thanks. I need the exercise. This is nice over here, on the creek. I'll just walk back by the water."

"It's no trouble. Looks like rain."

"Thanks, anyway," I said, and so he put down his beer and led me through his dark hall and let me out his front door. He touched my shoulder almost into a squeeze, so that my breasts jumped a little, in surprise, and then he said, "You let me know if I can do anything, Mary Faith. I always thought very highly of Michael. You were good to—"

"Thanks," I mumbled again, and set off toward Constitution. Mr. Dugan probably thought I cried myself to sleep every night over Michael Jagger, and I hardly thought of him at all.

It was late when I got home, and I set to work cracking crab claws. Momma always used the cans, but I knew Daddy liked the fresh stuff. I was hoping he'd make it home for supper, but by seven I knew he wasn't coming.

I couldn't eat by myself, and the oven had made the house too hot, so I got out my wine and mixed it with a little orange soda in case Daddy did walk in on me. It was then that I started to think about calling Mr. Dugan back. *He* was a Catholic. He'd know where to find those nuns. He wouldn't tell my father where I'd gone. It would be the most embarrassing thing I'd ever done in my life, but the more wine and orange soda I drank, the less embarrassing it seemed.

Finally I looked up his number in the book and dialed it. When he answered, I told him I needed to speak to a Catholic.

"I'm not a Catholic anymore, Mary Faith," he said. "I'd be glad to help you out, but I'm not a Catholic anymore. I'm what they call a bad Catholic." He laughed a strange laugh, and in the background I could hear his wife asking him who it was.

I said I was sorry, and tried to say thanks anyway, but he kept on: "Don't worry. Don't you worry, Mary Faith. You are probably wondering to yourself what I was doing in that church if I am not a Catholic. The answer is this. I came to see my father's grave in the churchyard and the sun got to me. So I came into the cool for a minute."

"Me, too," I said. "It was real humid on the street. I just stepped into the cool."

He didn't answer, so I said again that I was sorry to bother him and he answered, "Mary Faith, I can tell you want to talk. I'll come right over."

"No," I said. "No, please don't. My father will be home soon."

"Then you come right over here," he said. "You get yourself over to this house as quickly as you can. You have a bike?"

"Yes, sir."

"Does it have a headlight? It's getting misty out."

"Yes, sir."

"You know you go all the way down River Street to Constitution? Then cut off on Freedom? It's number forty-seven."

"Yes, sir," I said, and hung up before I remembered to say good-bye. I was thinking about balancing myself on my bike with all the extra weight. I was wondering if I should leave my father's crabs in the oven to stay warm, or whether I should rest them on top of the stove so they wouldn't dry out. I was imagining what Mr. Dugan's wife would think of me, coming over to her house that way.

The bike ride sobered me up, and when I went to ring the Dugan bell I was damp from the drizzle that had followed me.

His wife answered. She was tall, about as tall as I am, but thin, with tiny wrists and a flat stomach and no breasts that *I* could see. Her hair was brown and frizzy, and her eyes were dark in a long, horsey face that was as tanned as the rest of her. She looked like one of those women my cousin Betsiann makes friends with. They take turns minding each other's children so they can golf and play tennis; they wear shorts starting in March, and bathing suits starting in April, and they are always rubbing cocoa butter into their bony elbows.

"Uhmhum?" she said.

"I'm here to see Mr. Dugan," I said. I was still standing in the rain.

She let out a broad grin and hollered, "Stephen! It's one of your little groupies!" and then she said, "Don't mind me. Come on in."

She went back to sitting with her little girl on her flowered couch. The child never looked up, but Mrs. Dugan grinned back at me and picked up a big green bottle of wine off the coffee table.

"Care for a drink?" she said. "Or are you as young as the rest of them?"

"Marygail! For Christ's sake!" The minute Mr. Dugan walked into the room I could see that he was drunk too. His eyes were red, and he looked as if he'd been lying down or sitting at his desk with his head propped up on the typewriter. "I see you met my *wife*," he said.

"Oh yes," she said. This time she didn't turn around.

"Come on back to the study," Mr. Dugan said.

"Yes, y'all go on back to the study," said his wife. "I wouldn't want to disturb you."

Mr. Dugan's face reddened. "Marygail," he said slowly, "this is Mary Faith *Rap*ple. You met her father the other night. Remember?"

His wife turned to face us then. "Oh yes," she said. "Oh, *yes.*" Her voice floated out cool and sharp, and finally their little girl turned to look me over, too. She was about four and took after her father more than she did her mother. She was pale and blonde and had that thin strip of mouth her daddy did. When she saw me, she turned back again quickly to the television set, and put her hands over her ears.

Her mother went on: "You wouldn't be*lieve* the number of times Stephen helps people out of trouble. Although I hope he's not too intimately involved with your trouble."

Mr. Dugan took a single step toward his wife, but before he could raise even his voice the little girl spun around again and said, "Don't fight! Don't fight!" She skipped up to circle the living room rug, humming and holding her hands over her ears, and her parents glared at each other over her. Mr. Dugan was having trouble just hanging on to the arm of the couch, but finally he stepped in and scooped his little girl up. First she buried her head in his shoulder, and then she slid down and went back to the television as if nothing had happened.

"I better be going," I whispered, but Mr. Dugan barked out: "No. Stay."

His wife shrugged, turned her back to him, and leaned over to turn up the television volume. She sat, and the little girl nestled back in her mother's arms.

"Really, I better be going."

"No," said Marygail, in that same sharp voice. "I a*polo*gize. I had a shotgun wedding myself, and I don't suppose Stephen had anything to do with knocking you up." It was hard to hear her over the television. Mr. Dugan told her to watch her language in front of you know who.

I followed him back to his study and collapsed into the same chair as before, listening to hear if his wife was coming down the hall to check on us. Mr. Dugan stood by the window looking out at nothing, at the rain, the pines, and said, "I'm sorry she was such a bitch. She's not usually that way."

I tried to remember the speech I'd memorized pedaling the bicycle, and I took a deep breath. "Mr. Dugan," I said, "I was just wondering if you might possibly know of some kind of religious home, something nuns run in Charleston or Savannah that might take in a teenage girl to have her baby. And wouldn't mind if she's not Catholic. Or Christian," I said as an afterthought. "But I could pretend I'm still Baptist if that's what it takes."

First he whirled around and stared down at my face for a long time. Then he came over to the armchair and knelt in front of it, and then he took my hands in his. He reeked of gin. He had never even brushed my hand before, and I couldn't help but stare at his big white hands circling mine. He didn't say a word.

Finally I said, "My daddy wants me to have an abortion."

He started a sentence—"My little girl"—but he never finished it. He got up, went to the window again, took out a cigarette and stared out. Then suddenly he said, "I was halfway through my dissertation when Marygail got pregnant. I don't know what you can tell your daddy."

"Do you know of a home?" I said.

"A home? No, I don't believe I do." He stroked his beard as if he were really considering it. "You know, my sister had her baby alone. She was sixteen at the time. It's hard, Mary Faith."

"I guess it is. Did she go to a home?"

He laughed. "You might say that. She came to *my* home. I took her in when my mother threw her out." Somehow I didn't think he'd be offering to take me in, too.

"I've got to find someplace," I said.

"Do you need money? I could lend you a couple of hundred." He was beginning to slouch down, drunker, lighting cigarettes one after the other.

"I've got to get going," I said.

"Mary Faith, I wish there was something someone could *do* in a situation like this," he said, and before I knew it, he had come to the low armchair and was trying to hold my hands again. When I got to my feet he circled his arms around my shoulders, and I slid out. I couldn't be*lieve* he didn't know where some sort of nuns' home was.

Marygail was friendly on my way out. Her little girl was asleep on the couch, and she offered to drive me home in the rain or get me a Coke, but I said no thanks. She said she was sorry if she'd sounded nasty, but it was so hot already and only the beginning of May. "You know, there's a doctor on the

Calhoun Road might help you out," she said. "You could get it done right in Due East."

"I'd best be getting home," I said.

"From the looks of you, you'd probably need the salt by now, but it's quick," she said.

I was inching toward the door. "My father's probably home," I said. "I usually put his supper on the table."

She shook her head and grinned. "You call me if you need that number. I was *twenty*, and having a baby was the worst thing that could have happened to me. She's a doll now, look, but you call me if you change your mind."

I backed out of the door and onto the bike. The drizzle had turned to steady spring rain that glued my jumper to my belly, and the night shone gray-blue. I didn't want to go down River Street, so I took the back loop around town, down the Calhoun Road, across Oysterbed and up Division. When I passed Our Lady of Perpetual Help I could see a dark figure in the cemetery, gliding in the rain.

I was drenched by the time I walked into my own kitchen. The crabs were cold on top of the stove and the dinette table was as shiny clean as when I'd left. I could feel the night breeze crawling along my wet arms and legs, and I took a dish towel to wrap around my ponytail. There was nothing to do but climb the stairs and go to bed: my father was going to be out for another late night.

Upstairs I pulled the wet clothes off and looked down at my belly. Five and a half months. I was a fool to think nobody could see it. I remembered Mr. Dugan's little girl running around the living room rug, and I wondered if those home abortions, hot baths and epsom salts, worked when you were this far along. When I pulled on my old white summer nightgown, it stuck to me, like gauze in a wound that hasn't closed. I went to fetch the phone book from the hall, but there were three doctors listed on the Calhoun Road, all of them new to Due East, and I didn't know which one took care of things.

I came back to my narrow bed and lay on it without even taking down the old spread my mother had put there. I was chilled but I didn't want to be covered, didn't want anything touching the ache of my legs where they'd pedaled to Mr. Dugan's house. The baby kicked me, hard, and I rolled over on my side. It was the first time I'd been aware of the kicking all day.

The phone rang and I sat up to go answer it, but the baby kicked again, three times, fluttering, harder, and I lay back down in the luxury of it. The phone was probably Mr. Dugan, with the name of the doctor, or my father, drunk, too, or Aunt Lizann. It was easier to lie all alone, until the kicking and the ringing subsided together, until the chill that had passed over me stopped.

The rain tapered off, and I looked at the calendar. Tomorrow was Thursday. The library was open late: I thought maybe I'd go there around suppertime, when there was only one clerk on, and steal the Savannah Yellow Pages. Maybe they would have a home for unwed mothers listed.

8

Lovers

When Jesse Rapple stooped down to put his shoes under Nell Dugan's bed, he saw a pile of *Raunch* magazines there, the top one sliding off the neat stack. He was not even surprised. Beered up as he had been every night for the past two weeks, nothing Nell Dugan could say or do would surprise him.

When he'd finally worked up the courage to lift her sleeveless shirt up over her bony arms, she'd mumbled, underneath the shirt: "It's about time," and when he'd turned his back to her on the bed and asked if they shouldn't do something about birth control—he didn't know anything about what people did for birth control nowadays, not after a lifetime of trying to make Faith pregnant—she said, "Jesse Rapple, I am fifty years old and I am not likely to have a baby *now.*"

That hadn't surprised him, either. He'd known she was older than his forty, at least ten years older—if anything, he would have guessed she was fifty-five or fifty-six. Those years in the boat, in Chessy Creek, had aged her.

It took him three minutes to make love to Nell Dugan once they were naked. After, they lay back on the new pink flowered sheets in the air-conditioning. Every time he closed his eyes his head seemed to jiggle in tiny circles, so he opened them again and tried lying on his side, his stomach, his other side. Nell lay rigid on her back, staring at the ceiling, her mouth stretched in a wide grin.

"What you smiling at?" he said.

"You," she said. "You're shy."

His head stopped swimming when he was on his right side, facing her. "I'm not shy so much as preoccupied," he said.

"With Mary Faith," she said, in a flat voice.

He rolled over on his other side. He hadn't been going on about Mary Faith's situation; he didn't know why she had to have that *at*titude about it. He'd been leaving his little girl to eat supper alone in that big house so he could come get drunk with Nell Dugan and make love to her and find out she kept magazines under her bed that half his friends would blush to look at. He thought of rising to drag on his pants, to go home to Mary Faith, but his head was heavy and foggy and dull, and he decided he'd better lie for a few more minutes before he tried to drive.

"It *is* Mary Faith." She was accusing him.

Jesse took a deep breath. He couldn't believe he'd done this, couldn't believe he'd gotten hooked up with an old woman, a skinny, wizened old woman who touched him in places Faith wouldn't have even *looked* at, who had netted him like he was some tiny helpless shrimp. He had a sudden panicked feeling that she did this often, that he wasn't the first man to be lured in here since her husband died, that she'd bought the apartment just so she could seduce any man in Due East who was fool enough to come knocking on her door.

"Yeah, it's Mary Faith," he said, and tried to make his voice as flat and as even as hers. "It's Mary Faith I'm preoccupied with because I've got to figure out how to get an abortion for her and I don't know how to go about getting the money or getting the doctor or getting her to do it." He'd held back even talking about his daughter to Nell the past two weeks, and Nell hadn't brought it up, either. She'd just gone on opening beer after beer for him, and when he was sotted on that she'd ply him with her beer-batter fried chicken and her beer-batter fried oysters and her beer-batter fried shrimp and pork chops and ham steaks, and when she was done he felt so doused with beer and oil that every visit to this woman's house left him with a greasy coating all over his skin.

"Well, for pity's sake, why didn't you say so?" Nell said, and before he knew it, she was sitting up and rubbing his back while she talked. "Why didn't you say that's what you been worried about? You can *drive* her to the clinic in Williams, it doesn't cost but a couple of hundred dollars, I can *give* you a couple hundred dollars if you need it."

His whole back stiffened under her fingers. "How do you know about all that?" he said. A clinic, in Williams, thirty miles away—nobody'd told him. He hadn't paid any attention to the abortion news flashes before.

"I know about that because every old lady in the Catholic church is getting ready to march on the Williams clinic and tear it down brick by brick," she said, and then she giggled.

Jesse didn't giggle: he could see Mary Faith in the clinic while the women of Our Lady of Perpetual Help massed outside, knocking on the windows, looking in to see her on some operating table. Maybe they'd enlist the ladies of First Baptist of Due East, too, and half the females in town would be able to march on Mary Faith.

"I don't know," he said. "A clinic. What do you do? Call them?"

Nell dug her fingers deep into his shoulders. "Of course you call them. They'll think you're the father!" She giggled again.

"I am the father," he said, morosely. His head was beginning to clear: he could picture himself in the gas station, early, before any cars were on the road, calling up the clinic. "I don't know about a clinic."

"Well, I thought you were worried about money," she said. "You can always go to a private doctor. Stephen's wife says there's a new one over in the medical building does abortions, but you'd probably have to sell your house to pay him."

"I don't know how I'm going to get her there," Jesse said. "She watched her momma go into the hospital too many times."

"It's not such a big deal," Nell said. "Don't you know every family in Due East has watched somebody go in a hospital and never come out? You're not helping her being so soft on her. She doesn't go into a clinic now, she's going to be going into a hospital a little while later, and carrying out a bundle she doesn't want."

They lay in silence after that until Jesse said: "What about Ruthie?"

"My Ruthie?" said Nell. "I never could talk any sense into my daughter. She was going to have that baby and that was that. But with Ruthie it was different. Her daddy was Catholic and he wouldn't have *let* her get an abortion. And Ruthie is stubborn. And they didn't have clinics then."

"That's right," Jesse said. "They didn't have clinics then." He closed his eyes. The awful swirling had stopped, and he could take a deep breath now without the bed churning. He could just drop under for a minute, take a catnap, and still be back home by midnight. He felt the pink flowered pillow beneath his hand and drifted off to sleep, a sleep that was as unsteady as the waking drunkenness had been, and he dreamed of Faith. Again. This time he had to carry his wife off to an abortion clinic before the rains started, but his wife wouldn't go. He covered the floor of his pickup with piles of soft newspapers, a paper bed, and still Faith clung to the kitchen table. The bed in the pickup was soaked. Finally he tied her into a sack and carried her out into the rain in his arms, as if she were the baby.

He woke after midnight. Nell, beside him, had thrown off even the thin sheet that covered her and lay curled on her side. He covered her quickly, and pulled on his own pants, and drove himself home without a trace of the light-headedness he'd felt before.

He felt it the next morning, though. His head ached and shimmied, and every time his thoughts drew him back to being at Nell's the night before, or bending down to put his shoes under the bed, or getting a first glimpse of her brown nipples —like boys' nipples, almost, flat on her chest—he made himself concentrate on how much money was in the checkbook or whether he could persuade Lee Mac to take two weeks off without pay. His pants smelled of beer, even his socks, Lord, even his *shoes*, and he dressed warily. He was going to have breakfast with Mary Faith this morning.

He hadn't taken a meal with his daughter in two weeks. Every morning when he got downstairs she had something waiting for him: corn bread, cereal, boiled eggs, runny grits, greasy sausages. Something. And every morning since he'd met Nell he'd said, "Sorry, honey, I've got a mess of work down at the station. I'll just pick up a box of doughnuts at the 7-11." She would say that it was okay, and ask him if he'd be home for supper, looking at him with that hurt blank look of her mother's, her lips just starting to purse, and he would answer: "Well, I guess so. I have to work things out. I'll give you a call."

Then every night he'd gone to Nell's vowing he'd get home for supper, swearing he'd call her if he was going to be late, and every night Nell poured the beer faster and faster. By eight o'clock it would be too embarrassing to call Mary Faith, so he'd stay and have a fried supper with Nell, and sneak into his own house at one in the morning.

But today he was going to face her. He pulled on the smelly socks from the night before; Mary Faith had told him, three weeks before, that he'd better give her five dollars to get some new socks, but he hadn't had the five dollars to give her. She was using the ones with holes as dust rags. He could hear her stirring downstairs. She'd be dressed in school clothes by the time he got down there, her hair pulled back in the same ponytail she wore every morning because she could comb her hair and tie it back in fifteen seconds, her books on the counter opened to some homework she hadn't finished the night before. She'd have the coffee ready, and she'd look at him with that blank sharp face, lips barely pursed, and she'd say, "There's breakfast if you want it, Daddy."

He came downstairs practicing different ways to let her know he was staying for breakfast, but when he walked into the kitchen her back was turned and finally he just said: "That bacon smells good."

She didn't even turn around from the stove.

"I saved on the other meat this week," she said. "I just eat a couple of slices in the morning."

"Mind throwing a few slices on for me?"

"Oh," she said, "you're going to *eat* with me?"

"Mary Faith."

She put on more bacon for him, and poured him his coffee, and set a place for him at the dinette table without ever once meeting his eyes. Finally it was all on the table, white toast and a jar of grape jelly, coffee and bacon, and when she sat down opposite him, still averting her eyes, he said, "Mary Faith, I've found out about this abortion thing."

She didn't answer.

"There's a clinic in Williams where you can get it done, baby."

She chugged down her coffee, wiped her mouth, and said, "Well, *I* know you can get it done in Williams. That's the one the Catholic ladies are trying to close down. I knew you could get it done in Williams before I knew I was pregnant." And then she met his eyes with her face erased of all the blankness, straining now, and she started to cry. She hadn't cried in front of him since her mother went into the hospital for the first operation. She hadn't cried at the funeral. She hadn't cried telling him she was pregnant.

"I could drive you up there next week," he said softly, and she cried harder, crumpling her napkin in her fist.

"It'll all be over soon," he tried, and her crying trickled off. She sat with her napkin held to her eyes, and Jesse picked at his bacon and jellied his toast, waiting for her to stop.

When she did, she said: "Where have you been?"

"What?" he said.

"Where have you been every night, out drinking? Momma would've died."

"Mary Faith, leave your mother out of it. Keep a civil tongue in your head."

"Well, I want to know where you've been."

Jesse stared hard at his daughter, at the light, intense eyes. "I've been out trying to arrange things for you," he said, and filled his mouth with bacon sandwich.

She picked at her food for a minute and then said, fiercely, "It's been *lonely* here."

He swallowed his sandwich.

"It's been lonely," she said again, and threw the wad of paper napkin across the table. "When I lie in my bed I can hear Momma in the sewing room. I shouldn't have to listen to that."

"Mary Faith!"

She started to cry again. "Well, I can," she said, wiping her eyes. "I can hear her making me a maternity dress."

"Mary Faith," he said quickly, "I'm going to take care of things for you. You're not going to have to worry about a maternity dress." About a year after Faith was gone, she'd said she could hear her mother in the kitchen, cleaning out under the sink, or that she could hear her in the garage, straightening. That was when he'd taken her to Dr. Black, who had said to take her to a psychologist. "Mary Faith, you didn't mean you could really *hear* your momma, did you?"

"Oh, Daddy," she cried. "Do you have to be so literal?"

"I just want to make sure—"

"You leave me all alone in the house and sure I hear things. I can hear things in her room and in your bedroom and in the kitchen. And I start imagining that for the rest of my life I'll be lying alone in bed or cooking for myself. Only I won't. I'm not going to be alone anymore, don't you see, because I'm going to have a baby. And I'll tell you something else, when I have this baby I'm not ever going to leave her alone at night, not ever, not to go out drinking at some stinking bar. And don't you ever ask to have breakfast with me again, because me and my baby have been doing fine at breakfast all alone without you." She ran to the counter for her books.

"Mary Faith! You get back here to this table." He thought she hesitated at the counter.

"I mean it, Mary Faith."

She picked up her books and looked back at him, her face smoothed into composure, the same face that had met him these past weeks. "Daddy," she said, "I have to tell you one more thing. I'm sorry to have you worrying about money. Don't worry about money, because I'm going to address envelopes at home, or something like that, and we'll get by. But if you don't want my baby in the house, then I guess you don't want me. So please don't say it one more time, because you *know* Momma wouldn't have wanted me to have an abortion." She walked out the back door.

"Mary Faith!" he called out, one last time, sharper than all the rest, but she was gone. He rose and banged his plate down on the counter and unplugged the coffee pot. He decided to clear the table for her, and put the jar of grape jelly back into the refrigerator. "I didn't *ask* you to go out and get pregnant. I didn't *ask* you to keep the boy's name secret."

He scraped the plates into the garbage. "You think your momma would be so upset about the word *abortion,* well how do you think she'd feel about your sleeping with some boy in the back of some car?"

He didn't know where she dumped the bacon grease, so he opened the back door and threw it beside the steps. She had already walked out of sight.

"How do you think your momma would feel about me sleeping with an old widow lady, huh?" he said, slamming the door shut. "How do you think she'd feel about that? I never cheated on her, Mary Faith, not once, never once, never once, and it's not your business to tell your father what to do." The dishes looked up at him from the counter, covered with crumbs and smears.

It was only nine o'clock in the morning, and Jesse found himself turning into Pinetowne again. He hadn't *planned* to drop by Nell's; the truck seemed to turn in of its own will. After he had washed all the dishes for Mary Faith, and wiped the table for her, he'd gone upstairs to his wife's sewing room and opened the closet. Lizann had told him to throw all the clothes out, had said she'd do it for him, but he had saved them stubbornly. "Maybe Mary Faith will want them one day," he had said to his sister-in-law, when what he meant was that it helped him to be able to open the closet door and look at them from time to time, helped him remember what she'd looked like, how she'd passed the time. He hadn't been in her sewing room for a year now, and when he'd opened the door this time he'd been awed by the volume of the dresses. There must have been two dozen maternity dresses hanging in there—every time she got pregnant again, she'd made herself a new wardrobe. The old clothes, she said, just reminded her of the baby she had lost.

He'd stood in the closet door for a while, and finally fingered one of the tent dresses. He'd never imagined that he would be able to remember the pattern, but the faded blue flowers rushed back at him, and he could smell the cologne she used to splash on, and picture her sandals. It was one of the earliest, probably one she'd worn with Mary Faith. There were bound to be five or six dresses, maybe even ten or twelve, that would fit Mary Faith: his wife and his daughter were both tall women.

But then he had shaken himself away from the dresses. He had time to make the phone call to Williams, away from the station and whoever might hear him there, but instead he'd gone out to the truck and let it drive him to Nell's place.

He was fidgety as he rang her bell—the station was losing money every minute it stayed closed—and he didn't know what he'd say when she answered, aside from "I can't make it tonight." But she solved the problem for him by fluttering to let him in and saying: "What in God's name are you doing here at this hour of the morning? Sit down, I'm on the phone."

The phone was in the living room, and he could hear every word Nell spat out. "Stephen," she was saying, "I don't care if your sister wants to visit Due East with the National Guard escorting her, she's not staying in Pinetowne." She was furious.

Jesse fumbled for a cigarette and realized he'd left them, the night before, in Nell's bedroom. After he'd fetched them from the night table and come back down the hallway, he could hear Nell's voice still raised: "She's so worried about that little boy's safety, she shouldn't be bringing him into Due East. Now let me speak to your wife. That little Rapple girl's father is trying to fix up an abortion for her and I need the name of the doctor on the Calhoun Road." Jesse gestured frantically, waving his arms in a no!-no!-no! sweep, but Nell smiled sweetly at him and went on. "It's none of your business what I've got to do with it, Stephen, now go call Marygail to the phone. Well, have her call me, hear?"

Jesse sat on the sofa with his mouth open. "You shouldn't be telling your son that," he said.

Nell sat beside him and ruffled his hair. "Don't be silly, Jesse. I can see what needs to happen. You need to have somebody take *over* for you, somebody to push you out on the road. You *know* what's best for your daughter."

"I'm not sure I do," Jesse said.

"Well, you let me handle the details," Nell said. "You hear what Stephen was telling me? Ruthie has finally decided to grace Due East with her presence, and she's gone and called Stephen and told him she wants to stay with me. With her *husband.* Like there's nothing I'd like better than having some rednecks shoot me dead with a rifle for having a daughter married to a black man. And staying in my apartment! What's the matter with Stephen's house?"

"Well," said Jesse. "Please don't go telling your son what's going on with Mary Faith that way."

Nell grinned. "Okay, okay," she said. "I can tell you're real worried by *my* troubles. But you let me call this doctor in Due East and find out how much he charges."

"Oh, I don't know," Jesse said. The room rocked as badly as it had the night before. "I just don't know, Nell."

"Let me get you a cup of coffee," she said. "I'm going to take *care* of you," and she went off to the kitchen humming and smiling.

Jesse closed his eyes on the couch and groaned. He didn't know if he'd ever make it to work, and suddenly he remembered the edges of his dream the night before. Why was Faith doing this to him, popping up in his dreams and at the edges of his waking and just when he was struggling to make the right choice for Mary Faith? He opened his eyes, stood up, and followed Nell into the kitchen.

"You better make that call," he said. "I guess you've got the right idea."

9

Running Away

I was in English 3, where Mr. William was reading aloud sections of *Light in August*, when the assistant principal's voice crackled over the loudspeaker. "Mary Faith Rapple, report to the office." A bored crackle. "Mary Faith Rapple, report to the office immediately." Well, of course the whole class turned around to watch me squeeze out of my desk and slump up the aisle and across the classroom. I had a feeling we were doing *Light in August* for my benefit. I was pregnant, and they all suspected it or guessed it or knew it, and the only thing we were all wondering was whether somebody in the office knew it, too. Mr. William gave me a sympathetic look.

But when I got to the office, it was only Aunt Lizann waiting for me. "Hush," she said, and pulled me aside to a corner. "I told them it was a family emergency."

"Daddy?"

"No, Mary Faith, it's not exactly a family emergency." She looked around her nervously. The secretary was black, and the three student aides were black. The door to the assistant principal's office was open, and she could see that he was black, too. Aunt Lizann started to whisper.

"Mary Faith, your Uncle Zack and me have been planning our vacation, down at the car lot, and his secretary—you know, the one who looks just like a doe with those big brown eyes— well, she says her sister works at the travel agency and Mary

Faith, this is getting complicated. Is there any place we can go?"

I led her outside the office and into the hallway, aiming for the benches out front. "Don't you have to get a hall pass or something, Mary Faith?"

"I don't think so. They know it's an emergency."

"Goodness!" said Aunt Lizann. "Due East High School certainly has changed."

"Come on out front," I told her. We passed the principal in front of the library, and Aunt Lizann brightened. The principal is white. "He looks like he has his hands full," she said.

I led her out to a stone bench under an oak tree and sat her down facing the road instead of the school. The school is only twenty years old, but it's too shabby-looking for Aunt Lizann. It has five halls that come together in a brick I, and from out front the line of windows makes it look like an ocean liner— only nobody here is planning on going abroad. Paint is peeling off the windows and doors, and rust weighs down the gutters. It was early in the day, so Aunt Lizann got the whole scraggly front lawn to herself; if she'd come half an hour later she would have run into a lunch break and found herself surrounded. The black kids take the front yard; and the white kids go out on the breezeway or in the parking lot. It's always lunchtime for somebody, because the school is too crowded, and they run students around to lunch or recess or study hall in the gym to get them out of the classrooms.

"Well," said Aunt Lizann, and stretched out her freckled legs, in sandals. "This is better. Where was I? Mary Faith, your uncle and me have got a chance to go to the Bahamas for two weeks, very cheap. I've been begging Uncle Zack to take a cruise for a long time, but he never did want to leave the business alone that long. But this secretary got us such a cheap deal that even Uncle Zack couldn't resist, and Mary Faith, the only trouble in the whole world is that we have to leave in three days. And I said to Uncle Zack, I said I wasn't going to leave Due East until I found out what my niece was going to do and if she needed me to take her to New York after all. For, you know."

"And that's why you're at school?"

"And that's why I'm at school, to find out from you direct what you are planning to do." Now that her speech was out, Aunt Lizann looked around gaily at the school buses, the stragglers coming in late, the faculty's sports cars parked out front. Finally, she looked back at me. "Well, Mary Faith?"

"Well, Aunt Lizann, I thought you knew what I was going to do."

"Oh," she said.

"Thank you for coming by."

"Well, I want you to know, Mary Faith, that it's not so easy for me to come to Due East High School, not after what they've *done* to it."

"Well, thank you for coming by."

"Mary Faith."

"Yes, ma'am."

"Mary Faith, are you really going to *have* that baby?"

"Yes, ma'am."

"Are they going to let you stay in school?"

"I guess so."

"Are you going to *keep* the baby?"

"Yes, ma'am."

"Where?"

"In Momma's sewing room."

Aunt Lizann puckered up her lips. "That makes me want to cry," she said. "Poor Annie." She picked up my hand and held it in hers. Her nails were covered in a deep red, the same color my mother used to wear on her lips. "Mary Faith," she said, "you have probably been wondering why Uncle Zack and me gave up on getting you to have an abortion, why we stopped coming over to the house. Well, I'll tell you why. We could see that night that your daddy was *real* determined. I should have known he would just let you go this way. Has he been home?"

"Yes ma'am."

"Mary Faith?"

"Well, he's been home for supper," I said. I could hear the bell for third period ringing. I'd have to go back to Mr. William's class and walk through a roomful of strangers to get my

books. With my luck he'd have a remedial class and the obser-
vant ones wouldn't even whisper, they'd ask me right out loud
when the baby was due. It had already happened, twice, in the
hall.

"Mary Faith, what are you going to do about school after the
baby's born?"

"I thought maybe I could go at night."

"With that Mr. Dugan? Your daddy's been worried about
him, and I don't blame him. Goodness, Mary Faith, I can't
believe this is happening. There *is* your daddy's reputation to
consider, too, you know. You're making it real hard on him."

"I know."

"Mary Faith." She put her arm around my shoulder, and
drew me close. Her moist arm sucked me up better than a
vacuum cleaner. "Mary Faith, I'm going to be around for three
more days, and I want you to know if you change your mind
that I will cancel that cruise to the Bahamas and take you up to
New York. You know, you are finally getting big."

"I know."

"Mary Faith, with that *at*titude nothing is going to get done
about this baby. Now, are you going to walk me to my car?"
She pulled her arm away with a pop, and I followed Aunt
Lizann to her black Oldsmobile, big as Uncle Zack's but more
subdued. I even let her kiss me on the cheek. She tooted her
horn driving off, and when she waved she looked like a beauty
queen in a parade down River Street.

I walked back to the stone bench and waited for the fourth-
period bell to ring. The guidance counselor pulled up in his
white Fiat, but he didn't ask me for a hall pass or tell me to go
back to class. I had been his biggest hope in the sophomore
class. He said I could probably get a scholarship to Radcliffe or
Yale or Princeton or at least Wellesley or Bryn Mawr. Now he
waved at me nervously, and hurried away.

At lunch Reba McFee and her friend Beth found my table
and sat with me, waiting for me to confide my troubles. For the
past few weeks, since I'd started to show, they'd been seeking
me out. Two or three times a week I'd see them carrying full

trays out of the cafeteria line and consulting in low voices until they found me. Then they sat like confessors, and since I never said much until I said I had to go the library to study, it was a quiet lunch. Once Reba asked me if I thought they should give Michael Jagger a full-page or a half-page memorial in the yearbook, but she just seemed to be trying to make conversation.

We ate our fish cakes, and they asked me why I'd been called to the office during second period, and then we ate our applesauce, and Beth asked me if I thought Sam Byrd, the student council president, was cute. He was passing by on his way to the garbage window with a full lunch tray. I said Sam Byrd made me throw up, the way he was always slapping people on the back. Beth poked at her tray.

We had almost finished what little we could eat of our lunches when the p.a. sputtered. This time it was the principal's voice, and when he repeated the same message we'd heard in the morning—"Mary Faith Rapple, report to the office. Mary Faith Rapple, report to the office"—Reba and Beth hung their mouths open in oh my goodness! sympathy.

"I must have left some books in English class," I said.

"Hope you're not in trouble," Beth said cheerfully, but Reba poked her with an elbow. I could feel their shaking heads and clucking tongues following me out of the cafeteria. They were getting to be just like their mommas.

In the office, the secretary pointed me in to the assistant principal, and the assistant principal pointed me in to the principal. I tried to stand straight, walking through this line of offices, but I could see my belly protruding without even looking down. I'd been wearing the same loose jumper, with a different blouse, every day for a week.

Mr. Anderson was writing when I walked in, and when he felt me in front of his desk he said, "Yes?" You knew from the sound of his *yes* that student aides and secretaries and parents and assistant principals and student council presidents walked into his office all day long to interrupt him.

"You called me on the loudspeaker."

He looked up, a man almost as big as my Uncle Zack but

seeming not so much massive as just fat. "Oh, yes," he said. "Mary Faith Rapple? Well. I recognize that name. Aren't you the one who did so well on the state math exam?"

"Yes sir," I said. "I like math."

"Well, that's *good.*" While I was waiting for him to say *And aren't you going to have a baby?* he bent down over his writing and said, "I called you in because Mr. Dugan here is setting up the fall schedule for the GED classes and wanted to talk to the student tutors about getting some more of our *better* students involved." He looked behind me, and when I turned I saw Stephen Dugan sitting in a big plush chair in the corner, smoking a cigarette. He raised his eyebrows at me.

Mr. Anderson rose, and papers fluttered to the floor as his belly brushed them from the desk. He ignored them. "So, Mary Faith Rapple," he said, "you don't mind missing lunch period for a cause like this, do you? Mr. Dugan can't get over here all that often. Why don't the two of you just sit in the p.a. room and talk out some ideas and let me know if you need me." He hitched up his pants and led us into the little room that adjoined his office, gesturing vaguely at two hardback chairs by the p.a. "I'll just see to those absentee forms," he said, and closed the door behind him.

Mr. Dugan smiled and put a finger to his lips. "Is that thing on?" he said, pointing to the p.a. board.

"I have no idea."

He stuck his cigarette in the corner of his mouth and walked softly over to the board, reading every switch until he'd satisfied himself that the whole school couldn't hear us.

"Pretty tricky way of getting you out of class, huh?" His voice was still low.

"Out of lunch," I said. "Why are you whispering?"

"I don't want Anderson to hear me."

"What, are you planning to blow up the GED classes?"

"You sound just like Jagger," Mr. Dugan said, and flashed me a sympathetic smile that could have been Reba's or Beth's or Mr. William's or Aunt Lizann's. They'd all been practicing at the same mirror.

"Mr. Dugan, what are you doing here?"

He took me by the hand and led me to a window that looked out on the breezeway, the farthest spot from Mr. Anderson's doorway. His expression didn't change, but mine tightened, and so did my breath.

"This doesn't have to do with the GED classes," he said. "I wandered around the breezeway for fifteen minutes looking for you and then I bumped into Anderson and had to think of a reason for being here."

"And what *are* you doing here?" My voice came out very, very small. He was still holding my hand, touching it with the lightness of a man patting a dog's head without knowing he's doing it.

"Mary Faith," he started, "this might not amount to a hill of beans." He let go of my hand. "Look at that, not a black kid out there on that breezeway. It looks just like the Due East High School *I* went to."

I waited. He ground out his cigarette on the windowsill.

"I spoke to my mother on the phone this morning," he said. "And it seems she's been talking to your father."

"*My* father?"

"Uhmhum," he said, and slowly took another cigarette out of his pocket. "It seems the two of them have been spending some time together."

"Your mother and my father?"

"Uhmhum," he said again, and gave me time to think about it. I knew Mrs. Dugan. I knew her from the time my mother was dying, just after her husband died. She was an ugly old woman, with dried leather skin, and she walked around downtown stinking of whiskey in the middle of the day and talking too loud. I'd see her in the graveyard of the Catholic church when I passed by on my bike, and she'd be crying loud enough to be heard from the street.

"I think they've been spending a *lot* of time together," he went on calmly. "And it seems that between the two of them, they are going to talk to a doctor on the Calhoun Road about getting you an abortion. I remember from the other night how much you did not *want* an abortion." He exhaled a beautiful funnel of white smoke, and for a minute I couldn't see him through it.

"I don't think Daddy's been spending time with anyone," I said. "I think he's been out drinking alone every night."

Stephen looked at me without saying a word. This time he kept the sympathy but dropped the smile.

"He's been drinking with *her?*"

He nodded. "I knew she'd been keeping company with somebody, and this morning it all fell into place. This morning when I was on the phone with her she answered the door to him."

"Oh, *no,*" I said. "My daddy never even *drank* before, he never came home late. My mother would've just *died* if she thought he'd take up with somebody, with her."

Stephen led me closer to Anderson's door, away from the window. He put his arm around my shoulder and brought my head down on his chest, and I tried not to let him hear my breathing. I was breathing very, very quickly. "She *is* my mother, you know," said Mr. Dugan. "But I came to warn you because I feel the same sort of revulsion you do. Maybe not revulsion. Distaste. I don't trust her. I thought you should know she was pushing your father into this." We could hear Anderson scraping his chair back in the next room, and when Stephen pulled his arm away from me I thought I could hear how fast *he* was breathing. The room was filled up with breathing. I walked back to the window and saw Reba and Beth on the breezeway, talking to Sam Byrd. Stephen Dugan's mother had gray hair and laughed like a sailor and always had on a pair of shorts, never a dress. My mother didn't own a pair of shorts.

"Ironic, isn't it?" Stephen said. "After my father died, she converted, and now that she's a Catholic she's pushing you into an abortion. She regards herself as a strict disciplinarian. She used to beat my sister Ruthie across the legs with a leather belt."

"I've got to get out of here," I said.

"Why don't you go back to lunch?" he said. "Sorry to upset you. I just thought it would be better for you to know than not to know. To—anticipate them."

"I've got to get out of here," I said again.

"Go on back to lunch."

"I've got to get out of Due East." In another couple of weeks, they wouldn't be able to force me into an abortion. Not a legal one.

"Oh, shit," Mr. Dugan said. "I didn't think I was going to push you in *that* direction. Now listen, you don't need to start talking like Michael Jagger just because you're carrying his baby."

I stared at him.

"Mary Faith," he said. "Listen, if it gets too bad, come stay at my house. Marygail would be glad to have you."

"No she wouldn't."

"That's true," he said, calmly again. "She might not be *glad*, but she'd do it. There are ways out of these things."

"There's a road north out of this thing," I said.

"Come on, Mary Faith. *I'll* talk to your father for you. I'll even talk to my mother."

"I've got to get out of Due East," I said again. "Mr. Dugan, do you remember the couple of hundred you said I could borrow?"

He flushed. "Sure," he said. "I remember."

"Well, I only need to borrow about fifty," I said. "Could I have it today?"

"Mary Faith. Do you have any idea what kind of trouble that could get me in? You're only, what, sixteen?"

"Fifteen," I said. "Don't worry, I can get it from my aunt if I can't get it from you."

"Hold your voice down," he said. "Mary Faith, you don't have to run away because my mother is involved with your father."

"I've been planning it anyway," I said. "I got the name of a home in Charleston and all I have to do is get there by the bus. They'll take me in." Suddenly I could picture myself standing in line at the Greyhound station. All around me would be Marines playing video games, and when I got off the bus in Charleston I'd hear the same *blips* on different screens. I would call a Catholic church from the station. I'd catch a taxi out front.

"Jesus, Mary, and Joseph," said Mr. Dugan. He began to pace a small circle in front of the p.a., and I stayed by the window, staring out, wishing I had one of his cigarettes. I'd never had a cigarette, but I thought breathing one in deeply would calm me and set me on my way. I thought maybe I'd buy a pack at the station.

Finally Mr. Dugan stopped and said, "Mary Faith, you must know I wouldn't come here for just anybody. You've become—very special to me." He wasn't watching how loud his voice was anymore. "I care very deeply for you," he said, and finished in a mutter. "Fifteen." He shook his head.

"I'll be sixteen in July," I said. I didn't know how he meant *care very deeply for you.*

"Mr. Dugan, I'm sorry I asked you for any money. I can get it from my aunt."

"No, wait. Never let it be said that I didn't contribute to the delinquency of a deserving juvenile. *I'll* give you the fifty bucks."

"Thanks," I said. "I'll pay it back someday."

"Ha!" he said. "You don't know how much money it takes to keep a baby in those plastic diaper things. You take that fifty dollars as a gift. Make me the honorary godfather or something."

"I'm not going to baptize my baby."

"I'm only kidding," he said gently. "I was only kidding."

And then we agreed that I should go back to lunch and then classes, and that I should meet him at the bank at three-thirty. He was concerned that I get a bus before my father was due home for supper, and I said I thought for sure there'd be an afternoon bus. He made me swear that I'd be doing this anyway, even if he didn't give me the money, and then he made me swear that I'd been planning to run away anyway, that finding out about my father and his mother didn't have anything to do with it. I could see the two of them out at night, in the mist, going from graveyard to graveyard with bottles of whiskey, leaving the bottles on the markers. I could see my father taking that woman's short bangs and pushing them aside on her forehead. I could see him kissing her.

We had to leave through Mr. Anderson's office. He didn't look up when we came through, but smiled down at his papers and said, "I hope y'all came up with some bright ideas."

"Yes sir," said Mr. Dugan, just as smooth as you please. "I think we'll get some good tutors in the fall."

"Well, *good,*" said Mr. Anderson, and finally looked up. "I'm glad to meet you, Mary Faith. Didn't I give you some awards last spring?"

"Yes, sir."

"Well, I hope I'll be giving you some more this spring. You look different, though. I guess you little girls grow up fast when you get to my high school."

Mr. Dugan and I went back out through the assistant principal's, out through the main office, back into the A hall and the crowds who weren't supposed to be there in the middle of lunch. A typing teacher stood in her doorway chanting "Clear the halls, please clear the hallways."

When we neared the front door, I heard a boy behind me say, "You reckon that's the father?" I tried to hurry on, but Mr. Dugan reached out and held my elbow back, and I felt like the rubber end of a slingshot being tested for aim.

Behind me burst a cackle of giggles, fourteen-year-old boys slapping each other on the back and doubling over with the fun of my belly. Mr. Dugan swiveled me around and bore down on me with his blue eyes. "You're almost out of it," he hissed. "Don't let them get to you."

The bell rang just as we reached the front door, and he held me back again. "You take care for the rest of the day. Have people been saying things to you?"

"I'll be all right."

"Well, watch out. Don't let them trip you. I'll see you at the bank, then. Three-thirty. Maybe you better wait out back."

"Yes, sir."

"And don't call me *sir,* hear?"

"Okay," I said. "Thanks, Mr. Dugan."

He shook his head dubiously and wandered off, pushing his

way against the crowds coming through the front door. I let myself get swept up along A hall until I got to my locker, and then I carried every book I owned to trig class. I looked like a library pushcart gliding along the floor, but that wasn't what was on my mind. I was seeing the bathrooms on the bus, and the bus driver, and the priest who would answer the phone, and my father putting his hand on that woman's skinny little breast until it made me throw up.

10

To the Rescue

When it crawled out of Pinetowne, Jesse Rapple's truck was *supposed* to take him to his gas station, so that he could open it up for the day, let Lee Mac in, pump some gas, tune an old Volkswagen bug. Change his own distributor cap, if there was time. But the truck—missing, jerking out onto the highway—took a right toward town instead of a left toward the Plaid King, and it wasn't until he was already on Oysterbed Road that Jesse Rapple knew where he was heading. He had to talk to somebody sane, and the truck was leading to the beach road. Miles Seafood was on the beach road, and he was willing to take a chance on finding Buddy in the office.

He had to talk to Buddy because the minute Nell had closed the door on him he had begun to see again the blue flowers on Faith's maternity dress, plucked from the material he'd held in his hand an hour before. The flowers were following him; Faith was trying to tell him something. Now he swung the truck down Division Street, heading for the bridge and the long, flat, green ride, the ride he'd taken with Faith a thousand times. When she was pregnant the first time she'd wanted to go to the beach every night. He'd been a mechanic for Mike McCarthy then, aching with tiredness at six o'clock, but they would take the little Chevy over the bridge, edge it past the fields and packing sheds and marsh, and park it at the beach before dusk set in. It was the only time she'd appear in public with her legs bare, and it had tickled him to see them, white and plump, wading in the water. Nell would never set her feet so delicately in the ocean; she'd show up at the beach in a pair of old brown shorts, probably, and bare feet, carrying a fishing pole. She'd go charging out into the waves until she'd set herself up to catch more fish than her husband or any other man on the beach.

But Faith would hold back if they met anyone else on their beach walk. Her dress floated before him again, its billows in the ocean air making her look as if she were carrying triplets for him. Maybe Faith was leading him on, telling him to go slowly, to take care of important things. To breathe salt air. To see Buddy again. What was losing a day's take at the gas station compared to letting a friend slip away? It had been a month since he'd seen Buddy, and he hadn't answered the messages left with Mary Faith and Lee Mac. He'd been too busy at Nell's. Buddy didn't even know about Mary Faith. He'd been too busy to tell him, too busy letting Nell run her fingers through his hair.

Faith had never run her fingers through Jesse's hair, or even through her own hair, because Myrt sprayed it into a helmet that set like plastic and stayed where it was for a week, until it was time for her next appointment. Faith was not the type to take liberties with anybody's hair, with *anything* attached to a body. When they made love, they did it in the dark, in the bedroom. They didn't *watch* each other undressing, and half the time they kept the sheet over them in case Mary Faith walked in and surprised them. Faith was plump, and her breasts were big, big and white and ending with pale nipples; the sight of her breasts had made him grow large enough to fill three women, one after the other. In the beginning, he would roll over at night and climb on top of her to take her with a sudden fury that he knew left her cold, but as the years went by they'd developed rhythms, she'd learned to shift and move beneath him until he'd want to burst three, four times before he came. When they found the cancer, he'd worried that it was just the *size* he got, making love to her, that had diseased her somehow, or maybe it was the way they always started back in again too quickly after the miscarriages. Those nights he had been scared to enter her, scared to go near the wound, but she had pulled him over, wanting to get pregnant again soon, she'd say. He didn't think it was wanting to get pregnant so much as just wanting the sex. She was never so passionate as when she'd just lost one. Twice before Mary Faith—the early miscarriages, the ones that didn't count so much—and three times after. And then the sicker she got with the cancer, the more they both wanted it. Until she was lying in the hospital and it was only he who wanted to crawl into bed with her when the nurses had their backs turned, only he who wanted to force her, hurt her, only he who wanted her to say, "You did this to me!" She was so soft, so shaded by her long days in the curtained house and the air-conditioned grocery store and the darkness of the church. He *must* have hurt her, torn at that softness, but she would never say so. When Lizann brought her a copy of *The Joy of Sex* as a joke birthday present, she'd blushed and giggled and kept it lodged between the headboard and the mattress so they could sneak looks at it when they went to bed. But they'd never tried any of the positions in the pictures, just stuck to the same old force of his seeing her breasts, her grabbing him over, his climbing on heavily, her pulling him down, down, down.

With Nell it was all *Joy of Sex,* and beyond. She knew every trick he'd ever fantasized, and more besides, ones she'd probably culled from *Raunch.* What bothered him most about Nell was not what she did—he'd always *wanted* to use his mouth, he'd always wanted a woman to use hers—but that she seemed to push him into it, that her skinny body clutched like a monkey's on the organ grinder's back. He wasn't going to be the organ grinder. What bothered him most was that he wanted it so badly, that before he was aroused he'd think *She's disgusting, and old,* and that as soon as he'd had a couple of beers he'd be ready to act out whatever scene she had planned for the evening. When he remembered Jesus drawing the line and challenging the Jews to cast the first stone, he wasn't sure whether he was praying for forgiveness for himself, or for Nell. He just hoped heaven didn't mean that Faith had to *see* what was going on with him now.

Now if he were to tell Buddy about what went on between him and Nell, Buddy would roll his head back and laugh, and ask him what time he was through at Nell's, so Buddy could get himself some, too. He crossed the last creek before Miles Seafood and knew he wouldn't tell Buddy about Nell. Faith had never trusted Buddy about sex: he'd never told her that Buddy fooled around and egged him on, but Faith seemed to sense it, and she was watchful and quiet, almost mean, around him. Buddy knew she didn't like him and treated her with big false gestures of politeness, and Faith got quieter and colder. The blue flowers. He couldn't shake them.

Buddy's car was parked outside Miles and the woman behind the counter in the retail shop sent Jesse into the back. Buddy was there, his beer-bellied long body slouched on a straight-back chair, a long net spread on his lap and bunched at his feet. He feigned crazy surprise, seeing Jesse, hid under the net, said, "Hey, Jesse, grab yourself a chair. The shrimp aren't gonna run this year and I'm fixing my own goddamn nets. Sit *down.*"

So Jesse pulled over another straight-back chair and picked up the end of the net to hold in his lap. Buddy said they looked like a couple of old women at a quilting bee.

"So you been making yourself scarce?" Buddy said. "Lizann told me about Mary Faith. I'm sorry to hear it."

"Lizann told you?"

"She called me up one night at home. When she says can she talk to me, Becky thinks we're having an *affair* or something, and then she gets me on the phone and says Mary Faith's pregnant and will I help her persuade you to make Mary Faith have an abortion."

"And what'd you say?"

"I told her to mind her own goddamn business. Then I told Becky I'd been balling Lizann for over a year."

"You did not."

"I did. I said I'd been mussing up that starchy little hairdo of hers back here in the shed. I said we did it underneath the nets."

"You did not."

"I did. And then I started to think about what it'd be like to screw Lizann and it wasn't any fun anymore."

"Well, it's true."

"About Mary Faith?"

"Yeah. She's pregnant. She won't tell me who the father is."

"Is she going to have the baby?"

"She wants to."

"And you don't want her to?"

"No," said Jesse. "I don't want her to. I don't want her to be stuck when she's fifteen. She's already living in her own little world. She doesn't need to be *that* far away from every other kid in town. She needs to go to dances, drive-ins. She needs to be a kid." He didn't say he didn't know how he'd feed another mouth, and he felt guilty, not saying it, because somehow he believed that Mary Faith would never go to dances and drive-ins *any*way and that it was the money, the idea of another face staring up at him at supper, another set of doctor bills to pay, that really made him want the trouble over with.

"It might fill up the house," said Buddy, and Jesse started at the idea of someone thinking the baby would be a good idea. Buddy had bent his slick black hair down over the net again to concentrate on a knot, and Jesse watched him the way he used to watch Faith sew. Buddy loved babies. He had four kids at home, fourteen and under, and another one he supported in Georgia that Becky didn't know anything about. Buddy loved women having babies. He'd told Jesse nothing made him hornier than the sight of a woman in her fifth or sixth month, when her breasts swole up and it wasn't just lying on top of her, it was *mounting* her, it was like you'd climbed a little stepladder to get atop her belly. Buddy made sure he spent plenty of time out of the house, but when he was there he was playing with one of the kids, yelling at Becky if she let the baby cry too long in the crib or the high chair. The front office of Miles Seafood was a gallery of school pictures. "You might get to like the little bugger," Buddy said.

"Aw, Buddy, I can't let her do it."

Buddy considered. "I guess not," he said. "She's awful young. But she's a pretty one."

Jesse froze in his chair. Buddy would have to say *that*, about Mary Faith being pretty. Not that Buddy would ever think of Mary Faith that way, just that he had this *ease* talking about women, about girls, about whether they were pretty or easy or good lays and whether they might have babies you might get to like. Jesse felt the way he'd felt when he found out about Buddy's eighteen-year-old cashier. "I better go open up the station," he said.

"You mean you hadn't opened up today?" Buddy said. "Jesus, Jesse, you are letting this thing weigh heavy. Hell, half the girls in this town get pregnant before they get out of that high school. It's not such a big deal."

It's a big deal to me, Jesse almost said, but he didn't. He had put off seeing Buddy too long. He rose to go, but before he was out the door Buddy said suddenly: "You still seeing that Nell Dugan?" and there was nothing for him to do but laugh hard.

"Lizann tell you that too?"

"Yup."

"She must have been following me around at night."

"She probably bugged your telephone. You having a good time with her?"

Jesse laughed again, a high-pitched laugh he couldn't seem to control. "I don't know," he told Buddy. "I just don't know."

"It's *good* for you," Buddy said. "I knew there was some other reason beside Mary Faith you'd been lying so low. *Laying* so low."

"I'm not sure it's not all the same thing," Jesse said, but Buddy wouldn't have any of it. If it was a woman, it was all right. If it was lying in somebody's arms when you didn't know what to do, it was just all right. Of course, it was kind of a surprise after *Faith*.

The ride back from Miles mesmerized him. There were a few pickers out in the tomato fields already, Mexicans plucking up hard green balls that didn't even resemble tomatoes yet. He drove past them almost in a trance, so that by the time he drove past the bridge and back into town, past the bank clock that said 88°F/12:15, he was already driving back to his own house and not even knowing he'd turned off onto the Point. He couldn't imagine what he had in mind to do at home, but he turned into his driveway, went into his kitchen, called Lee Mac and told him he wasn't feeling well, and went upstairs to fall into a deep sleep he hadn't even known he needed.

He dreamed about Nell, about Buddy climbing a little stepladder and *mounting* her, about a line of boys they'd known together in high school following Buddy. He was on the line, but after Buddy and the others he just couldn't get it up. Nell laughed at him. She was lying in satin, white satin, and he slipped off it and tripped on the stepladder. The phone rang in the middle of his dream—a siren, an alarm that sent the high school boys into a scurry, pulling up their jockey shorts.

He shook himself awake and picked up the phone by the bedside. The little alarm clock said 4:15, and he thought it was the middle of the night.

"Mr. Rapple? This is Stephen Dugan." It came to him that there was still light at his bedroom window, that it was still day, and he began to remember coming home and climbing heavily into the upstairs bed. He hadn't fallen asleep in the middle of the day in twenty years.

"I've just left Mary Faith," Stephen Dugan was saying, "at the Greyhound bus station."

"What?"

"She's planning to run away, Mr. Rapple. She bought a ticket to Charleston and the bus leaves in twenty minutes. I'm calling from the pay phone in the bowling alley."

"How did you get there?"

"I walked across the street."

"No," Jesse said, kicking his shoes out from under his bed, "how did you get to the bus station?"

"Mary Faith asked me to meet her," Dugan said shortly. "I'm not going to stick around, though. Listen, Mr. Rapple, do me a favor and don't tell Mary Faith how you found out."

"Dugan! You're the father of that baby, aren't you?"

Stephen Dugan hung up on him, and Jesse Rapple pulled on his shoes and careened down the stairs. Now the whole day made sense. Now Faith coming back in the maternity dress and his ride to the beach, now even his dream about Nell Dugan— the *whore*, his dream had been telling him—now all fell into a pattern as regular as the blue flowers printed on that tidy cotton cloth. The whole day had been a warning that Mary Faith was on the verge, on the edge, and that he had to pull her back. And he had been so blind that he not only didn't *see* it, he had fallen asleep on it. Who else had fallen asleep? Simon Peter? What other traitor?

He was three minutes away from the Greyhound station, and he didn't know if he'd reach her in time.

He could hear them calling the bus as he jumped down from the truck: Walterboro, Charleston, Florence, Fayetteville. The man's voice droned on and on until it reached *New York*, and Jesse had reached the ticket counter. He didn't need to inquire, though: he could see Mary Faith edging out the back door, between crew-cut Marines. The bus driver had his door open, and Jesse had a vision of his daughter in a Greyhound seat, shifting on the hour's ride, unable to swing her legs around so that they were comfortable. Looking like her mother.

She was third in line, and he came up behind her and pulled her gently by the elbow. Her eyes barely registered his presence, and she followed him to the corner of the loading area. They were under an overhanging roof, out in the open, and he could feel the line of Marines and mothers and fussing children turn to stare at him and his business.

"It's better like this, Daddy," his daughter said to him. She wouldn't even look up; she was carrying nothing, carrying her *pocketbook*. What did she think she was going to do for clothes?

"Where are you going?" he finally said.

"Charleston," she whispered. Then louder, "There's a home there."

"A *home?*" he hissed. "You've got a home."

"I mean nuns," she said. Five people were already aboard the bus.

"Nuns? Mary Faith, are you crazy? Did Dugan talk you into this? He's the father of your baby all along, isn't he?"

Then she looked up. She looked up at him with her gray eyes and said, "He is not."

"Well, what are you doing running away to nuns then? Who put that kind of crazy notion in your head?" There were only two more passengers on line.

"Daddy, I'm going," she said. "They'll let me have the baby." And she pulled away from him and stood behind the last Marine boarding the bus.

He wanted to slap her silly. He wanted to grab her from the end of her bus line and shake her and hit her hard across the face and say, "You are a little girl. You do not need a baby. You've got no idea. You don't know what it's going to be like, waking up five times in the middle of the night. You don't know what it's going to be like quitting school. You don't know what it's going to be like, giving up college. College! You'll be damn lucky if you can find yourself a husband ten *years* from now." He found his voice and said loudly to the driver: "You can't let that little girl on the bus. She is my daughter."

The driver—forty, fat, tired—rolled his eyes and handed Mary Faith back her ticket. "I'm sorry, miss," he said. "I can't let you board the bus."

Jesse heard Mary Faith say: "I'm eighteen years old. He can't hold me back," and he shot forward to grab the back of her jumper. Mary Faith! Talking to him like that! But the Marine in front of Mary Faith had turned around to come to her rescue and was holding out a hand for her to grab, to hoist herself into the bus.

"Do something," Jesse hissed to the driver.

"Miss," said the driver. "Miss." The Marine had tugged her up to the top of the steps, and Jesse could barely see her in front of the driver's seat, her face obscured in the dark of the tinted-glass.

"Miss," said the driver again. "I'm going to have to see some identification." He wouldn't look back at Jesse.

"You don't need identification," shouted Jesse. "Look at

her. She's fifteen years old!" He knew, saying it, that she looked almost eighteen.

Mary Faith twisted her pocketbook around her arm, stalling for time. Finally she said to the driver, "He took my driver's license away from me." Jesse breathed out a torrent of air. His smart little daughter, who'd always had him so twisted around her every heart's desire, had gone way beyond manipulating him now. Now she was standing at the top of a Greyhound bus accusing him of stealing her things.

"Mary Faith Rapple!" he shouted. "You get down from that bus this instant." The little Marine was standing still behind her. He couldn't have been more than seventeen himself, but he extended his hand like a brace to support the small of her back. Mary Faith stood looking at the driver with a wide-open blank stare, and the driver put his hand on his hip in frustration.

"All right," Jesse said. "All right, Mary Faith." He took a deep breath, and then he took two steps back from the bus and told himself he was doing the wrong thing. "You can have the baby," he said. "You can have the baby and I'll take care of you both." He saw the Marine slip his arm around Mary Faith's waist, protectively, and then he saw her slip out surely, with a smile turned backward on the little Marine. She made her way down the steps of the bus. The driver muttered something after her, but Jesse didn't stick around to hear it; five steps ahead of his daughter, he walked back through the swinging rear doors of the Greyhound station and didn't pause to hold the door for her. He knew, without a sound telling him it was so, that she was following him through the station and back out through the front door to the parking lot. He opened the passenger door of the truck for her, but let her climb in herself. He waited until they were both in the truck, silent, until they were backing out of the Greyhound parking lot and on their way home to turn to her and say, "Don't you ever do anything like that again, Mary Faith." She didn't answer, and he didn't care. In the morning he would take her to the closet and give her her mother's maternity clothes. The blue dress. She could cut them down if they didn't fit right. And tonight, whore or no whore, he was going back to Nell Dugan's apartment, and get himself some of what the rest of the world had been getting for the three years he'd been dead to it. And tomorrow he would ask Mary Faith for once and for all if it wasn't that Dugan who was responsible, because who else but the guilty party would give her the money to run off, and tomorrow he would call Buddy and let him know there was going to be a baby after all, a mewling, puking baby he was already beginning to visualize with dismay. Strange tugs of affection. Mary Faith sat on the seat beside him without a glimmer of rebellion or contrition, looking serene and taken care of, and he knew Buddy was right. She was pretty. He was even beginning to settle down to the idea of swollen breasts and swollen belly, and he could almost remember a little patch of his dream about Nell and Buddy and the high school boys. The patch when Nell's eyes for a second turned into Mary Faith's eyes, gray and wide and knowing.

11

In Love

I tried to work up some remorse for telling the bus driver that my father had taken my driver's license, but I couldn't make it all the way to guilt. He took me into my momma's room the next morning and showed me all her dresses, not knowing that three months before I'd been through them all and picked out which ones fit and didn't look entirely like 1966. I cringed a little bit the first time I felt them on my skin—I could see her own skin, flaking and covered with bed sores—but I knew I couldn't go on about a thing like that. I'd need the dresses to get me through the long haul.

Besides, it wasn't me who should have been feeling the guilt, it was Stephen Dugan. He was the one who'd turned on me, who'd promised not to tell a soul and then had gone straight to my father. Somehow the bus station, and the twenty people watching what happened to me there, had taken away all my pride and it didn't seem strange to me that the next night, when my father went out to see the old lady, I called up Mr. Dugan to tell him he'd done the wrong thing. His wife answered the phone, and I didn't have any pride about that either. I told her it was Mary Faith, the pregnant one. I could hear Mr. Dugan in the background, telling her to say he wasn't home, but even that didn't hold me back. I called back a half-hour later, and that time he answered, and I hollered at him just like an old fishwife and then I said it was all right, I'd wanted to be home all along anyway. So he asked me if I wouldn't come tutor the summer session of the GED classes, which just happened to start the next Monday night, and I said yes, because once you throw away shame that way you don't care about walking naked down River Street, much less showing up pregnant to teach a slew of not-too-bright Marines' wives who live in trailers.

Monday was the start of exam week for regular school, but since I was in all the advanced classes I didn't have much studying to do. The teachers in those sections tended to give what they thought were creative exams. That morning Mr. William had had us write, for our English final, an autobiography in Faulknerian style. He had just about strutted around the classroom after he'd put the question up on the board, he was so proud of it. I told Mr. Dugan about it in the car riding back from the first night of classes, about how I'd described myself as lush and fruitful and bovine in a sentence eighty-five words long. I said that since my father had decided to let me stay and keep the baby I was changing, getting bolder. I couldn't seem to keep my mouth shut.

When Stephen pulled up in our driveway, the house was dark. My father was at Nell Dugan's. I started to open up the passenger door, but Stephen reached over and put a hand on mine. "I'm glad you think of yourself as fruitful," he said. "I'm especially glad you think of yourself as lush. But I'm not crazy about bovine."

"I was thinking of Lena."

"She never struck me as realistic," he said. "Bovine, yes. A cross between a cow and the Virgin Mary. Listen, are you going to ask me in?"

I couldn't imagine that he'd want to see my father if he showed up, but Stephen said: "I have a feeling to wait for your father. He still thinks I'm the father of that baby."

And it turned out that I hadn't lost all my shame, because when he said that, my face flamed, and I let him come round and help me out of the passenger seat, and then I let him into the house. *I* knew my father wouldn't be back before the middle of the night, so I dug out the wine bottle from underneath the sink and brought him into the den and gave Stephen a full glass and myself a half.

Before the wine we had nothing to say, but after he'd finished his first glass, Stephen said, "Lush, huh?" and leaned his head way back to laugh. I said I hoped Mr. William had the same attitude.

I poured him another glass, and another half for me, and Mr. Dugan asked me how I liked the new batch of GEDs. I said most of them didn't have a prayer of passing, and then I said, "You know, my father probably won't be home until late. He's at your mother's."

"I know," Stephen said, and then tacked on: "I mean, I know he's at my mother's house, but I hope he'll be here soon so I can have a word with him."

"I don't think he really believes it," I said. "He just can't think of anyone else."

Stephen poured himself another glass of wine: he was chugging them. "I'm not offended by the suggestion," he said.

I could feel the flush spreading across my face again. His own face was down, so that I couldn't see his expression, but I could see his chest rising and falling fast, the way it had done in the p.a. room. I was afraid of what he would say next. With Michael Jagger, I had always been afraid of saying something hurtful, something innocuous that would crush him. Now I had the feeling that Stephen Dugan would do the same thing to me, that I would wait and listen and hover over everything he said, and that I would find most of it hurtful. I had known it when I called him back after he told his wife to say he wasn't home: I was in love with him. I was ten years younger than his wife, and I could talk to him better. His wife had never told him she was lush and fruitful.

"So you don't think he'll be back until late?"

I said I wasn't sure. I said he *might* come home early. I faced those stairs alone every night. A week back, I had bought myself a nursing bra, and now I had a picture of myself lifting up my shift and my blouse and unsnapping the panel over my right breast so that it gleamed naked over my big belly. His eyes were still down on the old braided rug, unraveling its threads.

"Suddenly I don't think I should be here," Mr. Dugan said. Still he wouldn't look up, and I didn't answer him.

"You know what's going through my mind, don't you?" he said. There was a quickness about his speech that the wine brought out, a vividness.

"I don't know," I said.

"What?" Finally he looked at me.

"I said I don't know."

He took a deep breath and said, "I've got to get out of here, Mary Faith."

I took a deep breath and told him not to go. I had been sitting opposite him in the lounger, but now I crossed over and sat next to him on the couch. I didn't care. No pride, no shame left.

Mr. Dugan put his arm around my shoulder and said, trying to pretend to be fatherly, "Mary Faith, it's just not right. Not when you're fifteen years old."

"I'll be sixteen in July."

"I remember that. July what?"

"July first."

"Mary Faith, in July I'll be saying it's just not right, not when you're sixteen years old."

"And you're married." I had *known* that would hold him back.

"And I'm married," he said. "I haven't cheated on my wife in three years, not since she was running around and just asking for it." He slammed down another glass of wine. "And I'm going to stick to it. And you're a little girl who shouldn't be hearing these things."

No shame at all. "I'm not so little," I said. "I'm going to have a baby, and I'm smarter than she is."

It didn't work out quite the way I had planned. He shook his head back again to laugh, and I thought the laugh might even veer off into hysteria. "That you are," he said. "That you are."

I sat very still and hoped he wouldn't move his arm away. I couldn't bear the need I had to have it there, the wish that he would move his head down and nuzzle my breasts. I had read about that, too, about how pregnant women sometimes want sex all the time, but the books hadn't said anything about not being able to *bear* it, about wishing I'd bought black stockings and a garter belt to go with the nursing bra, about holding my body so rigid that my neck and shoulders ached, about knowing that if I so much as reached a hand out to him it would repulse him, that he would be gone out the door and back to his wife. After a minute locked into that stillness, I suddenly realized that his arm was that stiff, too, that his shoulders must ache and that he must be trying to picture what I would look like with the shift pulled up, to picture how big the baby had pushed me out and whether my breasts were sagging under the new weight. I could tell by his breathing, by his rigid body, that he wasn't one of those men who can't see pregnant women as sexual beings. He was one of the others. I turned my head just a few inches toward him, almost knowing what would happen, and he kissed me hard, his beard so rough against my face that I stiffened tighter. When he felt the stiffening, he squeezed my breast, my right breast, the one I had wanted to uncover, only he hurt it: he pulled the nipple so that it stung under three layers of clothes, and I wanted to squirm out from underneath him and run across the room. I didn't. I pushed him away and stood to pull the shift up over my head, so that I was covered only by the orange blouse that didn't button and the little pair of white bikinis. I knew my legs and arms were long, and my thighs still thin, and I could have stood in front of him for an hour that way. He leaned his head down into his open hands for a second, but I knew that this time it didn't matter if I went to him, that it was too late for him to be repulsed. I circled my arms around his head until he buried it between open buttons, and when my blouse was off I snapped down the panel and held the breast for his mouth. I was standing in front of him, one knee bent on the couch, and he was half-sitting, half-stretched out from the couch, holding on to me and making noises that sounded a little like suckling and a little like gasping. He sucked at my nipple until I thought I'd cry out in pain, and we were posed that way when we heard my

father's truck pull into the driveway, which runs right by the
den. He didn't even move away, just held me around the belly
as he listened to the door slamming outside in the night, but I
popped out of his arms and pulled the shirt back over my head
without even trying to button the buttons of the orange shirt.
It was too late to hide the bottle of wine, but I took one glass
and spun it under the couch, and tried not to look at Mr.
Dugan, who sat still, his face limp. I could have killed him for
not getting up to help me.

   The next morning, during the first exam period—Latin for
me—my name was called out over the p.a. system again and I
was told to report to the office *immediately following exam session
A*. Mine was the last of a long list of troublemakers, the rest all
hoodlums and dopers. I was almost done with the translations
anyway, and I spent the rest of the exam period wondering if
my father had changed his mind. The night before, he'd come
in looking dazed and acted cold and polite to Stephen and
didn't say a word about the wine bottle. When Stephen said
he'd just wanted to reassure him, that he'd just called him the
other day out of *concern* for me and that he'd explained all that
to me, my father looked at him with a tired, puzzled look and
said thanks, he was just heading up to bed. Stephen ran so fast
out the back door he almost tripped, and I was left with lumps
of clothing bunched up underneath my shift.
   But it wasn't my father calling me into the office, and it
wasn't Aunt Lizann this time. After the secretary had herded
the rest of the bad boys into the assistant principal's office, she
told me to go in to see Mr. Anderson himself, and I knew by
her pitying look that it wasn't some award he wanted to see me
about.
   Mr. Anderson wasn't there alone. He'd brought in the guidance counselor, who had just arrived through the back door
and who tried to smile at me and look at his shoes, both at the
same time. Mr. Anderson lumbered out from behind his desk
and shuffled around the room until he'd dragged me out a nice
soft chair to sit in, a big chair, the biggest chair in the room,
and the only one that was upholstered.

"How are you, Mary Faith?" he said.

I said I was fine.

"We understand . . . you may have a little—problem," he said encouragingly, and the guidance counselor began playing his feet up and down and across each other, so that he'd have something to watch.

"No sir," I said. "I don't think I have a problem." If I'd boarded a Greyhound bus in front of twenty people *and* thrown myself at a married man, I didn't have so much to worry about from these two. I knew exactly what they were up to.

Mr. Anderson looked me straight in the eye. "Miss Rapple," he said, "are you expecting a baby?"

"Yes, sir," I said.

"We thought so. We had a little complaint from one of the older GED students. Who didn't think it was quite *fitting*. But we'd like to offer you a little help," he said. "I asked Mr. Young to be here so he could tell you about the plans Due East High School has for—cases like yours."

Bobby Young looked up in alarm, and cleared his throat, and began to tell me about the special series of classes for young women in my—state: that the classes were held at the tech school and that girls could attend right up to the time they delivered their babies! except that of course it was going to be summer right now and that they had a little day care center so the girls could come back when their babies were six months old and didn't need such *constant* attention and that all the basic courses were offered but that my case was unusual because I was taking so many advanced courses, and foreign languages, and hmmm things like that, but that maybe when my baby was six months old we could all sit down together and map out some kind of independent study plan, and that if I wanted to I could go ahead and prepare for the SATs and National Merit. With old test books.

I knew about that program. They segregated all the pregnant girls down at the other end of town and then they taught them nutrition and how to fold diapers. I would have to *talk* to them. About babies. I had no interest whatsoever.

I told Mr. Young and Mr. Anderson that I'd just been planning to finish up my exams and have my baby in the summer and then go to the GED classes to work on my own until I was old enough to take the exam. "And anyway," I said, trying to sound modest and shy, "I'll be *teaching* the GEDs up until the baby comes, so I'll be keeping my hand in that way."

Bobby Young and Mr. Anderson looked at each other, Mr. Young in a panic and Mr. Anderson in weariness. "Mary Faith honey," said Mr. Anderson, "I'm afraid you don't quite understand. We can't let you go back to tutoring those classes when the class members are complaining. We have a standard set of arrangements for girls who get pregnant, and we're going to have to follow them. As of today, you're not supposed to be sitting in the regular classroom, you're supposed to be down at the tech school in the special classes."

"But I'm taking my *finals,*" I said.

Mr. Young managed to get his hands underneath his thighs and sit on them. Mr. Anderson said: "I know that. How many more have you got to go?"

"Three," I said. "French and trig and world history."

"Technically you're not supposed to be taking those exams," he said.

I waited.

"But with only three to go, I don't see why you shouldn't just go ahead and take them. What do you think, Mr. Young?"

Mr. Young beamed and nodded.

I guessed I was supposed to thank them. I asked if that was all, and then my mother's training got the better of me and I *did* thank them. I went back into the hallways with two hours to kill before trig. If I didn't tutor the GEDs, I would never see Stephen Dugan again. If Stephen Dugan didn't drive me home he would never come by the house, and when he saw me in the street he would turn his head away in shame for kissing the breast of a fifteen-year-old girl.

I went into the bathroom on A hall, which should have been crowded between exams. It was almost empty. There was one girl standing by the sinks, standing by *both* sinks, she was so big. She looked to weigh about three hundred pounds, and she was wearing bedroom slippers for shoes. She was taking a long drag on a cigarette, and a good stare at me to see what I'd do about it. I'd seen it happen a hundred times: a black girl would be standing alone in the bathroom, smoking a cigarette, and three white prisses would come in to put on their *eye*shadow, and after their lids were some lurid blue they'd flounce out, saying, "There's no smoking in the *bath*rooms, you know," and they'd beat the hell out of there so that maybe they didn't even hear the girl behind them calling: "Oh, yeah? And what you going to do about it, white girl?"

I walked over to the mirror and pulled my hair out of its ponytail. If they didn't let me teach the GEDs again, I'd have two more months of that empty house. The girl's cigarette smelled good: she smoked my father's brand, Marlboro, and I asked her for one.

She pulled a cigarette out of the pack that balanced on the sink and handed it over impassively.

"Can I have a match?"

She lit the cigarette for me, and I choked a little on the first puff. She didn't laugh, though. She said, "When you due?"

"August the first," I said. That was what I had calculated from the chart at the back of *Your Pregnancy Can Be the Happiest Time of Your Life.* It was the first time I had said the date out loud to anyone.

"Ha," she said. "I'm August thirty-first. You know it's going to be *hot* for having a baby then." Her voice was soft and high.

I knew I didn't have to worry about her getting all sympathetic. I asked her if they'd tried to kick her out of school, into the program down at the tech school.

She laughed. "They don't notice me. They can't *tell* I'm pregnant."

"I couldn't tell either," I said. Then I thought I'd better add on, "You carry it real well."

She laughed. "You mean you don't see it with all the fat. What you want, girl or boy? I want a boy. I want to name him after my boyfriend. Josephus. He's in the Army. He don't want to marry me now, but he sees that little boy smiling up at me, he'll change his mind."

I took a long drag on the cigarette the way she did, looking up and out, and she said, "So what you want?"

"A girl," I said. "I don't know about boys."

"You just got to be meaner with them. What your boyfriend want?"

I went up and out. I could almost see telling her about Stephen Dugan. "My boyfriend's dead," I said.

"*Dead?*" she said. "And you due in August, too. Well, you get your momma to soak you down until you got to go into the hospital. Get her to rub you with a wet cloth. Your momma'll be more use around than some boy don't know what he's doing, anyway."

I could see standing with this girl in the bathroom until the second exam period. I could see telling her it was all right, that I was in love with a different man now. "My mother's dead, too," I said.

"You'll get somebody to soak you down," she said. "It's going to be *August*. It's going to be *hot.*" Then she gave me two cigarettes to take for the rest of the day and said not to inhale so much and asked me to reach down and pick up the matches off the floor. She couldn't bend over.

I walked out of the bathroom feeling dizzy and sick and hungry, and wandered around B hall and C hall and D hall and E hall and the breezeway, where I found the cigarette butt still stuck to the bottom of my shoe. I came back through A hall, where the pay phones were, and after I passed them by three times, I called up information and asked for the number of the Due East *Courier*. I had no shame left.

Mr. Dugan got on the line after three or four minutes, and I held in my breath and tried to remember what it had felt like, the night before, when he had twisted my nipple until it hurt.

"Mr. Dugan," I said. "Stephen. They're kicking me out of school." There was a pure, empty silence at the other end of the wire, until he said: "Bastards." And then I knew everything would be all right.

12

Madly in Love

Driving Mary Faith home from the Greyhound station had released a brake for Jesse. That night, when he went over to Nell's, he was free of all thoughts of Faith, and all he could concentrate on was a perfume Nell had put on, some musky odor that smelled almost as thick as a man's aftershave. She'd never worn perfume before, and after he'd made sure it was her, that it was coming from her neck, he said something *he*'d never said before: "Let me give you a massage."

Nell looked at him with a strange purse of her lips, but laughed her hoarse laugh and led him back to the bedroom, where she pulled off her blouse and bra and tucked two pillows under her belly. He had no idea how to start a massage, but it was the kind of thing couples did all the time in made-for-television movies, the kind of image that had stuck in his mind so clearly that it seemed easy enough, and he kneaded down Nell's bony shoulders and into her spine. There was no extra flesh on her back, nothing to squeeze, nothing to linger on. He had gotten so accustomed to her skinniness already that he couldn't stand to see fat women anymore, couldn't understand how they lost self-control so completely. Sometimes it seemed every woman over forty in Due East was fat, every woman but Nell. So when he had worked his way down her back, he started up at her shoulders again, digging deeper into her skin until he was back at the bottom of her spine. He stopped. She had worn perfume, and now he was making all the first moves. None of her scenes out of *Raunch.* He tugged at the elastic waist of her pants and heard her groan into the bedclothes when he'd pulled them down. He rubbed her firm bottom with both his hands, scooped it up, squeezed it. There was nothing about her tightness that reminded him of Faith: they might have been different sexes. When the bath towel slipped loose from Faith, he'd caught glimpses of a puckered white expanse that fanned out from beneath her waist and led down to her thick legs. But Nell's bottom was like a twenty-year-old girl's, and his hand slid down to the top of her thighs.

Nell rose quickly from the bed and tottered off to the bathroom, the pants legs still gathered around her ankles. She brought back a bottle of baby oil, and wouldn't look him in the eye: the first time ever for that, too, as if *baby* oil were the most perverted thing she'd ever thought of. She settled back onto the bed, and he slathered the oil over her back and then turned her over and slathered her breasts, and didn't even stop to think that he wasn't feeling the tugs he usually felt: the tug that she was fifty and wrinkled, the tug that Faith would weep if she could see him this way, the tug that Mary Faith felt something as sharp as hatred when she thought of him with this woman. He just wanted her.

The next day at the station he found himself chatting for five minutes with every driver who came in, kidding Lee Mac about a girlfriend, calling up the weather every half-hour to see if it would rain by the afternoon. It was hot and damp, the end of May, but the heat felt good to him. Not remembering Faith felt good to him. Again and again he found himself rerunning the image of Nell tottering back from the bathroom with the baby oil, averting her eyes, and a few times he laughed out loud at the thought. He was running little dialogues too, throughout the day: talks with Mary Faith when he sat her down at the supper table and told her she didn't *know* Mrs. Dugan, she had no right to resent her before she'd had so much as a decent conversation with her. Then he would become expansive: he could see telling Mary Faith that Mrs. Dugan was a *relief* after all the old bitches in Due East, that he *liked* to be with a woman who was blunt and knew just what she wanted. A thin woman.

At three o'clock he decided to call Nell—not his usual call to set up a time for that night, but a call just to say hello. To flirt on the telephone. When her phone rang ten times without an answer, he dialed the number again. She was always home in the middle of the day. She barely walked out in the sunlight. Still there was no answer, and he could not resist the urge to dial a third time. His fingers sweated his anxiety onto the receiver. He hung up convinced that she was at some other man's apartment. He just didn't know where else she could be. She was with some other man who lived in the condos, some retired officer who'd seen her at the poolside and wanted to squeeze her tight bottom. He could see her getting out the baby oil: hadn't the bottle been half-empty?

By four o'clock, when he'd made four more calls that weren't answered, he told himself that it wasn't her fault, that he'd never made any promises to her, never told her that he loved her or liked her or even thought she was *worth* spending all the time he'd been spending with her. A sudden loosening of his whole body, a sudden vision of peace descended on him when he realized what he had to do. He had to marry her. He had to move her out of the condo, take her back to the Point. It was a wonder the thought had never emerged so full, so complete, so clear before. It might be hell at first between her and Mary Faith, but the baby would be coming along in a few months, and by then Mary Faith would be grateful to have somebody else in the house, somebody to spell her with walking the baby, somebody who gave her a chance to get outside once in a while.

The new plan was so definite, so precise, that he even managed to stay away from Nell's for a few nights, holding back and tempting himself with pictures of baby oil and stretch pants gathered around Nell's ankles. He ate supper with Mary Faith and they talked about her exams. She told him she was going back to the tutoring—Monday nights this time, so he wouldn't have to worry about the service—and he said she could do it, thinking that Stephen Dugan, as much as he didn't trust him, was going to be his son-in-law. He'd never *really* believed Dugan had slept with Mary Faith, he just wouldn't be surprised if he'd *wanted* to. But that wasn't enough to keep him away from Mary Faith over something so innocent as those night classes, and he told his daughter that she could let Stephen drive her there.

On Monday night he made a point of eating spaghetti with Mary Faith and waiting until Stephen had come to fetch her before he left for Nell's. Nell had called *him* at the station, and he'd made her sweat it out a little bit, telling her he couldn't see her until after the weekend. She'd be ready for him by tonight. She'd laugh at him when he first asked her, maybe make him wait a few days until she gave him a real answer, but she'd come round. He knew it. He'd just known it since the minute he'd decided to marry her. Her hair was changing color —there was a little brown showing through the gray now—and Nell dyeing her hair, as far as he was concerned, was just another sign that she was looking for the same kind of permanence he was looking for.

But the minute she answered the door he knew it wouldn't be the way he'd planned. She wasn't wearing any perfume, and she was running one hand through her hair, itching with something. "Come on in," she said, grumpy, and got him a beer without asking. "Don't forget where the *ashtray* is," she said, seeing ashes dangling. She asked him if he wanted some ice cream for dessert, and then didn't get up to get it.

"Did I do something wrong?" he said. "Are you mad at me?"

"Oh, aside from not calling for five days, I guess not," she said.

He considered. "I'm sorry about that," he finally said. "I've had important things on my mind."

Nell glowered. "So have I," she said. "So have I had important things on my mind."

He put out the cigarette and watched her on the couch. He'd imagined she'd be greeting him in a nightgown, or those same stretch pants again, but she was in an old pair of jeans and another one of her husband's fishing shirts. What was that supposed to remind him of? She probably *had* been at the pool —her face was darker than ever, and the wrinkles around her eyes and mouth were ruts now. He wouldn't be surprised if she were fifty-five. But it didn't matter: she was mad because he hadn't called her, and that made her look old, but he was going to ask her to marry him and she'd strip off the old clothes and get down to her thin brown body and she wouldn't look so old anymore. When she moved in to the Point he'd drop some hints about her wearing dresses once in a while. Maybe he wouldn't even have to: maybe she'd see the closetsful of Faith's dresses and just know he'd like to see her smoothed out once in a while.

"I'll get you that ice cream," she said, and still didn't move.

"Nell, what is the *matter?*" He had a little twinge of desire to hear her say that she'd been miserable without his calls, that she'd been waiting for him every night, that she couldn't live without him. That would just swing ever so naturally into the proposal.

She looked down at the rug and pouted and said, "It's my damn daughter, that's what's the matter."

He leaned back and rubbed out his cigarette. Her daughter. "Ruthie?" he said.

"Ruthie," she said. "She's been calling me up night and day bugging me about this *visit* she wants to take. She's coming next week. I don't want to see her. I told her she's staying at Stephen's and still she calls me up night and day trying to make *plans*. She's driving me out of my head."

Jesse took a deep breath and got up to fetch himself his own ice cream. In the kitchen, spooning it out, he told himself that she hadn't said a *word* about missing him. She hadn't even bothered to brush out her *hair*. He slowed himself down, putting the spoon in the sink, and decided she was just bringing Ruthie up as a cover. He'd just let her talk about Ruthie, and then they'd bring the talk round to themselves, and it would all come out while they were lying on her bed together, slathering baby oil on each other.

He found her stretched out on the couch when he came back

into the living room, her fat cat curled up at her chest. She started in again before he had even sat down: "Can you imagine?" she said. "She thinks she's going to stay here with those two little children, not black and not white? What the hell does she think she's going to do with them all day? Sit with them by the pool until they're black as the ace of spades? I told her, I said I'd be glad to have Stephen with me again, but I've never even seen the baby and I'm not about to try learning to love a whole passel of Ruthie's kids that she is having to get back at everybody in Due East. If her father was alive."

Jesse ate his butter pecan ice cream. "It's not like it was when we were kids. People won't even notice. They're your grandchildren," he said mildly. He knew he could give up talking to her about marriage for the next half-hour at least.

"*I* know they're my grandchildren," Nell spat out, and the cat jumped off the couch in alarm. "But what are you going to do if your little Mary Faith's baby comes out black? Have you got any plans for that, Mr. High and Mighty? Two weeks ago you couldn't stand the thought of her having *any* baby, and tonight you're fussing with me because I'm not so wild about playing grandmamma to two children people in Due East would be all too happy to take potshots at."

Jesse took another spoonful, as slowly as he could. His first urge had been to say, "Mary Faith's not going to have a black baby," but he held himself back. Instead he said: "When's Ruthie planning to get here?" If Ruthie's visit were in two or three weeks, he and Nell might be married. She and her children might be coming to visit the Point.

"Next week," Nell said morosely. "Ten days. She's taking the train down."

"And how long's she staying for?"

"Lord knows," said Nell. "Two weeks. Three. As long as she can drive me crazy, she'll stay."

They could be married with her daughter there. With both their daughters there. Ruthie and Mary Faith could be bridesmaids or something. It was all meant to be. The timing. School out. Ruthie there. "Nell," he said, "I've got something to ask you."

"What?" She didn't look up.

He stared at his empty bowl.

"What?" she said again. "Something about not seeing me while Ruthie's here? I don't blame you."

"No," he said. "No! I want to marry you."

She swung her legs down to the floor and pushed herself up to sitting. "Say that again," she said. "I'm not sure I heard you right."

"I want to marry you?"

Nell stretched her thin lips over her wide gums, leaned her head back and hooted. Jesse watched her warily: she could just as easily have been making fun of him as laughing for joy.

Finally she stopped, and wiped her mouth with the back of her hand, and said, "Jesse Rapple, how long have I known you?"

"Well," he said, "I guess it's been a couple of months."

"It's been about six weeks," she said. "Now do you think knowing somebody six weeks is a long enough time for getting married?"

He tried to calculate back. It had to be longer than six weeks. There was the time when she'd put on the dirty movie on the cable channel, and the time she'd been wearing black stockings with a garter belt, and the time she'd taken off his belt and handed it to him with a leer—the time he'd come before she had unzipped his pants.

It had to be more than six weeks. "I don't care," he said. "I don't care how long it's been, I just know what I want."

She hooted again and said: "Who would've thought?" and slapped her knee. Jesse rose with his dirty ice cream bowl and walked into the kitchen. He could feel his ears reddening, and listened for the sound of Nell laughing in the living room. Faith! Damn her: all he could picture now, standing in another woman's kitchen, was Faith in some tidy little housedress, making some tidy heavy little meal, hearing this coarse old woman laughing at him, *taunting* him from the side of her plastic-covered couch. Faith would have cried. Faith would have wept gently at his humiliation.

Automatically he went to rinse the bowl out in the sink and

started when he felt Nell's hand on his shoulder. She was touching him lightly, and when he turned around she was smiling coyly up at him. She didn't come up to his shoulders.

"Come on back into the bedroom," she whispered.

"No," he said, surprising himself, and withdrawing from her touch. "Not until you tell me what's so funny about my wanting to marry you."

She licked her lips and batted her eyelashes up at him. There was more brown showing in her hair tonight. "Nothing's so funny," she said, "except that I didn't think you were so romantic. But nothing's so funny. You just can't rush a lady. You just have to give her a little more time than *six* weeks."

Now he smiled, at the thought of her calling herself a *lady*. A lady she wasn't: and that was why he wanted to marry her.

He didn't see Nell on Tuesday—he didn't want to seem *that* eager, now that he'd opened himself up completely to her— but on Wednesday morning she called him early at the station, and asked if he'd seen the morning paper yet. He said no; he never read the *Courier*, especially since Dugan had taken to writing half the liberal money-spending crap that was in it.

Nell asked him if he had a copy there and he said no, he didn't even *buy* the paper, and she said he'd better go out and buy one now if he wanted to know what was going on with his daughter.

"*What?*" said Jesse. "What?"

"There is a letter from your daughter in the Letters to the Editor column, Mr. Rapple," Nell said. "And I've got a pretty good idea who arranged to have it put there. Stephen!" she said. "Between him and Ruthie they're trying to drive everybody around here nuts."

"What?" he said again.

"It says she's seven months pregnant. Your daughter just announced to the world that she is seven months pregnant. It says she's not being allowed to tutor the GED classes that Stephen teaches anymore and that she doesn't think it's fair. It makes her sound like a crackpot, Jesse."

"Oh, my God," said Jesse.

"I mean," Nell went on, "I mean Ruthie didn't exactly *hide* her condition either, but she didn't go writing letters to the editor about it. She's going to be kicked out of the high school at the rate she's going. She's sure not going to make you any friends."

Jesse sat down at his desk, and asked Nell what she thought her son had to do with it.

"Well, I don't know *exactly* what he's got to do with it," she said, "but I know he saw that letter before it went out. I just know it. I mean, he's the one who teaches the class and he's working right there at the paper, and you just *know* he saw it."

"You don't think?"

Nell crackled over the phone. "No, for God's sake, Jesse, will you leave that alone? No, I do *not* think he had anything to do with your daughter getting pregnant. I just think he's using more of the same goddamn bad judgment that gets him and his sister into hot water all the livelong day, is what I think."

Jesse said, "She's got her last exams today. Her last two exams. She walked out of the house all bouncy."

"I'll bet she did," said Nell. "I bet she did walk out all bouncy. I bet she knew there'd be a fight coming when she got to the high school and I bet she was raring for it."

Jesse moaned. "Let me go, Nell," he said. "I've got to go get me a copy of that paper."

He heard her tense on the other end of the wire. "And thanks for calling, Nell," she said.

"And thanks for calling, Nell," he said absently, and hung up on her. She didn't scare him so much now that he'd smelled her perfume. She'd have to get used to him putting Mary Faith first *some*times.

The paper said just what Nell said it said:

To the editor:
    I am a sophomore at Due East High School. I have been on the honor roll every semester, and have won several awards for my classwork. This year, I was chosen to be a student tutor at the evening GED

classes, which are given for students over eighteen
who wish to complete their high school requirements
by taking a special exam.

This week I was told that I would not be allowed to
tutor the GED classes, and that I will not be allowed
back in the regular classroom after I finish my exams.
The reason is that I am seven months pregnant. I
guess the powers that be in the Due East schools
think that I will not be a good influence on the other
students. But I do not think a girl should be made to
go to a special program just because she is pregnant.
After all, my mind still works the same, and it probably has more influence on the other students than the
size of my belly.

I hope Due East High School will reconsider its
position about my being allowed to tutor the GED
classes.

Sincerely,
Mary F. Rapple

Jesse read the letter ten times during the day; by the fifth
time he was a little proud of Mary Faith. He liked the way she
used phrases like "powers that be," phrases that she had
learned from him, from his distrust of anybody in charge. But
by the seventh or eighth time he picked up the paper, after
Buddy had called to say his little girl had some nerve, wasn't
she *some*thing?, and after Nell had called back to say maybe he
should get her to write a letter of apology, and after three
women who had their tanks filled at his station for the first time
in months looked up at him through the windshield with sympathy that churned his stomach, he left the station at five
o'clock thinking this might be it. This might be the first time
he'd spanked Mary Faith since she was five. He felt ready to do
it. She was out of control now: he should have punished her
when she lied the way she did at the bus station. He should
have made her tell who the father was two months ago. But
now, anyway, he was going to make up for that lost time, that
lost punishment.

Then, when he walked in the front door at five o'clock, he could smell the shrimp creole she was making. It took her hours to make creole. All he could do was march into the kitchen with the folded paper in his hand and hold it up at her with a face he tried to make look wounded and threatening all at the same time.

She didn't blink at the folded paper.

He tried fanning it around, but still she wouldn't acknowledge it, and finally he said, "Did they call you into the office over this?"

"No, sir," she said. She was making croutons for a salad. She told him that nobody had said a word to her all day, that she'd finished her world history exam at noon and come home, and that it didn't matter because she wouldn't be able to go back to the high school during the day *anyway*, she just wanted to have something to do on Monday nights. She ran it all into one sentence, and then turned back to her bacon fat melting on the stove.

"Mary Faith," he said stiffly, "it is Wednesday night."

"Yes, sir," she said. "Are you going to Mrs. Dugan's?"

"I am not," he said. "I am taking you to service."

There was no answer. They hadn't been to Wednesday service together since long before she'd told him about her troubles.

"Mary Faith," he said again.

"Yes sir."

"After supper I want you to go up and find one of your mother's dress-up dresses. And put on a pair of those flat black shoes. And we're going to church together."

"Yes sir."

"Maybe you can get some comfort out of your religion now," he said. He thought she mumbled something sharp about *that* religion, but he didn't hear it clearly. What he did hear was what she said for him out loud: "If that's what you want, Daddy."

He threw the Wednesday *Courier* into the trash by the sink and asked her if she wanted him to set the table, but she looked up at him in such surprise that instead he went in to watch the local news before they ate.

He was too early for the news, and flicked the dial around until he found the Merv Griffin show, Nell's favorite. There was a very skinny young singer on, drooping her mouth over the microphone, and he stopped on the channel for a minute, transfixed. The singer wore a white dress with a plunging neckline, but the camera settled on her thin mouth drawn in red. He'd never been aware of mouths before, but since Nell he'd seen everyone's face anew. This one, this singer, had a Nell Dugan mouth: lips as thin as pencil points, lips that drew back on an important word in the song to show her pink gums. He tried to imagine Nell as a young woman and couldn't do it. They were not even of the same generation, really: they hadn't grown up together in Due East. He wondered how wild *she*'d been at the high school. The time she had taken his belt off before she unzipped his pants she had wanted him to tie her hands up with it. He wondered if she'd be willing to change from Catholic to Baptist, now that she'd changed from Methodist to Catholic. He wished he had her for tonight, for the three of them to walk down the aisle together like a proper family. It would give Lizann and Zack something else beside Mary Faith to stare at. It would give Mary Faith something else to think about. He pushed the Off button on the TV and listened to his daughter cooking in the kitchen.

13

Services

My father and I walked into First Baptist at eight o'clock sharp. He was wearing his blue suit and I had on the black dress with the white collar that I picked out from the closet. It made me look smaller, but the ushers stared at us anyway, with tight little smiles, and Uncle Zack and Aunt Lizann hurried in before we could catch up with them, and we could feel the whole choir —from the seven-year-olds up—leaning over the railing to watch my father escort his pregnant daughter down the aisle. A year ago I'd been part of that choir. Now I was just the high school slut, but even *they* didn't know how far I'd gone. My father walked me down to the front, and I made myself tall and thought about making love to Stephen, to a married man.

We sang about fifty hymns while I tried to think about when it would be safest to call Stephen back. I knew he got the letter in the paper for me because he wanted to see me on Mondays, too, because he was all ready for the sin that would have made every Baptist in the church faint dead away, but I knew I couldn't call too soon. I watched Dr. Beady mouthing the words to "A Mighty Fortress." Everybody in the whole damn church knew he didn't sing along, but he still moved his lips to pretend he did. He was an anemic-looking little man, with square black glasses and a bald spot he tried to cover up by parting his hair down close to his ear. He had the eager air of a rodent. My father and Buddy Miles had talked about dumping him as preacher because he gave every third sermon on money, but they lost interest in it, or my father did, anyway.

Dr. Beady fussed with his big sleeves and gazed out over the congregation. He looked out of place at the front of the church —everything in First Baptist is fifties-modern, from the walnut-veneer empty cross to the walnut-veneer pulpit that looks like it was made by the Zenith Corporation after they were done making television cabinets—but Dr. Beady is straight out of the nineteenth century. He is the kind of preacher who tiptoes into choir practice, wearing a cheap black suit and his hungry rat's smile, and pulls up ten-year-old boys by the collar if he finds them acting up. That night I had a feeling he had his small black eyes directly on me, but I told myself not to play up the paranoia. I was trying to decide whether to wait for Stephen to call me. I could wait forever, with his guilt.

Finally the choir had done its bit, and Miss Christobel Hawkins had sung her solo (flipping her blond hair over her shoulder at the end of every bar), and the deacon had done *his* bit, and Dr. Beady rose to preach. The last few Sundays he had been pushing faith: faith that there would be a good tomato crop this year, faith that the building fund would grow tenfold by the end of the summer, faith that California would not fall into the sea. The bulletin board outside had given the title of the Wednesday night service—the short sermon—as "Our Duty in the Community." I was pretty sure it was another tidy way of getting at money. But as soon as Dr. Beady began to speak, I knew I was in trouble. When he was seated, listening to the choir with one finger pressed against his temple, I had had the sensation that he had picked me out to stare at. Now I had the sensation that he had picked me out to avoid. His eyes darted around and up, to everyone in the congregation but me. He started in his low nasal whine, the whine that would work up to a fever pitch.

"The sinner," he said. "What must we ask of the sinner?" All around me I could feel the electric buzz that Dr. Beady set off when he began to speak. In a few minutes, people would drift away, would stop listening to him, but for now, he had them; he had them lined up naked with their legs spread apart and they were trying to shield themselves. He loved those words *sin* and *sinner:* he sloshed them around in his mouth like wine and then spat them out, all over the congregation.

"The sinner has a debt to pay to the community," said Dr. Beady, and all the Baptists of First Baptist snuck peeks at their neighbors out of the corners of their eyes. "The adulterer," Dr. Beady went on, and we all settled in, anticipating the best. "The adulterer must go back to his spouse and beg her forgiveness." He paused. "The employee who has pilfered must go back to his employer and make restitution." Big pause. "The fornicator" (here he took a deep cleansing breath and came out of it at the other end with a bellow) "the fornicator must stop his immoral actions and begin anew on a pure path." He swallowed gasps of air, and so did the congregation. We had made it past fornicators. Dr. Beady squeezed his eyes up again to circle them over the sinners below, and again I felt that he met everyone's eyes but mine.

Suddenly he began again, off-beat, catching us off-guard. "But *what,*" he said, "but *what* do we do when the sinner not only refuses to pay off this debt to those he has sinned against? What of the sinner who refuses to say to the community: I am sorry? What do we do with the sinner who is proud of his low deeds? *What* do we do with the drug addict who parades his weak character through our streets?" We all tried to imagine junkies marching down River Street. "What do we do with the drunkard who will not give up his bottle?" Winos parading down River Street! "*What* do we do with the adulterer who will not return to wife and children, but goes on in his sinful ways? Or the teenager who *flaunts* her promiscuity?" I felt my father stiffening beside me. No one had drifted off this time: we all followed Dr. Beady like sheep, and he was building up for the slaughter.

He pulled in another cleansing breath. "*I will tell you what we can do,*" said Dr. Beady. "We can confront that sinner. What has become of us, in 1981, that we are afraid to confront the sinner? What has become of us that we can no longer say to those who have gone astray: 'You are wrong. You are doing e-vil. You re-pulse me.' Why can we no longer say that?" We all shrank back in our pews. "I will *tell you why*. We can no longer say that because we are afraid. Because our society, yes, our media, our schools, tell us that it is all right for our children to drink liquor, to pop pills, to engage in the sacred marriage act when they are fourteen and fifteen years old. They have *frightened* us into acquiescence." He mopped his brow, but didn't look at all acquiescent. His face had the glow of proud red anger it took on for all his sinning sermons, and the glow shone out among the congregation.

When he began again, he dropped his voice, and I could feel my father's stiff arm lean forward, as if to catch his words. All over the big white church women leaned their shoulders forward to hear how they could regain their righteousness and lose their acquiescence. "We have an example," said Dr. Beady. "We have an example," whispered Dr. Beady, "of this in-ab-il-i-ty to face sin in our community today. I mean *today*, this very day, this Wednesday, in this hot June when we are thinking of our air conditioners and our sprinklers and when we should be thinking of bigger things, of sin that must be confronted." People leaned back an inch or two: it was one thing to confront sin, but another to be made guilty about an air conditioner in Due East, South Carolina. Dr. Beady rolled on, unperturbed. "We have this very day," he said, "witnessed the local media giving coverage to, giving *encouragement* to, what it should have been deriding." There was a sucking in of breath all over the church. The local media consisted of three radio stations, two of which played country-western and one of which played easy-listening; the educational TV station on UHF that nobody ever bothered tuning in to; and the Due East *Courier*. Dr. Beady meant the Due East *Courier*. For a minute I thought that even Dr. Beady couldn't do *this*, that he had never gone so far as to point a finger at an individual from the pulpit. He had hinted at those who didn't support the church, but he had never dropped hints about one who sat below his nose. About me. My father's hand had knotted into a fist. He was leaning forward again, almost to the next pew.

Dr. Beady looked around him and made a great show of relaxing his shoulders, of relaxing his whole body. We all knew this phase: when he was out of the buildup, out of the anger, and down to the conversational, I-don't-mean-to-scare-you-by-any-of-this-I'm-just-one-of-you-folks-too phase. Now his voice would be as smooth and as thick as treacle. "I don't know how many of you know exactly what I am talking about," he said. Conversational. "I'm not one of those preachers who thinks we should point the finger directly at anyone. Remember Jesus! Remember what he said about casting the first stone! Read your Bible. Read John, Chapter Eight, verses one through twelve." He laughed a little conversational laugh and hung his hands over the edge of the pulpit. "You know," he said, and now he stared directly at me, eye to eye, Dr. Beady's beady black eye thinking it was boring through me, thinking it was *scaring* me. "You know, when I was a boy, the preachers did not hold back at anything. When I was a boy, if you were caught chewing gum in church, the usher would come over and pull you up by the elbow and escort you down the aisle for all to see. Once," and he laughed again, mirthlessly, "once a young visitor to our small town upstate arrived in the middle of summer." We all of us realized we were in for a detour—Dr. Beady would take us back on a ride through his boyhood—and there was settling in all over the church.

"We were not a proud community," he went on. "Our fathers were farmers mostly, eking out a living from soybeans or peaches, but when this young visitor arrived at our church we all took notice. We were all dressed in our best—maybe not a very fancy best, maybe our shoes were run down, but they were polished; maybe our suits were worn thin, but they were pressed—we were all dressed in our best, but this young lady arrived at the front steps of our church dressed in shorts. Dressed in *bermuda* shorts." He calmed himself back into the conversational. "It was a hot day, a hot Ju-ly day, but I remember the look of my mother and the other good women of our community as they spied this young girl coming up the steps in her bermuda shorts. My mother, and all her friends, were wearing white gloves, and modest dresses with long sleeves, and their best shoes, and they blushed when they saw this young thing coming up the steps of the *house of our Lord* in her bermuda shorts. I will never forget the blushes, the shame those good women felt. When the one who should have been feeling shame bared her legs on a Sunday morning for all to see." He bowed his head in shame, and we all bowed our heads.

"I'm sure the good people of this community would blush, too," said Dr. Beady soothingly. "Even in the nineteen-eighties. Even in this day when anything goes. Even in this day of the drug addict, and the drunken driver, and the topless dancer, and the pregnant teenager." He bore down on me again. "*What do you think our preacher did?*" he roared. Then he stopped and composed himself. "This is what he did. Our minister was just arriving to enter the back of the church, but when he saw this young girl outside *the house of our Lord,* dressed in bermuda shorts, he had one of the ushers call her aside, and he took her back with him to the side entrance of the church. I suspect he told her she would have a special place for listening to the sermon, because she was a visitor. I suspect, in her pride, that she was flattered by his attention. Imagine that scene, if you will." He paused to let us all picture it. "Perhaps you can *imagine* what happened when the choir of our little church had finished singing. Perhaps you can *imagine* what happened when it came time for our minister to deliver the word of the Lord. Can you imagine it?" He let us imagine it. "Can you see our preacher bringing this young girl out in front of the congregation, and telling her what he thought of her disrespect? Perhaps you can't imagine that in 1981, but that is what happened. That is indeed what happened. Our preacher told this girl what he thought of her immodesty, what he thought—and he wasn't afraid to say it, not in nineteen *fifty*-one—what he thought of her *sin* of coming to Sunday services dressed in a pair of bermuda shorts."

Suddenly I was aware that my father had put his arm around my shoulder, lightly—not leaning me toward him or squeezing me, but just resting it there, something he'd never done before —and I saw Dr. Beady's eyes veer away from us. All the tension that my father had put into listening to the sermon, fighting the sermon, was gone. He just had his arm around me. I had never felt that sensation before, the sensation of being borne up by him.

But Dr. Beady was droning on: now he told us that he was not going to drag up anyone in front of the congregation, that it was not his intention to shame or disgrace anyone. I stopped listening. A phrase or a word would seep into my consciousness—I would hear *confronting* or *admitting* or *the wages of sin being met with the life, not the death, of forgiveness*—but I did not have to listen to Dr. Beady any longer. I did not even have to think of Stephen. Even he could not do what my father was doing, what my father had never done in his life; even he wouldn't defy Dr. Beady this way. Not with this arm, this loose arm draped around my shoulder as if it practiced being there every day. Not even my mother would have flown in the face of Dr. Beady's sermon *this* way; she might have squeezed my hand, her face aflame with shame for me, shame as red-hot as Dr. Beady's mother's shame, but she never would have put her arm around my *shoulder*. We were in the seventh or eighth pew back. My father had to know that most of the church could see him holding me this way. I tried to catch his eye, to smile at him, but he stared straight ahead at the hymn racks, not up at Dr. Beady, not sideways at me.

I began to tune back in to Dr. Beady's sermon when I heard it winding down. I thought I could sense defeat in his voice, a defeat my father was engineering with only his arm. Dr. Beady sounded listless now. "So what must we do?" he was saying. "What must we do when we know that one of our number is sinning in the eyes of the Lord? Here is what we must do. We must *confront* the sinner. We must tell her we know of her sin. We must offer forgiveness, but *firm* forgiveness. Forgiveness that says this community will not tolerate a flaunting of the sin. We are willing to forgive the error, an error that any one of us might make, but we will not *condone* the sin. We will not allow the sin to be *publicized.* Remember the prodigal son! Jesus has exhorted us to forgive, but it is the sinner who must come forward."

Suddenly I could sit in my seat no longer. My father was beside me: he would understand when I jumped up. He would follow me out of the church. It was a feeling so strong, so confident, so immediate in its descension on me that I could not distinguish between the second when I was sitting meekly next to my father and the second when I rose, rose and stretched myself out tall, thinking about my height, about Dr. Beady's little body and little eyes and little smile. I rose and stood silent, knowing that my silence would silence Dr. Beady. That little smile began to appear at the corner of his mouth: he thought I was rising to beg his forgiveness, to come forward, to be the prodigal daughter. My body had risen to take me out of the church, but now it could not leave without speaking. Now that Dr. Beady waited, now that the deacon waited and the choir waited, now that the congregation waited for me to beg their forgiveness, now I could bellow out louder than Dr. Beady. No insinuating little conversational asides from *my* tall body.

"Dr. Beady," I began, and was surprised that my voice was not as clear, not as low, not as loud as I thought it would be. "Dr. Beady," I called again, and this time it was firm and steady and bounced off the big white pillars in the big white church. "I do *not* beg your forgiveness, Dr. Beady," I said clearly, and then I stopped. I did not know what else to say. My body had propelled me up out of my seat, but it had not told me what to do next. So I repeated it: "I do *not* beg your forgiveness, Dr. Beady." Then I turned and made my way out of the pew, walking over the ankles of the two old ladies who had sat to my left and striding down the center aisle so tall, so steady, sure that behind me my father was following, my father who had put his arm around my shoulder, my father stretching out his arm perhaps to bear me up again, sure that now it was the two of us defying this minister. I could not see a single face as I walked the long aisle: even the ushers were a confused blur along the back aisle. They could have been a row of soldiers. I swung the great doors open—two at once—and it was not until they had stopped their swinging shut and I was in the vestibule alone, hot, shocked to find my shoulders trembling and my fingers stinging with the exertion of what I had done, it was not until then that I realized that no footsteps had followed me down

the aisle, that no arm had brushed against my shoulder to hold
me back or go with me. That no one had stood beside me when
I stood. That my father had not followed me. That he was
sitting, still, in the same pew where he had stretched his arm
out around me, and that he would sit there until Dr. Beady
finished his sermon, until Dr. Beady calmly exhorted the
crowd to remember forgiveness and to remember righteousness. I pushed open the big oak front doors now, sure that the
ushers would come after me if I did not leave.

Our truck was parked in the center of the parking lot across
Church Street, illuminated by the deep yellow glow of the
street lamps. It was hot and damp and still outside. Suddenly
all the twinges I had felt in the last month—in my legs, in the
small of my back, in my groin—became deep aches, and it hurt
to walk across the street and climb into the truck. I let myself
think that my father would be along any second, though I knew
he really would not. I knew he wouldn't budge from his seat
until after the sermon was finished and the final songs sung,
that he would stay firm in that seat until long after every other
member of the congregation had left, that he would let his ears
flame when Aunt Lizann came by to press his hand, a flame
more cowardly than my *mother* would have ever felt, that he
would sit until he was sure that the last gossiper had left
Church Street, until our truck was the last car in the parking
lot, until Dr. Beady left by the back and it was just the two of us
in the dark of night.

Soon the organ's rumble reached me, and soon, as I slunk
down in the seat, I could see the congregation bubbling out of
the church. They floated down the front steps and across to
their cars. They looked elated tonight. Tonight had been *in-
spiring.* Soon I caught glimpses of them unlocking their Buicks
and their Mercurys and their Pontiacs, getting into their cars
all around me. I was as low down in the seat as I possibly could
be, and like my father while he listened to the end of the
sermon, I would not let myself look up or around or to the
side. I stared straight ahead, at the lock of the glove compart-
ment, and counted to sixty again and again until the scratchy
sound of ignitions being turned on had died away, until the

rustle of voices from in front of the church had faded away, and the mothers of the junior choir had hushed their daughters who were pointing to the top of my head and asking what I'd *done*. Until my father trudged down the steps of the First Baptist Church of Due East and crossed the street and opened the door of the truck wearily, like an old man, and sat in the driver's seat without looking at me, and sighed. A long, tired sigh. Not a sigh of regret or sadness or shame. A sigh of resignation. He pulled his keys out of his pocket and said: "You shouldn't have done that, Mary Faith," and then he sighed again. I *made* myself look at him, tried to remember how he had put his arm around me, watched him shift the truck into reverse and start us on our way home. It wasn't the same man who had sat beside me in church. He was back to being the man who never remembered to wash his hair, who left me alone every night to go see Mrs. Dugan, a woman as small as Dr. Beady, as tight-eyed.

I thought again of Mrs. Dugan's son, of his getting the letter published in the *Courier* for me, of his saying *bastards* when he heard what they did to me, of the way he took my breast in his hand and sucked it though it pained him, squeezed it though it made him groan. My father was nothing next to him. Nobody. My father wouldn't even walk down the aisle and pretend he was going to talk sense to me.

It was two days later, Friday, when I got the call from Mr. Anderson. I was lying in bed, afraid to roll over because then the twinge at the top of my groin would turn into a digging, twisting pain. The last two mornings I had slept late, later than I had slept the whole pregnancy, and then I had lain in bed not wanting to roll over. I had been dreaming of my mother and of Dr. Beady, and of the ushers standing at the back of the church waiting to spear me. I would not get out of bed until long after my father had slammed the kitchen door shut. I would not get his breakfast or look at him, because he could only remind me of Dr. Beady.

But when the phone rang on Friday morning, I jumped up, thinking it was Stephen, and in jumping pulled my groin and my abdomen and every muscle there was to pull in my legs. By the time I had made it to my father's room and to his night table, the phone had rung eight or nine times, and the voice on the other end sounded sharp and itchy.

"Mary Faith?"

I knew who it was right away.

"This is Mr. Anderson," the sharp voice said. "Your principal." As if I'd forget. At least it wasn't Dr. Beady. "Mary Faith? Are you there?"

I told him I was there, but I hurt so much, felt so cumbersome and bulky standing by my father's bed, that I could barely pay attention to the phone.

"Mary Faith," said Mr. Anderson, "this is to inform you and your father that you will be allowed to tutor the GED classes as long as you are able."

All the pulled muscles went limp and I sat on the edge of my father's unmade bed. I forgot entirely about Dr. Beady and my father deserting me. Stephen in three nights. I had not heard from him, had not called him to tell him about my scarlet letter treatment in the First Baptist Church of Due East, had not called to ask him to please come back and start on the other breast. And now I wouldn't have to call him. I wouldn't even ask him for a ride; I would walk down to the high school if I had to, and I would wear my mother's green dress with the blue smocking, and brush out my hair so that it hung lank and straight down my back, and he would drive me home and know it wasn't wrong. Not with that wife.

"Mary Faith, are you there?"

I told Mr. Anderson I was still there.

"I suppose you're a little curious about the change in policy, Mary Faith."

I said I supposed I was. I *tried* to sound polite.

"I don't guess you had anything to do with the Civil Liberties Union getting involved in this thing?"

"No, sir!" I said. If only I'd thought of it. If only I'd told Mr. Anderson and Dr. Beady and every usher at the back of the church that I planned to sue them for millions of dollars.

Mr. Anderson harumphed on the phone. "I *told* Mr. Young I

didn't think you had anything to do with that," he said, and in his vindication that I was really sort of a good girl after all, even for a bad girl, he eased in close to friendliness. He told me that the Associated Press had written a little article on my letter, which had been picked up by Thursday morning's *State*, which had been read by the Columbia office of the ACLU. "They didn't get in touch with *you?*" he said.

I said no, they didn't get in touch with me. I'd been inside the whole day yesterday, cooking and thinking of ways to pull down Dr. Beady's pants on River Street, and waiting for Stephen to call me.

Well, anyway, he said, they'd told him they *planned* to get in touch with me if there was no change in the policy and that having Due East High School involved in a civil liberties suit while it was still fighting the latest busing order was not what he wanted to get bogged down in. He'd talked it over with the superintendent, and they'd agreed that it couldn't do much harm. "So I'm letting you go back," Mr. Anderson said, "against my better judgment. If you want to know the truth, Mary Faith, I think you're going to be more comfortable staying at home and getting plenty of rest on Monday nights."

"No, sir," I said. "I'll be glad to get back." I'd be glad to have my ride home again.

"Mary Faith?" he said. "Bobby Young told me about what happened over at the church Wednesday night."

It didn't matter what he said now. It didn't matter how much he reminded me of what Dr. Beady had done, how much he sympathized with me or warned me. I would be seeing Stephen Monday night.

"We wanted to let you know how sorry we are about that sort of thing," said Mr. Anderson, and then confused silence came over the wire. Finally he said, "Mr. Young thinks you can *still* get a scholarship to Radcliffe if you put your mind to it."

"Thank you, Mr. Anderson," I said, and he must have heard the way my voice warmed without my willing it, the way I almost smiled at the thought of me going to Radcliffe! while my father filed for bankruptcy and my baby pulled over the potted plants in the TV room. Stephen. Stephen would be seeing me.

I hung up and made my father's bed in a trance. I hadn't been making his breakfast since he'd turned his back on me, but I was still keeping the house in order for him. Now I was ready to forgive him, too. I squatted down to pick up his socks, and put them in the pocket of my nightgown so I wouldn't forget to darn the holes in the heels. His clock said nine-thirty. I still felt tired, but the aches were gone as I stretched around his room, and I could imagine curling up atop the corduroy bedspread and spending the day in my old white nightgown, drifting in and out of sleep and knowing that I would be seeing Stephen on Monday night.

When I did ease myself down on the bed, I could see Dr. Beady again, but this time I could see his humiliation. I could see the AP coming to interview him. I could see the Civil Liberties Union stringing him up right on Church Street. I could see a "Sixty Minutes" crew coming in to film him and watch him squirm. And I could see Stephen, with his arm around my shoulders, watching the whole thing.

14

Younger Women

The first time he saw Ruthie Dugan, Jesse Rapple ducked his head in embarrassment. He had been thinking of his own daughter, and when Ruthie opened her mother's door to him, all he could imagine was what she must have looked like pregnant. He was embarrassed, and wished Nell would hurry out of the bathroom. What was he supposed to say to Ruthie? Her children were with her in the living room, the little girl stretched out on the couch sleeping in a dirty pink pinafore and scuffed black patent leather shoes, the boy scrunched up on the rocker reading comics. They were black, all right—they had an even-toned, almost honied skin, but they were unmistakably black. The boy's hair was inky, the girl's brown, both of them wearing it in wild masses of curls. They needed to go to the barber. And their mother, Jesse thought, needed to go to the beauty parlor and get her red hair dyed again. Her dark roots fanned out like prickles in the short hair cut to frame her narrow face, and the fingernails she pushed through it were chewed.

Ruthie sat again as soon as she'd shaken his hand, and seemed content with their silence. Neither she nor the boy spoke to him, and she didn't bother with looking busy: didn't pick up a magazine, or fret with her nails, or even smooth her shirt. She just sat, still. Jesse was relieved that she was not like her brother, that she did not have that gift for easy, superficial, soothing talk that Stephen did. She resembled him in her height and her skinniness, even around her mouth, but it was her eyes he was drawn to. They were big and round and churned green as the ocean, and they turned what would have been an ordinary, skinny kind of prettiness into a beauty he found arresting. Shocking, even. It was hard to imagine her being *Nell's* daughter. She was dressed in slim black pants and a big shirt, clothes so colorless and shapeless that it was hard to tell whether they were fashionable or just unaware. But he guessed, since she was coming from New York, that they were fashionable.

Jesse watched her boy, who looked to be about six, reading his Thor comic. He was absorbed in the book, but preoccupied, too. There was no light of excitement as he turned the pages. He was a strange-looking child, with crooked teeth and a pair of black glasses that were too big on his face. His head looked misshapen. Nell had said something about that, about his being born with water on the brain. Now it was hard to describe what was wrong with the shape of his head, because it wasn't too big anymore. It looked like an egg about to wobble over on its side.

The little girl didn't seem to be good-looking either, at least not sleeping. Her cheeks were too round, puffy as an adder's. She was chubby even for a toddler, and she looked indulged to Jesse: if her mother was in a pair of black pants, and her brother in blue jeans, what was she doing in a party dress and shiny shoes? He wondered idly where the father was, whether the family often sat in this kind of unbroken sleeping silence.

He found sitting in Ruthie's presence alternately calming and unsettling. Usually Nell jabbered away at him when he sat in the living room, and that squared more with his knowledge of women as the talkers, the probing ones, the ones who had to ask you every three minutes what you were thinking and why did you look preoccupied, and did you still love them, and why didn't you answer the last question they asked. Faith had done it, too. Even Mary Faith, in these last months when she'd gotten so demanding, had slipped out of her silence and wheedled him more and more. When he realized that Ruthie had no intention of asking him how long he'd known her mother or whether he knew her brother or what he was thinking, he felt a great burden, the responsibility to come up with some conversation of his own. Every line he imagined, though—how did she like this southern weather or what was it like to be back in Due East—was fraught with difficulties, loaded with connotations that might remind her how conscious he was of her children being black, so he followed her cue and stayed still himself, and wished again that her mother would hurry out of the bathroom and rescue him.

Finally Nell appeared, dressed in a pink pants suit with a floral blouse, the kind of outfit he'd never have imagined her wearing. He was taking her to the movies to see *The Best Little Whorehouse in Texas.* She winked at him without looking at her daughter or grandchildren and said, "Well, what do you think of my daughter?"

It was too direct a question, but it put him at ease, having a woman take over the conversation again. He answered, without pausing to consider, "I think she's beautiful," and realized after he'd said it that though he thought women were beautiful all the time, six or seven times a day, he'd never said it about a woman in front of her. Having said it, he tried not to look at Ruthie, tried not to calculate how old she was—twenty-two, twenty-five?—tried not to see how high or how small her breasts were. But in avoiding her, he had to look Nell straight in the eye, and Nell had stiffened when she heard the word *beautiful* breathed about her daughter, had tensed her mouth into a hard little smile.

"Have you had a talk with Mr. Rapple?" She didn't seem to direct the question to her daughter—she croaked it out to the room in general—but Ruthie sat up even straighter and said, "No, we haven't really talked too much."

Her mother winked again at Jesse, good humor restored. "You mean he hadn't told you about his plans?"

"No, ma'am," said Ruthie, and Jesse could see the tension her body had taken on when her mother entered the room. Now her neck was stretched out tight, and her knees were pressed together. Now she was being badgered out of her silence. Watching her, Jesse forgot to react to Nell's question, forgot that she was hinting about his proposal, and when he remembered it, was not as surprised as he should have been. He took another long look at Nell, trying to compare her with her daughter. She was carrying a little square black pocketbook by the handles, and the pants suit gave her the look of one of those old retired sergeant-major's wives, lady golfers and fishers who had seen too much sun and too much air and not enough washing machines and ironing boards. Nell's eyes were small, almost beady compared to her daughter's. Nell's hands weren't so long, so white, so expressive. Nell didn't carry herself with the unconscious straightness that Ruthie had.

"Well, we'll all talk some other time," Nell said brusquely, and Ruthie smiled at him vaguely. It was the first time he'd taken Nell to the movies—her suggestion—and he wondered what Ruthie and the kids were supposed to do while she was gone. He wondered how long they could hold that pose, family in the living room, and whether they would turn on the television set or talk to each other. He wanted to ask them to come along, but it was the wrong movie for youngsters and besides, Nell had made it clear on the phone that she didn't want that. "We don't have to do *everything* together," she had said. "I told her she can stay at the apartment for one week if we don't have to follow each other around like a pack of rabbits." He was relieved, too, that he wouldn't be escorting Ruthie to the movies. He could imagine her sitting in the back of her mother's car—because they wouldn't be able to take the truck—keeping her thoughts to herself and radiating that studied quiet.

He shook Ruthie's hand again, leaving, and she looked up at him gratefully. He could see she was a pained young woman, neither as soft as his wife had been nor as tough as his daughter was. And nothing like her mother.

He took Nell on a real date, a teenage date, with popcorn at the twin cinema and a drink after at the Ramada Inn. Nell had been dying to go to the Sand Dollar Lounge and said they'd find all kinds of people out cheating on a Friday night, but all they found were college kids home for the weekend, drinking airline bottles of liquor and dancing in their stiff clothes, chinos and alligator shirts and Bass Weejuns. They didn't talk much over the disco tape—when he brought up Ruthie and her children, Nell waved her hand as if to dismiss both him and her daughter.

They stayed an hour, and as Jesse was helping Nell into the truck, she said, "You know, I've been feeling sick ever since Ruthie got here. I wake up in the morning wanting to throw up or faint. Isn't that just like Ruthie, putting me through that?"

Jesse smiled a noncommittal smile, and closed her door.

Saturday, Mary Faith sent him for groceries. Usually he drove her to the Piggly Wiggly and waited outside in the truck, but she was coming down on him heavy since the Wednesday-night service. As if he were the one who had jumped up like a madwoman and run down the aisle. As if he hadn't had to sit there after service while twenty-three Baptist women came up to offer their condolences. As if he hadn't had to watch Dr. Beady wait until the women had cleared out to approach him with a slick "Perhaps Mary Faith misunderstood what I was saying," and as if he hadn't been forced to say back, "I think she understood just exactly what you were saying," thereby permanently cutting himself off from his religion, or Faith's religion anyway, the one rope that had kept him from floating away all through her sickness and dying and now through Mary Faith's trouble. Well, he wouldn't go in search of another church to sing in: religion was either there for you or it wasn't, and for him it had always just been there. There was no argument, as far as he was concerned, about whether Jesus Christ was the true redeemer of the world. If he wasn't, then there was no God, or only some sly malevolent God unwilling to extend even a pinkie to help the world to its feet. And since he wasn't willing to accept no God—not with the way the sun set over the Chessy Creek—and since he wasn't willing to accept a malevolent God—not after watching Faith forgive him at the end for all the hatred he felt toward her—he accepted Jesus Christ and didn't need any Baptist ministers, no Dr. Beadys, to tell him about it.

But Mary Faith wasn't going to know that he'd cut himself off for her. She believed he'd deserted her when he sat in that church, and in a way she was right, because he'd considered it. He couldn't *believe* she had to be so wild, that she had to hurt all her mother's friends with that crazy dash down to the back of the church, that it never occurred to her that she might shame him.

Now, on Saturday morning, she was talking to him again. She was moody and snappy, but she was talking. He saw her holding her back and squatting down to pick things off the floor, and he thought she exaggerated her new waddle, that she had seen some movie with a pregnant woman who moved that way and was copying her. Like her mother, though, she still had that good tall way of carrying herself when she wanted to, and she didn't have that squat enormous look that some women couldn't seem to avoid. But now she made little grimaces getting up off a chair. And for the first time since her mother died, she made out the grocery list and asked him to go fetch it so she could lie down for a couple of hours. She asked him without looking at him, in a tone that didn't expect him to say yes or think she needed to lie down, and if he hadn't felt guilty about leaving her *and* Nell's daughter alone the night before, he would have told her to do the grocery shopping herself when she felt more up to it. But he did feel guilty, so he did take the list, and found himself in the Piggly Wiggly on Saturday morning, surrounded by the working women of Due East, who had all come from the beauty parlor and who seemed to know exactly where everything was and pranced around behind their shopping carts delighted with their own efficiency.

Mary Faith had the list blocked out in little sections, so that once he found the aisle with cleaning goods he could stay put for a minute, pulling down Lysol and Clorox off the shelves. But he kept missing the aisles he was looking for, and in his third circle of the store searching for paper goods, he ran his shopping cart straight into Nell Dugan's. She was loading up six-packs of beer.

They grinned at each other. They had *finally* gotten to the point where they could relax enough to do that anyway, and she teased him about wearing the apron in his family and he teased her about buying six-packs.

"So how's Ruthie this morning?" Jesse asked, and then lowered his voice, knowing how prickly she was on the subject. "I meant to ask you last night where her husband is."

Nell looked around before she answered. "He didn't come," she said. "I don't know where he is. Why do you think I let Ruthie stay in the apartment?" She said it was a lot safer having them stay without him, and that she wouldn't be a bit surprised if he were deserting the family or had another woman at least, even if Ruthie did say he was just too tired to make the trip. "Too tired, after we've been *negotiating* this visit for the past three months. Anyway, I think the kids could pass for Indians or something, don't you? Arabs, anyway."

Jesse said sure, sure, they could pass for a number of things. "How are *you* feeling? Still queasy?"

Nell brightened, but she didn't look good. She was back to her regular clothes, baggy pants and a workman's shirt, and her hair was still stuffed into its tight permanent, getting a little browner by the week. Her face was sallow, her lips cracked, her eyes lackluster. She was beginning to look older and older and older. He thought maybe it was the brown hair coming back, the lack of contrast against her brown skin. She looked one unwashed color. It worried him, not enough to make him change his mind about marrying her, but enough to make him think that Mary Faith would have more ammunition to fire against Nell Dugan, that she could argue, "She's too old for you," and maybe even be right.

"I'm better," Nell said, and then, turning dour, "I guess. It's probably just Ruthie cooking in the morning. She fries eggs and bacon and stinks the whole apartment up. But I've been feeling weak all day, too."

"The heat," Jesse said.

She was indignant at the idea. "I feel weak in the air-conditioning!" She looked around and lowered her voice again. "If I didn't know better, I'd think I was knocked up as sure as your daughter is." Then she dismissed the idea with a cackle.

Jesse stared at her. She was fifty, she'd said. Fifty was too old. He thought. Actually, he had no idea. Faith hadn't had to go through a menopause: she'd died too young for that. He wanted to ask Nell if she'd passed it already, if they'd really been safe—God knew, they'd been at it like rabbits, five and six nights a week—but it wasn't the kind of thing you could say in the Piggly Wiggly. Women glided by them waving and saying *hey*, and besides, Nell didn't look in the least concerned that she could actually be pregnant. It *was* probably just the heat.

"So where's the paper napkins?" he said.

Nell pointed him down a few aisles.

"I miss coming over," he said, "at night." He whispered again. "I miss your bed."

"You dirty old man," Nell said. When she grinned, she didn't look so old. Her eyes brightened that way, he could see *some* resemblance to Ruthie. A little. He squeezed her side, going past her to the paper stuff, and marveled again at how little there was to touch. She could not possibly be pregnant. There would be no place for the baby to fit.

He was still considering a pregnant Nell when he and Mary Faith sat down to a late lunch that afternoon. Mary Faith was warming up to him as the afternoon wore on, and after she unpacked the groceries she made them grilled cheese sandwiches and poured him a glass of beer.

He was just telling her the sandwich was good and trying to imagine *two* babies in the house when they heard a car shut off in the driveway. Buddy Miles swung open the kitchen door and stuck his head inside.

"Hey, beautiful," he said to Mary Faith, and Jesse watched his daughter turn pink. She had inherited her mother's mistrust of Buddy. But she said, "Hi, Mr. Miles," dutifully, like a little girl, and rose to let him in and set him a place and make him a sandwich.

"What you doing here?" Jesse said, but Buddy was watching his daughter.

"You're getting there, honey, aren't you?" Buddy said, and this time Jesse stiffened a little with his daughter. There had been a time, a year or two back, when Buddy would have been sitting with the two of them at this table every Saturday, when he never would have directed a word at Mary Faith.

"I'm getting there," Mary Faith repeated stiffly.

"Well, don't take offense," Buddy said. "How about a beer for the old man. Listen, there's nothing more beautiful on the face of the earth than a pregnant female. You all get that glow. Turn around. Let me see that glow."

Mary Faith was bending down over the broiler, putting his sandwich in, and when she turned her face around it more than glowed. It flushed an orangy-red from the heat of the oven and her embarrassment, but Jesse could see what Buddy was talking about. Her skin looked stretched as delicate and thin as tissue paper, and her gray eyes were darkening almost to blue. He wished, somehow, that Buddy hadn't been right.

"So what you been up to?" Buddy said to him. "Nobody sees you around anymore. What say we go fishing next Saturday? The whole day."

Jesse tipped his chair back and considered. He couldn't have dreamed himself sitting in his kitchen with his best friend and his daughter, worrying about whether to go fishing or not. His whole life, up until the past few months, he had gone out when he needed to. But now he was worried that Mary Faith would go into early labor and now he was worried that Nell was pregnant and now he was worried about Lee Mac keeping open the station on Saturdays, a day's wages he couldn't afford to pay. "I'll have to see," he said finally, and watched Buddy chug his beer down impassively.

Mary Faith set the last sandwich down in front of his friend, and excused herself to do some housework upstairs. Her own sandwich lay half-eaten on the kitchen table.

"Jesus, she's beautiful," Buddy said when she was out of the room. Jesse knew she'd still be in hearing distance on the stairs.

"Oh, don't talk that way about Mary Faith," he said sharply, and Buddy looked at him in surprise.

"You know I don't mean anything like that about Mary Faith," he said with a laugh. "I like them young, but not *that*

young." Then his eyes narrowed. "Listen, Jesse, I'm glad she
went upstairs because I didn't really come over about the
fishing. I've got a hot little number lined up tonight and she's
got a friend and I thought you and me could go out together
like we haven't done in six months."

"Buddy, you ought to quit cheating on your wife." It was a
line Jesse had said a hundred times, over five years, over ten
years, fifteen years, but suddenly he meant it. Buddy had never
tried to bring him along before on one of his dates: they'd had
an understanding when Faith was alive that he just didn't do
that to her, and Buddy liked it that way, liked being the one
with the stories to tell on Sunday afternoon.

"I can't help it," Buddy sighed, and tried to look remorseful.
"You should see this girl, she's twenty-two, twenty-three. She
waits on tables down at the Rebel and she's got the curviest
little ass and a thing for older men. Old men like us. But she
wants to go out on a *date*. You know? Come on, Jesse, you need
a woman's company."

"I've got a woman's company," Jesse said.

"You can't stay home with your daughter every night."

"I don't mean Mary Faith," Jesse said.

"Nell Dugan?" Buddy didn't say another word, but he might
as well have, as far as Jesse was concerned. He might as well
have called her an old battle-ax for the way he rolled his eyes.

"It's getting serious," Jesse said.

"Oh, Jesus." Buddy whistled. "Oh, Jesus. Jesse, you're not
thinking about getting *married* again, are you? Listen, you're in
the best spot in the world. I swear, you get yourself a squeeze
of a young girl's ass and you won't look at Nell Dugan again."

Mary Faith's footsteps sounded on the stairs, and by the time
she was back at the table picking up her sandwich Jesse
couldn't get the words *young girl's ass* out of his head, couldn't
blank out the image he had of a tanned, blond, full-breasted
waitress at the Rebel who wore pants that curved up too tight
around her crotch and sandals with no backs and three-inch
heels. He hated Buddy for giving him the picture even, while
the woman he was going to marry was back in her apartment
with her *grand*children and while his daughter, who had a

young girl's ass, too, only one that was covered now by a big, flowered, puff-sleeved blouse, while his daughter picked up her lousy grilled cheese sandwich and went to do her house- work upstairs.

"Don't you stop looking for a man once you have that baby," Buddy was saying to Mary Faith, and Jesse stared at him in wonder. Had he been saying things like that for five years? Had he just never noticed before?

Now Mary Faith rolled *her* eyes, and Jesse watched her scoot out of the room. He didn't like that little self-satisfied grin Buddy wore, watching her, and he didn't like having a hard-on from just picturing waitresses down at the Rebel.

"I've got to see Nell tonight," he told Buddy again, knowing that Buddy would shake his head and tell him he was making the biggest mistake in the world and finish down his beer. Knowing that Buddy hadn't expected him for one minute to go along with him after waitresses.

"Jack'll go," Buddy said. "Jack'll go with me and get the pussy you should rightfully have."

"Let him go," Jesse said, and shook his head and grinned at Buddy. "You ought to quit cheating on your wife."

"And you ought to have some fun," Buddy said.

Jesse swallowed down his own beer. Two babies in the house. Grandchildren. Nell. A houseful. "I'll be having plenty of fun," he said to Buddy. "Don't you worry."

15

In Memory Of

On Sunday my father decided to borrow Buddy's bateau and go crabbing all the way out at Bay Point. By himself. He didn't say anything about not going to church, and I didn't press him. It never occurred to him to wonder what *I* was supposed to do all day, and I stayed in my nightgown. His room was the only one upstairs with air-conditioning, so I brought magazines and a cup of coffee into his bed and told myself I'd stay there all day if I felt like it. My only job would be steaming those crabs, and that would take half an hour.

Two of my magazines slipped to the floor when I went to put the coffee down, and I had to get on my hands and belly, and reach underneath the bed, to get them back. I could feel a book on the floor, and when I pulled out the magazines, I pulled out a hardcover copy of *The Joy of Sex,* too. I thought at first that it was my father's, but on the flyleaf was an inscription in ball-point pen: "TO MY STRAITLACED SISTER, WHO PROBABLY KNOWS MORE THAN THIS BOOK TELLS. HA!HA! LIZANN. P.S. I HAD TO ORDER THIS THROUGH THE MAIL!!!" The pages hardly looked touched, but the book flipped open to three or four spots, as if they'd been studied again and again. By my mother? I could hardly bring myself to thumb through a book like that, that she'd thumbed through, but I couldn't put it back. "Pregnancy Can Be the Happiest Time of Your Life" said that I might not feel like sex at all. Ha. But I could feel my mother watching me as I turned the pages, could feel Michael Jagger's breath on my neck.

The doorbell rang before I had time to block out my mother and Michael Jagger, and I grabbed my father's old flannel robe from out of the closet and went flying down the stairs. It wouldn't be Aunt Lizann or Uncle Zack, or even Buddy Miles ringing, since they all went to the back door. It had to be a stranger. Suddenly the day opened up. I remembered Mr. Anderson's words about the AP picking up my letter. It *could* be the AP on my doorstep. The Civil Liberties Union. The CBS Evening News.

It was Stephen Dugan. I did not open my mouth to say a word to him because I could picture myself in the robe, with the belt wrapped around me like a piece of twine around a mattress. I hadn't combed my hair or brushed my yellow teeth.

Behind Stephen stood another tall woman, and this one was not his wife. This one had short hair, dyed red and pushed back all crazy and wild from her face. There were great big black rings around her eyes, as if she'd been crying or punched, but there was none of the puffiness a crying woman usually has. Her face was gaunt, with cheekbones that jutted out, and her skin was as white and smooth as the pillars in First Baptist Church. She was wearing a loose black dress with just a hint of sleeves, and slinky black shoes, and I tried to tell myself that she was a reporter for the Associated Press, that Stephen wasn't bringing her by to scare me. She was the most beautiful woman I had ever seen in my life.

The first thing Stephen said was, "This is my sister Ruthie," and that saved me, that let me find my tongue to ask them in. I knew about Ruthie. All Due East knew about Ruthie. Ruthie had her baby when she was sixteen, too. Ruthie lived in New York. Ruthie was married to a black man. Ruthie looked at me and past me, with her lips parted in what might have been a smile. She didn't seem friendly, and she didn't seem un-friendly.

Stephen said that they didn't have time to come in, that they were on their way to his mother's apartment, that he wanted to know if Mr. Anderson had reached me. When I told him yes,

that I was teaching the GEDs with him again, he grinned and
put his arm around Ruthie and said: "See? I always said there's
nothing to sounding like a lawyer."

Ruthie's smile lightened.

I wasn't sure I got it. "Do you mean," I said, "that you called
Mr. Anderson and pretended to be a lawyer?"

Stephen nodded. Ruthie's smile broadened.

"You called Mr. Anderson and said you were the ACLU?"

Stephen nodded again. "Ruthie played the secretary. She
put Mr. Anderson on hold for thirty seconds. It was nothing. I
just sounded earnest."

Ruthie tottered on her slinky black heels, and Stephen
rocked back and forth on his heels, both of them embarrassed
to be on the front steps and just so pleased with themselves
that they could have exploded like shaken-up Coca-Cola bottles. My father hadn't even followed me down the aisle of First
Baptist, but Stephen had impersonated the Civil Liberties
Union to get me back into tutoring. We would be lovers. I knew
we would.

Ruthie said it was nice to meet me—her voice was soft, as
vague as her smile—and turned to go back to Stephen's car in
the driveway. I could see the outlines of two little ones
squeezed together in the backseat, could hear the older one
giggling and the younger one calling "Momma!"

"We have to run," Stephen said, and wouldn't look straight
at me. I could feel the robe working its way loose, but didn't
move to tighten it. I knew he'd be back.

"I wanted to give you this," he said, and thrust a folded
paper in my hand. "Ruthie wanted to go to mass," he added,
and then waved nonchalantly, and skipped down the front
steps to his car, and his sister, and her children. He never
looked back, but I knew it didn't matter.

I took the paper inside the house, and had to go all the way
back to the kitchen to find enough light to read it. It was a
church bulletin, from Our Lady of Perpetual Help. A church
bulletin. I sat down at the kitchen table to read through it. A
church bulletin. If Stephen wanted to convert me to *another*

faith. If Stephen had been going back to *mass*. If Stephen had decided lying with me was a sin.

The front cover showed a cartoon of a woman standing at a hospital bed, her hand extended. Underneath was a caption in purple letters: "The greatest of these is charity." Then there were two columns of text, a friendly little sermon on loving our neighbors and visiting the sick and the joy that comes with extending ourselves. Catholics seemed so *cheerful*. I didn't understand why Stephen had given me this to read. I couldn't understand him giving me religious tracts, not after that *sound* he'd made.

I opened the bulletin and read all the big blocks of print inside, but they seemed to be about meetings of the Holy Name Society and the Legion of Mary (at least Baptists didn't put up with *that* kind of mumbo-jumbo) and softball practice. It wasn't until I went back and found the week's mass listings that the name shimmied before my eyes. Michael Jagger. Michael Jagger's name was in the bulletin. Five o'clock Monday. Tomorrow. Mass for Michael Jagger. I didn't know what that meant, that they were giving a mass for him. Did it mean that they despaired of his soul, and prayed over him as a last hope? Did it mean they just went down a list, and gave a mass to everyone who'd died in the last six months? Was it just his turn?

I found myself tipping the coffee pot for another cup of coffee, even if the books did say I was supposed to cut down on caffeine, and I found myself coming back to the bulletin and reading the little entry again. Monday. 5:00. Michael Jagger. 5:00. Michael Jagger. *This Week's Mass Intentions.* For the soul of Michael Jagger.

And Stephen had wanted me to remember Michael Jagger, had slipped this bulletin to me the way Michael Jagger had once slipped me notes asking me to meet him at the marina. I slammed the coffee cup down on the table. I had been going on without thinking of Michael Jagger for weeks. For months. I had been able to go without remembering his crying, his looking at me with shame and guilt and doubt. I'd been able to take Stephen's face, the beard and the thin lips that had kissed plenty of women and knew how to do it, wouldn't cry out after they were done, I'd taken that face and plastered it over Michael Jagger's every time he tried to make me remember him. I wouldn't remember him. I wouldn't. It was like remembering my mother: there was no sense in it, no comfort, no peace. I wouldn't remember him. I would think of Stephen, and Mr. Anderson thinking the ACLU had called him. I would think about standing up to quiet Dr. Beady's voice. Five o'clock mass. Why was Stephen telling me about it? I just wanted to get on with my life.

On Monday I was ready for the mass at four-thirty. I wore the same black dress I'd worn to the Baptist church: that was what I thought of their masses, their services. I had decided that Stephen was going to be there. If I didn't go he would think I had no feelings for Michael Jagger; he would think I was cold and calculating, and when I saw him that night he would shrink away from me.

I walked down the back streets of the Point. It still felt like ninety degrees outside. There'd been no rain all day, and the air was a soft damp curtain to push aside. Nobody was out in the day's last haze to see me in my black dress and black flats. I'd twisted my hair into a bun on the back of my head, so that I'd look older.

I had to sit in the back pew of Our Lady of Perpetual Help for twenty minutes before anybody came in. I'd expected a big crowd to mourn Michael Jagger. If a Baptist had gone and killed himself, the pews would fill up at the mention of his name, and everybody would gather to remember the most gruesome details. But nobody was coming to this mass.

Finally the back door creaked open and three women made a big point of staring into my pew to smile. Then they walked up to the very first row and kneeled. They were nuns. I could tell even if they didn't have veils on. They all wore brown hair cut short and straight and not kept very clean, and they all had sturdy fat legs in tan pantyhose and stout black shoes. One wore gray and one wore brown and the one with the cleanest hair wore a sky-blue polyester summer suit. She had also given the biggest smile. In the front row their shoulders were too wide across, and their pleated skirts fanned out across their big hips.

After a few minutes of their praying, the back door creaked again, and an older couple, a man and woman in their fifties, walked in. I had turned around to see if Stephen was coming to the mass, but when I caught sight of the two, I sank to my knees and buried my face in my hands so that they wouldn't learn it. They didn't seem to notice me, though; they made their way up to the front, to sit behind the nuns. I was sure they were Michael Jagger's parents. He had never described them, but they would fit perfectly. The man could have been my father, a little older: he was a grease monkey, or a mailman, or a clerk in a hardware store. He wore a clean white shirt, with the short sleeves rolled up, and a polka-dotted tie. His wife was plain and stout—when she stood behind the nun in gray she blotted her out—but she had on a navy blue dress with a white fleur-de-lis pattern that made her look as if she dreamed of better things than Due East. It was the kind of material my mother would have seen in the back of a magazine and sent away for.

Finally, at ten minutes past five, Father Berkeley shuffled out onto the altar and got things started. He didn't seem surprised that there were only six people there to remember Michael Jagger. He kept his head bowed so low and his words muttered so fast that I wasn't sure he knew that there *were* six people there. He recited the prayers as if they were a grocery list, and the only words I could understand were the ones the nuns batted back to him in clear, loud, not-to-be-hurried voices. Lord have mercy, Christ have mercy. I confess to Almighty God. The Jaggers didn't seem to be responding the way the nuns were. They didn't look at each other or reach out for each other or cry or turn around. They just kept bouncing up and down—stand, sit, kneel, stand, sit, kneel. This didn't seem to be the type of service that had any singing or any sermon, and it didn't seem to have anything to do with Michael Jagger. Once they mentioned his name, midway through. The souls of the faithful departed. But he might as well have been Saint

Agatha or Saint Lucy or any of the other saints Father Berkeley
rattled off.

Even though twenty minutes had passed, I was sure that
Stephen would show up, and thought that if he did he would
sit in the back row with me and whisper explanations: why the
priest had zipped through the Bible readings and what he was
doing hoisting that chalice up to the sky while the nuns and the
Jaggers bowed their heads down as if golden rays of light were
shooting through the stained glass window behind the altar, as
if organ music were shaking the quiet little church.

But when the nuns rose to their feet and began leaving their
seats I realized that Stephen wouldn't be coming. At first I
thought the mass was over, and the nuns were leaving, but
when Father Berkeley walked down the three altar steps and
stood in the aisle with his chalice, I knew it was communion
time for the Catholics. This was the big number, the climax of
the mass, and Stephen wasn't coming. He'd sent me alone, to
pay my last respects to Michael Jagger, and I hadn't thought of
Michael Jagger once. I saw Mr. Jagger help Mrs. Jagger to her
feet, saw her raise herself slowly, painstakingly. In another
minute they would go up to the priest for their bread, would
delude themselves that they were eating flesh of god-made-
man while their son rotted in the ground, brain-dead from
chemicals. In another minute they would be on their way back
to their pew, and in the back row of Our Lady of Perpetual
Help they would see a pregnant girl in black, a girl their son's
age, and they would think about it, maybe not that minute, but
the next day, the next week, the next month. That was why
Stephen had sent me to this mass! He had known the Jaggers
would see me pregnant and would want to know me, want to
know their grandchild. Stephen believed that, seeing them, I
would remember Michael and forget about *him.* Leave him
alone. Keep him from his temptation.

I raised myself to my feet just as slowly and just as painstakingly as Michael's mother had risen to hers. I would not let
them see me. I would not let them try to meet me or take me in
or find out if their son was the father of my child. If Stephen
didn't want me, fine. But I wouldn't be taken over by ghosts

and people who prayed to virgins and martyrs and grew fat and thought there was some relief in a mass the priest barely knew he was saying.

What I hadn't calculated was how long it takes to give communion to five people. Father Berkeley just shoved the little round pieces in their mouths, lickety-split, and as I left my pew, Mrs. Jagger turned away from the priest and started back down the aisle. I could sense her standing still in the aisle, pausing at her pew, as I opened the back door. She had caught the biggest view of me—the side view, the great protrusion—and I knew just what would happen when Father Berkeley had rammed the last prayers down their throats. They would all gather outside—the priest, the nuns, the Jaggers—and they would ask each other: Now who was that girl? They probably wouldn't even say *pregnant* girl. They would just say: Now who was that girl? and the nuns would smile their fat smiles and the Jaggers would avert their eyes and Father Berkeley would shuffle off without adding anything to the conversation. But they would all have the suspicion planted in their minds. They would all tote up the months pregnant I looked and the months Michael Jagger had been dead. And Stephen would have his way: the Jaggers would know, and they would come after me.

I scuttled down Division Street. How could he, how could Stephen do this when we were coming so close? Didn't he know why I wanted to forget Michael Jagger? The week before we made love, Michael Jagger read me a passage from *The Brothers Karamazov,* a passage about the Turks killing babies, torturing children before their mothers' eyes for the pleasure of it. I still remember the phrase he repeated: *a voluptuous pleasure.* He said that the reason no one read Dostoyevski was that passages like that were exciting, that people couldn't bear to admit that they derived a *sensual pleasure,* as Ivan Karamazov called it, from descriptions of child torture. The next week he made love to me, and afterward, he wept. Did Stephen want me to remember that? Did he want me to bring a baby into the world all alone and then bring it up to be tortured, tortured like her father?

I cut off onto the Point and made my way home along the back streets, the way I had come. I would be tutoring in a few hours. I would be seeing Stephen. I didn't want him to rescue me. I just wanted to be with someone for a few hours of my day.

When Stephen picked me up for tutoring that night, he told me that my father was at his mother's house. My father and his mother and Ruthie and her children were all making plans to sit up and watch *Gone With the Wind* on television, and my father had told Stephen that I should come, too. My father. Invited me over to his *girlfriend's* house. His old lady's house. I said I'd rather not.

By nine-thirty, when he drove me home, it was murky night. He pulled into the driveway and we sat for a minute, dazed by the heat. The moss hung down like a string of furry animals tied together from the trees in the front yard, and the air muffled any sound. There were no frogs croaking tonight, no crickets, just the nasty, insistent whine of the mosquitoes. We couldn't sit in the car long with the windows open, so I would have to say something soon. Tutoring had been awkward. I had known somebody there had complained about me, probably the old bat sergeant's wife, but it made me look at everyone I helped with suspicion. They all worked quietly in their programmed math and English books and asked me questions about simple quadratic equations. They couldn't even *factor*. Stephen went from table to table, from book to book, making little jokes about the use of the subjunctive in the real world, and never once smiling at me or looking at me. It was as if he sensed danger there, that he expected whoever it was who had complained about me to start complaining about us. Either that, or he just sensed the danger from me.

He was quiet on the ride home, too, and as we sat in the driveway he said, "Well, I shall not compare thee to a summer's day. I can't breathe."

I couldn't repeat the last invitation, to come in for wine, but I thought fast and asked if he'd like a cool drink before he headed home. I could feel him hesitating on the seat beside me, but he said, "Yes. I'd like something cold," and came around to open my door.

I served him a beer at the kitchen table, and he drank it down in three long swoops.

"I went to that mass for Michael Jagger," I said.

"I thought you would."

I swallowed, and tried not to sound aggrieved. "Did you want his parents to see me?"

Stephen ran his finger around the rim of his bottle. "No," he said. "No, I've never seen his parents and I never thought of it. I just thought you'd want to know." He got up to get himself another beer.

I took a deep breath. I knew I should have gone slower, that I had every Monday night to see him until the baby came, but I couldn't stop myself. "I thought you might have wanted to remind me of him so I would forget about you."

He stood with the refrigerator door open, his back to me. He was wearing a long-sleeved plaid shirt and corduroys, even in the middle of summer. The back of his hair was plastered to his neck, and though I couldn't see his face, I could *feel* his glasses slipping down his nose. He didn't answer.

Suddenly I could see everything in the room that made me ashamed—not ashamed exactly, but embarrassed. Everything was plastic and tacky. Daddy painted the cabinets bright blue after she died, and used vinyl tape to repair all the dinette chairs. It made me think of how I'd do my own kitchen, if I ever had my own kitchen, of how I'd leave everything—the counters, the cabinets, the walls, the floors, the curtains—white, a shimmering white, a nice plain white. My kitchen table would be wood painted white. The chairs would be cane painted white. "The beer's behind the milk," I told Stephen.

He came back to the table and sat down warily. He didn't try to answer my question or start another conversation; he just watched me as I sat, hands folded on the table, drinking nothing, watching him. When he smiled a little smile, I said, "I'm sorry to say that. I didn't mean to be pushing you."

He opened his mouth to say something, closed it, took another long swig of beer, got up, went to the kitchen door, came back, sat down, and said nothing.

"I know I'm just fifteen years old," I said.

"Mary Faith!" It was hard to say whether he was angry or troubled, but his voice was *passionate*. Passionate toward me. I was tugging at him. "Mary Faith," he started again, in a lower voice. "The other night was a terrible mistake. The other night I had too much to drink and forgot myself entirely. You must put it out of your mind that there can be anything like that between us."

I had been expecting him to say something just like that. I had told myself that I would have to be braced for it, expect it, keep on getting him beers, hold him just a little longer. I had told myself beforehand that he wouldn't really mean it, that he would *have* to say that, that no grown man was going to like admitting he was falling in love with a teenager. Still, when he said it I reeled, and I stood up so that he wouldn't see the bright red spots on my cheeks. Having nothing better to fetch, I fetched him another beer. I knew he wasn't ready for it, and I knew that if I asked him he would refuse, but I knew that if I set it down in front of him he would drink it.

"I know, Mr. Dugan," I said softly. I knew I had to back off. "It's the funniest thing," I went on, "but when I went to that mass for Michael Jagger all I could remember about him was a passage he read me from *The Brothers Karamazov*. It used to make me not want to read the book, he was so troubled with it."

Stephen settled back in his chair. He was not so frightened of me anymore. "The Grand Inquisitor," he said. "He told me once that was why he quit the church."

"No," I said, "no, the part just before the Grand Inquisitor, I forget what the chapter's called. Wait a minute, I'll just run upstairs and get it." I thought it was a stalling tactic. I meant to get the book to hold him ten minutes longer, to hear what he thought about Michael Jagger carrying around Dostoyevski like a Bible. I had given up on his making love to me that night. I had given up on his making love to me anytime soon, not next month, maybe not when my child was a baby. I was starting to steel myself for years. But I would have liked him in the kitchen for ten minutes longer.

What I wasn't prepared for was his following me up the stairs, carrying his bottle of beer in his hand and walking slowly behind me. I was conscious again of parts of the house I'd long since stopped seeing. The strips of green carpet on the stairs were worn almost straight through, and the lineup of school pictures that my mother had staggered on the wall made me feel almost faint with embarrassment. There I was at six, at seven, at eight, my bangs cut across too short, my eyes too light and looking past the photographer as if I didn't even know he was there. I wasn't smiling in one of the pictures. I could remember telling myself that the photographer would *try* to make me smile, but that I wasn't going to fall for it. When I was little, I didn't think it was dignified to smile. But now Stephen would see what I'd looked like as a little girl, a little girl too serious, and it would remind him how close I still was to childhood.

He didn't mention the pictures, though. He said, "I know the part you mean. Perfect for Michael, hmmm? I told him then, and I still think, that Dostoyevski did too good a job in that part of the novel. No wonder he made Michael quit the church. None of that Father Zossima stuff could ever match the horrors of the Jesuits."

I didn't tell him that I didn't know anything about Jesuits, or that I hadn't been able to read through *The Brothers Karamazov*, not after Michael's weeping. When I had decided to forget Michael entirely, I had buried the book away, under the winter sweaters Aunt Lizann brought me back from New York, too heavy to wear in Due East.

So I didn't say anything as I led him into my room. Here, at least, I wasn't ashamed. I still used the old white bedspread, and I hadn't let Daddy touch the walls. Everything was plain, like a nun's room. There was a picture of my mother on the dresser, an old picture my father had of her when she was nineteen and still pretty, still shy in front of the camera. She was like me, afraid to smile for the photographer, and you could see how close she was to biting her lower lip. I had put

the picture in an old wooden frame I found down in the basement; I had stripped the black paint off it, so just the plain
wood was left. It was the only decoration in my room. If Stephen thought he would step in and see posters of rock groups
or movie stars, he was dead wrong. It hadn't been a little girl's
room since I was twelve.

He sat on the bed and finished his beer, his third beer if I was
adding them right. I hadn't seen too many people drinking,
but I didn't imagine most of them drank as fast as Stephen
Dugan.

I kneeled down to the bottom drawer of the dresser, where
the sweaters were, and dug out the two volumes of the Penguin
edition. When I turned around to hand them to Stephen,
though, he wasn't looking at me. He was staring at the picture
of my mother, and he looked troubled.

"How long ago did she die?" he said. "She had your eyes."

I thought *three years,* but I couldn't say it. Not to him. I
thought *three years* so hard I could almost imagine that I'd said
it, and then I did what I'd been doing only since I was pregnant, what I'd kept under control for the three years before
that. I cried again. I cried blankly, thinking not about Stephen
being in the room, and not about my mother, not about what
she looked like, or how her lips cracked and turned white
before she died, not about her vomiting for hours on end, not
about her never knowing I was in the hospital room, but just
about those words I couldn't bring myself to say. Three years.
Three years. Three years. It was a good long time. I couldn't
imagine I was crying after three years. It must have been the
hormones setting me loose. The sound of it echoed through
my body: three years, three years, three years. My weeping felt
like pure sorrow, and I didn't bother to cover my eyes but just
sat on the floor, facing the bottom drawer of the dresser, and
cried to the rhythms of the two words together. Three years.

I could feel Stephen kneeling down beside me, and then his
hands were on my shoulders as I'd always imagined my father's hands should be, after she died. He let me slope back
into his arms and never said *hush,* never said to stop crying.
When I started to shudder with the tears, though, he turned

me around, so that I could bury my face in his chest. When the crying let up he lifted my chin and smiled at me, a smile as clear as my sorrow had felt. I eased into him, into his long arms circling my big round body, and I will never be able to remember who starting kissing who first, because one minute I was crying and the next minute he was smiling and then, without any pause in the long fluid sweep time was taking, we were kissing, and then we had fallen together on the floor.

I unbuttoned the top of the black dress and tugged it off. Stephen was still lying on the plank floor, curled up and scrambling to pull his pants and shirt off, and we undressed ourselves in a fever. I knew he was drunk. I had tasted it in his mouth, and I could see it in the way he made himself naked. He was white and skinny, with a hairless chest and knotty arms, but I didn't dare do more than sneak a glance at him. I knew he didn't know what he was doing, and since crying, I didn't know what I was doing either. I thought he might faint dead away at the sight of my belly, but he circled his arms around me again —so we wouldn't have to look at each other—and took my breast in his mouth again, and then pulled me over on top of him. He closed his eyes, but mine were open, and when I slid down close to his body I could see his face tighten into tension, as if he were gritting his teeth. Then there was a look close to alarm. I was on top of him, crushing him down, for a long minute. He was soft against me. Impotent. I had heard of that, but I didn't know what to do. Michael Jagger hadn't been impotent. I tried to kiss him again, but this time his tongue was in his mouth, and he opened his eyes. I didn't know what to do. I pulled myself up so that he could take my breast if he wanted it, but he turned his face away. I rolled over, off him, and he took his arm away. I lay on my side on the floor, and he lay on his back. Now both our eyes were closed.

"Well," he said, "my body still seems to know what it's doing. *Some* part of me still has a conscience."

I didn't say anything.

Then he sounded angry. "This must never happen again," he said. "Mary Faith? This must never happen again."

Then I *wanted* to cry, but knew I wouldn't. I kept my eyes

shut and listened to the soft sound of his pulling his clothes on, his shoes on. I pulled the black dress over me like a blanket, and floated almost into sleep. The hard floor beneath my back felt like a good whipping.

Finally I could hear him finished and could feel him kneeling down beside me. He touched my shoulder, gently, and said: "I'm sorry. I'm going now." I stayed still, and I could feel his fingers tense with worry. "Don't you serve me any more beer or wine, hear?" he said, and I smiled a tiny smile, a little faint laugh at his joke, so that he would still drive me to tutoring and not hate me.

Then he was gone. I heard him making his way downstairs, and I couldn't move myself up off the floor. I didn't know whether to get out *The Brothers Karamazov* or *The Joy of Sex*. I didn't know whether to look at my mother's picture or get out Michael Jagger's letters. I didn't know whether to hate my father for leaving me, whether to hate Stephen for going. Finally I rose and kneeled just below the windowsill. Naked, I could watch Stephen get into his little yellow car and back out of our driveway. He never once looked up to my bedroom, and I held my breast myself, just for the comfort of it. Just to remind myself of his holding it and Michael Jagger looking away from it and my mother never even seeing that it had grown there, that I had passed from being a girl.

16

A New Home

By the end of June, the clouds of heat and stickiness pushed at Jesse Rapple until he woke at five o'clock in the morning. He considered putting the air conditioner on, just to clear the air, but the May electricity bill had been two hundred dollars. He would have to change the frayed wire on the little fan.

He managed to sleep fitfully until six, and then he knew he might as well get up. Sunday. Nell, pretending to be angry with Ruthie and her kids for staying on and on, was packing them all off to Savannah for the day, and he hadn't been invited to come along. He wouldn't be going to First Baptist this morning, either. He might as *well* fix the fan, and mow the lawn, and tend to all the other chores he had let pile up.

He knew there wouldn't be much talk with Mary Faith. She had been in a snit the last week, a deep and then snappy depression that kept him from coming home to dinner at all. He knew she had nothing to do all day since school let out, but the few times he called her, or came in to eat with her, she sulked in a nasty way. Two pimples were sprouting out on her face, one on her nose and one on her chin. He'd never seen a spot on her face before. Besides, he was working on Nell, trying to wear her down until she'd agree to the marriage, and once he had that settled, he wouldn't have to leave Mary Faith alone at night. Not ever again.

He went in for a cool shower and, drying himself, picked off little black balls of grime from his skin. The minute he left the bathroom, he was sweating again. Seven A.M. He called the weather. Eighty-four degrees. High expected in the high nineties. Humidity 87 percent.

He decided to make a stab at breakfast when he heard Mary Faith getting up. She couldn't sleep in the morning either—nowadays he heard her making her way to the bathroom at six or seven, but then she disappeared back into her bedroom so that she wouldn't have to make him breakfast. He tapped on her door and called out, "I'm making fried eggs if you want one. I'll put on coffee." There was no answer, but he trudged down into the kitchen anyway and got out four eggs and two cups and made toast and mopped his brow. The air outside was a gray soup.

She came down in her nightgown, and he pulled his eyes away from her. He wasn't sure of the word for how she looked: *slovenly, slatternly,* one of those. Her white nightgown had turned a dull gray, the color of their early summer days, and it wrapped itself around her swollen breasts. She didn't bother to cover herself with a robe or put slippers on or comb her hair. Or even to wash her hair anymore. He could almost picture her with a cigarette dangling from her mouth. She was still pretty—she couldn't hide her firm jaw, her sharp features —but in the last week she had cast off all the tidiness that had once made her so like her mother.

"You want juice?" he asked, but when he went to look in the freezer there were no more cans of juice. Neither one of them had done the Saturday shopping.

"Where you going today?" she asked him. He could hear her trying to sound bored, uninterested, and when he answered that he thought he'd just poke around the house, he thought he saw her straighten in the chair.

"Where's Mrs. Dugan?"

"She's taking Ruthie and the kids to Savannah," Jesse said, and wished he hadn't said it, wished he could take the words back and lie and say she was home but he'd just been planning to spend the day with his daughter anyway.

They ate the food quickly, as if finishing it off would keep them from noticing how much hotter hot toast and hot eggs and hot coffee made them. He thought Mary Faith looked bouncier as she cleared the table off, and when she said she was going upstairs to shower, he almost breathed a sigh of relief. She was lightening.

He wanted to tell her about him and Nell getting married, but that was impossible. She would sink deeper into her cloud if he did that. There was no way he could explain what it felt like looking at Nell now and seeing a little bulge in her stomach. He was sure she was pregnant. He didn't let himself think much about an actual baby, a baby on top of Mary Faith's, but he was sure she would be saying yes to his proposal, and soon they would be moving the two families in together. He had visions of Ruthie staying on in Due East—she didn't seem so eager to get back to her husband in New York—and every night before he fell asleep he pictured the house filled up with all of them. Ruthie's kids could have the den downstairs. Ruthie could have the sewing room. It was the first time in three years he was grateful for having a big old Due East house, the first time the seven rooms shrank in size for him. Things would change: Buddy Miles wouldn't set foot in his kitchen again, knowing there were colored kids sleeping in the den. But there would be two babies and Mary Faith wouldn't be poking around the way she did now. Seeing how Ruthie fixed herself up, she would follow suit. She would keep the refrigerator filled up again, and make his breakfast.

After he'd finished the front yard, the gas mower weighed eight hundred pounds beneath his arms, and the grass around the sides and back of the house looked seven feet high. He had done a lousy job trimming around the dogwood tree, and he didn't care. He couldn't remember ever pushing so hard or stopping so often, cutting the grass. They had a small yard for Due East: on O'Connor Street, the houses had been built close together, and while the rest of the houses on the Point had wide sloping yards leading down to the marsh, his front yard stretched only twenty feet deep, and in back, thirty. Faith had kept roses along the sunny side of the house and azaleas in front, but he didn't know anything about gardening, and he'd

let them go so that now, by the third year, only a thin scraggle
of rose vine came up in the summer. The azaleas had only
bloomed for a week.

He finished the left side of the house and started on the
back. Twice he went into the house for tea, and after he drank
the second cold glass he bounded back to the mower. If he
gave this a good burst of energy, he could be finished by ten-
thirty and spend the rest of the day out of the sun. He pushed
the mower three steps, and then thought he might pass out.
His chest tightened, a sudden spasm, and he leaned against the
mower's handle. His field of vision closed down to pinpricks of
light, and he wasn't sure if he was holding himself up or if the
mower was doing it for him.

It lasted less than a minute, and he remembered himself
telling Mary Faith as a girl that she shouldn't chug down icy
drinks on a hot day. It had just been that second glass of tea,
and running back out into the yard. It had given him a good
scare. But now that he had his breath back, the honeysuckle
from the neighbor's fence wafted toward him, and he sat on
the fat gas tank. He was breathing normally again. Normally,
for ninety-two degrees in the sun. He sat and smelled the
honeysuckle and the fresh-cut grass and, he thought, the roses
from the side of the house, until he knew he wouldn't be able
to finish the job in the morning. He would wait until six or
seven, when the sun was close to going down, the way Faith
had always told him to do it.

He had trouble getting to his feet. Both legs were shaky, and
his left arm ached. He reminded himself that he'd pushed
hardest on the left arm, that forty-year-old men didn't have
heart attacks. Maybe he could start worrying when he was
forty-five. He'd be damned if he'd start jogging down O'Connor Street with all the young lawyers and their wives. His heart
was fine.

He left the mower under the pecan tree and went into the
kitchen to sit. He could hear Mary Faith running the vacuum
upstairs, and the sound calmed him. He was fine now. He was
breathing fine. He had another glass of tea, his third, but
sipped this one slowly and felt it cooling him down. It was a

funny scare for a Sunday morning. He'd have to fill up the day in other ways——maybe ride over to K-Mart with Mary Faith, get a new plug for that fan.

He had almost finished the tea when the doorbell rang, and he moaned aloud. Who rang the doorbell at ten o'clock on a Sunday morning? It was bound to be somebody selling newspapers or Girl Scout cookies, and he didn't look forward to saying no again, the same no he turned on all the little tanned faces, the little armies of nine- and ten-year-olds who trooped through the neighborhood and looked up at him from his doorstep. He hoped secretly that it was an Avon lady, so he could call Mary Faith and *she* could say no.

Mary Faith bounded down the stairs at the same minute he went for the door, and he stood aside, breathing hard, to let her open it. A middle-aged pair of strangers smiled nervously at them: a stout woman with blowsy hair underneath a navy straw hat——a peculiar little hat that sat far back on her head, a hat Faith would have worn for Easter Sunday twenty years ago ——and behind her, barely visible, a wiry man dressed for church, in a white shirt and tie. Jesse felt his own black T-shirt clinging to him with sweat. Either they were Jehovah's Witnesses, in which case he'd send them packing, or they were long-lost relatives. They were not selling Avon, anyway. He couldn't imagine, really, what a couple like this wanted, and when they didn't speak immediately, he had a chance to see Mary Faith look back at him in agony. *She* knew who they were, and in a flash he thought he knew, too. He thought he knew that these people had something to do with Mary Faith's baby.

"Mary Faith Rapple?" said the woman softly. "Mr. Rapple?"

Jesse stepped forward, trying to block Mary Faith from their view. "That's right," he said, pleasantly enough. "What can we do for you?" He wasn't going to ask them in until he knew their business for sure.

The woman smiled hesitantly. "This is a little difficult," she said. "If we could come in and talk for a minute? Our boy was a friend of Mary Faith's, and we just wanted to . . ." Her voice trailed off, and her husband turned around and looked down the street, as if there were nothing *he* wanted from the Rapples.

Jesse felt Mary Faith's breath on his back, and for her he wanted to say *no*. No, you can't come in, we've already settled this. No, she wouldn't tell me who it was and we finally let it stay that way, that Mary Faith's baby didn't really have a father, didn't really need a father, *doesn't* need a father now. He could see himself telling these people that he could take care of things, that he was getting married himself in a few weeks, that there wouldn't be any need for any interference. But the woman's face stopped him. He could see she wasn't the whiny sort. She was wearing an old-fashioned red lipstick, and she reminded him of Faith in other ways, too: she probably looked older than she was, and she wasn't used to asking favors of people. But there was a solid look about her, too, the look of a person who has to do all the talking in the family, the look of a lady who would stay on the doorstep all day, sweetly, if she had to. Besides, maybe they wanted to offer Mary Faith money. "Come in," he said, and showed them into the living room.

He had almost forgotten his chest: the tightening there now could be just from the excitement of having these people in the house. Mary Faith muttered that she would get them all tea, and he was left alone with the couple in his living room. It was not a room he felt at home in—he almost never stepped foot in it. Faith had filled it with furniture from her parents' house, after her mother died, and the overstuffed armchairs and sofas, covered in a faded brocade, never seemed to belong. Faith had always wanted to buy a rug for this room, but they'd never saved that kind of money, and the floor was bare beneath the heavy furnishings. The room reminded him of Usher's Funeral Parlor, where Faith had been laid out.

The woman introduced herself as Moira Jagger, and said her husband's name was Mike. Their son was called Michael Jagger, she said, and looked as if she expected Jesse to recognize the name. It didn't mean a thing to him—Mary Faith hadn't let on anything as helpful as a *name*. "My son died last December," Moira Jagger said, "of a—pill overdose."

Now he remembered. Jesse could remember, in fact, a supper conversation with Mary Faith over the boy. She'd barely reacted when he told her about the way they found Michael Jagger in back of the Breeze. "You don't think?" he said.

Mrs. Jagger nodded, an abject apology, and her husband followed her nod. "We think," she whispered, "that Michael could have been the father of your daughter's baby. Has she mentioned him? Do *you* think?"

Jesse tried to sit back in the armchair, but couldn't. It was too fat, too big. He was short-winded again, and the idea of Mary Faith's baby being fathered by a dead, drug-taking kook was just too much for him. No, he didn't think. No, he didn't think Mary Faith could have been so calm when she heard about the boy keeling over. No, he didn't think she'd have been able to keep it quiet all this time if there wasn't anybody to protect, if the father was already dead. No, he didn't think Mary Faith could have gotten herself involved with the kind of boy who'd be popping pills in the first place. Although to look at these people—the Jaggers—it was hard to imagine them being the *parents* of a boy who'd do a thing like that. At least it wasn't Stephen Dugan.

He didn't have time to answer, though. Mary Faith was bringing in a TV-tray full of iced tea glasses, and he jumped to his feet to help her. Just due he needed. Another glass of tea. He took one off the tray and sipped it absently. Mary Faith served them all, and turned to go.

"Mary Faith?" he said, and when she turned around her face was a studied gaze of unconcern. She *had* taken care of herself, washed her hair that morning, and pulled it back into its ponytail, and dressed in a yellow sundress, but her face was such a skillful blank that he knew these people were right. The boy who had gotten Mary Faith into trouble was dead. And that was why she had wanted to call it a virgin birth.

"Mary Faith?" he said again, and she sat, obediently, in a little rocker next to him. "Mary Faith," he said softly, not looking at the other parents in the room, "these folks think their son might have something to do with—your baby."

Mary Faith continued to gaze in front of her. "No, sir," she said clearly. Then she looked Mrs. Jagger in the eye. "I was real sorry to hear about Michael," she said. Her voice was firmer than any of theirs had been. "Real sorry. We weren't that close, but I always liked him. Anyway, he didn't have anything to do with my trouble."

Mrs. Jagger stared back at Mary Faith with a trembling smile. Jesse could see that there was disbelief in her eyes, but doubt, too. He had to hand it to Mary Faith: she was the coolest liar he had ever heard. Mary Faith standing on top of the bus steps, saying he had stolen her license. "Are you sure, Mary Faith?" he said.

She nodded again, without any energy or force. "I'm sure," she said, and this time Jesse watched Mr. Jagger, watched him bow his head down to scratch the top of it. Neither of the Jaggers looked at each other, and all four of them sat in Faith's old living room, quietly, until Moira Jagger said: "I'm sorry, we're sorry to take up your time. I hope we haven't caused you any embarrassment."

"No, ma'am," said Mary Faith clearly. "Not at all. Thank you for coming by."

Thank you for coming by! Jesse couldn't believe how his daughter floated into that voice of her mother's, that efficient little tone that might as well have been wiping away dust as wishing people good-bye.

He was dizzy when he rose to show the Jaggers out, but he got through it, and came back into the living room to have it out with his daughter. This had gone on long enough. He wanted to hear the whole story, to know why she couldn't have just said from the beginning that the boy was dead. And he wanted to tan her hide for lying to the Jaggers, who looked like decent people, and who might have come over to offer help with the hospital bills, for all they knew.

But she wasn't in the living room when he came back from the front door. She must have slipped into the hallway behind him, and padded upstairs while he was saying good-bye. Suddenly he was nauseous. He made his way shakily to the red couch and sat, then lay on his belly, his head over the edge. All desire to chase after Mary Faith, to learn the truth from her, vanished. All he wanted just now was to lie in the darkened room, to feel the heat wash over him. That fourth glass of tea had put him under. When he had the flu, Faith had put him in bed and soothed his forehead. That was what he wanted just now: not to find out if those people had been right, or if his daughter popped pills herself, or if Nell Dugan was going to marry him. He just wanted someone to find him in the living room, in the dark, and soothe his forehead.

For two hours that Sunday Jesse Rapple had slept on the red couch. When Mary Faith finally stood over him, calling his name to waken him, he'd been groggy and barely able to hear what she said: "You might as well know, Michael Jagger was the father of the baby. And I don't want to discuss it. I guess it wasn't a virgin birth." Then she had marched out of the room, and by the time he had absorbed her speech, he had already decided to give her a chance to tell him about it on her own good time. He was so taken aback that she had admitted it freely, so let down, almost, that the mystery of this baby's fatherhood was so easily solved, he told himself that he wouldn't hound her for more of the story.

And for a week they hadn't discussed it. He had let their lives go on the way they had been going, he leaving early for the gas station and eating supper at Nell's, Mary Faith keeping to herself in the house. He hadn't told Nell yet, because he knew she would push him to find out everything, every sordid detail, and he wasn't ready to know everything yet.

He and Nell had floated into a family routine every night. Supper was punctuated by her asking Ruthie, "When are you going to get out of here?" and "Where is that husband of yours?" After they cleared the table, they watched an hour of TV together while Ruthie put the dishes in the dishwasher and her children into their pajamas. There was no more lovemaking with Ruthie's children sleeping on sleeping bags in the bedroom, but he wasn't entirely displeased about that. There was a discipline to it, a holding back he thought was hard for Nell, that he imagined was wearing her down when he whispered on the way out, "And when do I get my answer?"

By the weekend he was ready to try to talk to Mary Faith again, and he told Nell that he was spending two days with his daughter. On Saturday they did the groceries, and when the washing machine sprang a leak, he drove her to the Laundromat. She cooked him a fried chicken supper, better than Nell's, and after he watched the end of the "Game of the Week" he fell asleep in the den. He didn't know how to start.

Sunday he woke early again, to a muggy day, and heard Mary Faith stirring inside her room. Today was the day, he thought, when he could approach it. This morning, this Sunday morning, he could ask her to tell him the whole truth about this suicidal Michael Jagger.

He couldn't start it over breakfast, though. She had made french toast, and she was cheerful, and he didn't want to spoil their sitting together without fighting. When she asked him, shyly, if he'd like to drive over to Coosaw to do some fishing off the bridge with her, he almost reached over to squeeze her hand. She hadn't been fishing with him since she was twelve.

They were clearing the breakfast table together when the front doorbell rang again, and this time they looked at each other. He went, while Mary Faith stayed at the sink, and when he came back into the room he was leading the Jaggers.

He wasn't sorry to see them. All week long he had been calculating how much they would be willing to pay of the doctor's fee—which Dr. Black would never *ask* for, but which that new receptionist had already begun hounding him about —and whether they would put out for the hospital, too. He sat them at the dinette, and Mary Faith wiped her hands to come join them.

He wasn't prepared for what they said, though. They all sat awkwardly in silence until Moira Jagger leaned forward at her place and cleared her throat. She seemed tenser this time, fiddling with her wedding band, and she began in a formal voice. "We want to thank you, Mary Faith," she said, "for calling us and telling us you'd changed your mind." She looked at her husband, whose vision was focused on the back door and trees beyond. "Mr. Jagger and I appreciate what you must have been going through," she went on. "We appreciate your never bringing up Michael's name, until we came and asked you."

Jesse stared at them in wonder. Mary Faith? Called them up? After a week clammed up? After asking him to go fishing today? She must have known the Jaggers were coming back.

"Mr. Rapple," Moira Jagger went on, "I don't know if Mary Faith has told you about our offer."

Jesse shook his head, but calmed. The word *offer* sounded good to him. He could understand Mary Faith going behind his back to try and get some money.

"We would like to take Mary Faith in," the woman said, and Mary Faith bowed her head.

Jesse tipped his chair back, and when he felt his chest tightening told himself that it *had* been the excitement last week that had made him think he was having a heart attack. He could not have heard the woman right.

"Take her in?" he repeated.

"That's right," Mrs. Jagger said, and her husband nodded dumbly. "When we saw your daughter at the mass for our son, we knew right away that we had to do something. You see—our son was an unhappy boy. A very unhappy boy. And it was something we never felt we could reach. But now that your daughter is carrying his baby, well, perhaps we can reach the little child and somehow make up for all of our boy's misery."

Jesse looked at his daughter. Surely she would have told these people that she didn't need to be *taken in*, that she had a father to take care of her. But she wouldn't look up at him. He could see her breathing quickly, waiting for his answer. Did she want to leave home? To go with these strangers? These people who had let their son get hooked on drugs? Who had never made him happy?

"I don't know what to say," Jesse said. The trouble was, he did know what to say—he knew to say: Get out of here. This is my daughter. Your son is dead. I am taking care of things. I have been taking care of things. Let us be. But Mary Faith wouldn't even look at him, wouldn't confirm in her eyes, for just a second, that she wanted him to take care of things. It was as if she *wanted* them to take her away. Was this the way she got back at him for falling in love with Nell Dugan? Was this how a fifteen-year-old girl tried to show her father she wouldn't allow him to marry who he pleased? He wouldn't have any of it! She should be jumping up to his side, this minute, telling these Jaggers that she meant to stay with her father.

Finally Mike Jagger spoke, his voice rusty and hesitant. "Maybe we should hear from Mary Faith what she thinks about all this," he said.

Jesse searched for an answer in Mary Faith's face, but she kept her eyes lowered, her head bowed. "I haven't made up my mind," she said quietly.

Hadn't made up her mind! Then she was considering it, considering an offer to go away with these people, to make her child their grandchild and not his. When would he get to visit —on Sundays, like a divorced father?

"Mary Faith," he said, and the pain in his chest spilled out into his voice. Heartburn, he thought. Hell, heartache. Her name was all he was willing to say: if she were willing to run out again, after all she'd put him through, it would have to be her decision.

Then Moira Jagger started in again, and Jesse discovered that he couldn't bear the sound of her voice. She had seemed determined when he first met her; now she was a bulldozer. Couldn't she stop? Couldn't she let him get his breath? "We don't want to take her away from you," she was saying, and Jesse couldn't *stand* how self-assured she sounded, the further along in her plan she got. "We just want to give her a place to live, and some help with the baby. We feel it's our duty to pay the medical bills. We talked it over with Father Berkeley."

Why didn't you call the pope and ask him *his* opinion, Jesse wanted to say. Now, Mary Faith, he was thinking. Now, tell these people now that we don't need their help. But his daughter was rising, always the hostess. She would offer these people coffee or cookies, and they would see what a good little help she was around the house, and they would start hounding him day and night until he let her go. Well, they wouldn't have to hound him. If she wanted to go, out she went. She looked better in the yellow sundress than her mother ever had. Her arms were slender and tanned, reaching up for cups. If Faith could see her now, considering going off with another family.

They might as well have given her up for adoption when she was ten, and they started running into trouble with the doctor bills. They might as well have given her up when she was *born.*

"You three talk it over between yourselves," he said, and didn't care that his voice ripped through theirs. "I've got some things to see to down at the station."

The Jaggers looked alarmed, but even *she* couldn't think of what to say, and he left through the kitchen door without glancing back at them.

17

Birthday

On July the first, I turned sixteen years old, and not a soul in the world remembered my birthday. I *knew* my father wouldn't, but I thought Stephen Dugan might. I thought he might send me a friendly card—nothing romantic—but he didn't. When I went to the mailbox at noon, there wasn't even a card from Aunt Lizann, who has a book where she writes down everybody's birthday. I must have been scratched from the book.

The only letter in the noon mail was signed *Jagger*, and I didn't want to read it. I didn't want to move in with the Jaggers. Poor Mr. Jagger, a sweet old mailman, afraid to say a word when his wife was there to do all the talking. I'd only called them up because I thought they might help my father with the bills, but then Mrs. Jagger went off the deep end, thinking I'd come be with them and bring the baby. No wonder Michael went nuts.

I was in a trap now, though. When the Jaggers came over to the house, my father acted as if he *wanted* me to go. He hardly gave them time to say what they wanted, and then he ran out of the back door, to go to that old woman's house. He was probably glad for the idea of me being off his hands. He was probably glad that I wouldn't be here when he took Nell Dugan into my mother's house. If I were gone, she could turn everything upside down, turn my mother's sewing room into an upstairs TV room.

If only my father would give me a sign that he wanted me to

stay. But he couldn't even remember I was turning sixteen—sixteen, which is the birthday when my cousin Betsiann got a two-thousand-dollar party at the country club. I opened Mrs. Jagger's letter, figuring she had set out more reasons for me to come. She had been calling every day with a new one: first she said she thought she should take me in so that together we could make sure the baby wouldn't go crazy the way Michael did, and then she said she should take me in so that my father wouldn't be overburdened, that men were emotionally unprepared for that sort of thing. I had been leaving the phone off the hook for the past two days, trying to cancel out her pressuring me into a decision. I never thought I'd be considering going to live with the Jaggers, but unless my father said *something* to show he wanted me to stay instead of Nell Dugan, I'd have to go.

Mrs. Jagger's letter was written in a very neat hand, on yellow stationery with a big red rose in the corner. It was dated June 30, the day before.

Dear Mary Faith,
I have been trying to get you on the phone all day, but your number rings busy, so I have decided to write you this little letter. It is the kind of thing I would rather tell you in person, but it is weighing so heavily on my mind that I feel the need to get it down on paper. Please don't tell Mr. Jagger that I have told you any of this, he thinks we should keep it a secret, but I am not one for secrets, and Michael, God keep his soul, can't be hurt by this now.

You see, Michael was not our real son. We adopted him when he was a year old, after the doctor told me I could never have children. I wanted a baby more than anything in the world! My sister is a nun who works with adoption for the diocese in Charleston, and she told us she would try to get us a child.

Well, Michael was the child she got us, and he was a little boy nobody else wanted because he was so frail and skinny and hurt-looking. He never smiled. My sister wasn't supposed to tell me his story, but when I said I wasn't sure I wanted to take on such a scrawny child already a year old, she blurted it all out to me.

Michael's mother was a little girl at the College of Charleston who got pregnant and didn't tell a soul, she kept it all a secret until she was about six and a half months pregnant and started to show. Then she got scared and she took a wire coat hanger and tried to give herself an abortion. Mary our lady of perpetual help have mercy on her wherever she is today. She can't have known what she was doing. My sister said she was found in her room, bleeding and passed out, and when they rushed her to the hospital Michael was born, just over two pounds. They never expected him to live, but somehow he did, he fought to live, and then nobody wanted to take him, because he was so sickly. They let the mother name him, and she named him Buddy Holley, but of course we had to change that later.

I put her letter down and remembered all the letters her son had sent me.

Well, Mary Faith, after my sister told me that tale I just had to adopt Michael, of course I did! I adopted him, and I told myself he would never know he hadn't been wanted, he would never know his own mother had tried to kill him in the womb.

But, you know, it was just like Michael knew his whole life that something terrible happened to him when he was born. He never was a normal child, no matter how many baseballs and basketballs we gave him, he didn't want to play sports or be with the other kids. Mike used to take him fishing every Saturday, and do you know, in twelve years I bet he didn't catch but twelve fish? He was always playing alone in his room, and the older he got, the less we could figure him out. He started bringing home those Russian books and since he said they weren't communist I tried to read them myself, but to tell you the truth I could never get past the first couple of chapters they were so hard to follow.

Mike, Mr. Jagger, always said to leave the boy alone, but I never could see the sense in leaving a hurt child alone, and that is why I am telling you all this now. I think you are a hurt child, too, now that Michael is dead, and since I know that the Blessed Virgin herself would not stand in judgment of you, I want you to know how much we want to help you. We never could convince Michael that he was a wanted baby, as soon as he found out he was adopted when he was ten he got you might say cool to us, but this baby will be off to a fresh start, won't it! We can all love this baby and protect it from all the harm that comes to it. We will tell the baby that Michael died of natural causes, like cancer, so that the baby won't have to think his father didn't want him! Because I know Michael would have wanted him, only he was still just a boy himself when he died. And I have resolved in my mind, no matter what anybody says, that he didn't know he was taking all those pills, that he just got confused and didn't mean to kill himself at all.

I am sorry, I can see I am going on too long here. I didn't mean to burden you with these facts, but I just want you to know why it means so much to me to do the right thing by you and that little baby. That is my grandchild, you know! Maybe this little one won't run into his room after supper, the way his father did. Maybe he'll like fishing! Who knows?

Please think it over, Mary Faith. I have said a rosary three times a day for this, ever since we first found out from Mr. Dugan your name and address. Please take us up on our offer.

> Your mother-in-law,
> Moira Ann Jagger

There were three crosses underneath her signature, and if her wanting to burden me with the story of Michael's birth hadn't decided me, those three crosses did. I wasn't having any baby brought up in a house where they called on the Blessed Virgin to make all their decisions. Poor Michael. I bet he had tried real hard to love his mother. I bet he had tried real hard to catch those fish.

I felt like calling up Mrs. Jagger and telling her to keep her sad stories to herself. Between Stephen and the Jaggers they had gotten me to the point where I didn't just have to remember Michael crying after he made love to me—now I could remember him being miserable his whole life. I felt like telling her I had seen plenty of sad stories in the hospital when my mother died, and it was my sixteenth birthday and she didn't have to start giving me the gruesome details of Michael Jagger coming into the world unwanted.

But there was one good that came from Mrs. Jagger's letter, besides making me decide that I had to stay home whether my father wanted me there or not. The other good was the news that they got my name from Mr. Dugan. I knew that all along, but now I could carry the letter over to his house and show him I knew it. He hadn't shown up for tutoring on Monday; he'd called in sick and had the office call me, and we both knew why. Okay, okay, we weren't going to be lovers, but I had to convince him we were still *something* to each other. Friends, even. Somebody besides Moira Kook Jagger, with all her exclamation points, who knew Michael's secret.

I decided it would be a birthday present to myself, to see Stephen and tell him the latest developments. I decided to get myself dressed and take the bike over to Freedom Lane. I would bring the letter, and I would act as if nothing had happened between us.

When I rang Stephen's doorbell, Ruthie answered. She was wearing a cotton nightgown and a pair of rubber thongs, and it looked as if she'd just gotten up. The circles under her eyes were bigger than ever.

She told me that Stephen wasn't home, and all of a sudden I

realized what I'd done. I'd gone to his house on a Wednesday, in the middle of the afternoon, when he'd be at work. I'd been locked up in my own house too long to even realize that other people got on with their lives and didn't sit around waiting for a baby. I felt stupid, giggling in front of Ruthie, but she said to come in, nobody was home and Stephen had told her he might drop by to take her out to lunch. Her mother had her children for a few days, she said.

She padded around the house without saying much, fetching me water and going into the back to change. I knew Stephen wasn't going to show up, but there was something so quiet about his sister I just wanted to stay put a little longer. It was too hot to get back on the bike and face everybody's stares.

Finally Ruthie came back in an old faded pair of overalls over a shirt that was Mexican or Indian or something foreign. It had too many bright colors to be American. I could imagine what Ruthie had been like at Due East High School. I bet nobody there thought she was beautiful at all, and I bet everyone in New York did.

She sat down on the couch, and she chewed her lip so hard and so continuously that she got me to chewing my own lip. "It gets heavy toward the end, doesn't it?" she said, and it took me a minute to figure out she meant the baby. I nodded. It sure did get heavy. I turned from one side of the bed to the other at night, and my ribs ached and I couldn't catch my breath and my legs felt like sandbags tied onto me.

"I was nine months pregnant with Stephen in August," she said. She didn't seem to be *trying* to make conversation, the way Reba McFee or Betsiann did. She seemed to be really remembering. "I used to walk down by the trestle back here over the creek—you can see it from Stephen's backyard—and once I got there, I wouldn't know how to get home. I'd be so tired, and so hot, and the pine trees weren't enough to shade me. Finally I'd drag myself over to my mother's house, and if she was mad enough she'd beat me on the legs with my father's belt. I didn't care. At least it was cool enough in the house."

I looked down, in case she would be embarrassed by telling me something like that about her mother, about my father's girlfriend, but when I sneaked a glance at her, she didn't seem perturbed.

"I get like that," I said. "I get so I could kill for an air conditioner. I go in my father's room and turn it on, just for an hour. I could stay there all day if it weren't for the bills."

"You ought to try the movies," Ruthie said. "I used to see the same movie five days in a row at the Breeze. I gained forty pounds from popcorn."

I didn't want to tell her Michael Jagger went into a coma behind the Breeze, so I said, "People stare." It was true, too. I probably could have gotten over Michael falling down behind the Breeze if I didn't have to worry about people staring. I didn't mind people I didn't know, people who thought I was some ignorant little Marine wife, staring. I minded the girl selling the popcorn and the ticket taker and all the jocks from the high school staring.

"I know," Ruthie said. "But with me it didn't matter. I knew they'd stare worse once they found out my baby was black, so I didn't mind the staring when I was pregnant. Stephen says the father of your baby is dead?"

She didn't ask it with any pity. I told her yes, he was dead.

"And you're fifteen?"

I said I was sixteen, but I didn't say it was my birthday.

"Stephen really cares for you."

She didn't say *that* with any more emphasis than she'd said anything else, but I felt that a hurricane wind had blown into me and pinned me back against the couch. I wanted her to go on. I wanted her to say *He talks about you all the time* or *He can't get you out of his mind* or some other line from a Top Forty song. But she didn't say anything else about Stephen. She didn't say anything else.

Finally the quiet gave my lungs time to fill up with air again, and I said, "Do you like New York?" trying to cover up how I'd reacted to what she said, and how long I was staying. I was scared Marygail would be coming back home any minute, coming in and stopping me from hearing any more about Stephen. But Ruthie didn't seem to hear my question. She was looking over her shoulder, out into the front yard, and pulling thin loose strands of red hair from her head.

All of a sudden she said, "I have to tell you not to lose your heart."

This time I didn't answer.

"Don't lose your heart to Stephen. He's a Catholic, maybe a lapsed Catholic, but he won't leave Marygail. I know, anybody else in Due East would say he wouldn't leave her because you're sixteen years old, but I know Stephen better. Your being sixteen doesn't bother Stephen any. He won't leave her because he *married* her."

We both sat quiet while I tried to take it in. It wasn't just because he was drunk. It wasn't just because he had taken pity on me after Michael Jagger died.

Ruthie began again. "I don't know what you know about me," she said, but didn't wait for an answer. I didn't imagine she had many talks like this one. "When my boy Stephen was born," she said, "I'd lost touch with his father. His father didn't even know I was pregnant. But after he got out of the Marines, a few years later, he came looking for me, and he found me, and he took me out of Due East and back to New York. I can't tell him I miss Due East—I can't tell him I miss that hot trestle and pulling a crab pot from the water—because he could never live in Due East again."

I tried not to look at her. She was running her fingers faster and faster through her hair. The circles under her eyes *were* blacker. I didn't think she'd had much sleep.

"We live on the Upper West Side," she went on, her voice quickening. "I don't suppose that means anything to you. What it means to us is that there won't be any trouble about the children, there won't be any trouble about his being black and my being white. When we moved in, it was cheap, cheap and dingy and ugly, and now all of a sudden they put ferns in all the bars and everybody wants to live there. We pay six hundred dollars a month for a one-bedroom apartment. Ralph and I sleep in the living room, on a pull-out couch. We're always tripping over the stroller."

She faded for a minute, but then she went on. "But that's not the point. The point is about Stephen being Catholic and not wanting to leave his wife. My husband's a Catholic, too, a black Catholic in a white church, a black man with a white woman's family. He doesn't want to leave me either. Before I left for Due East he started crying one night because he fell in love with a woman at work. A black woman. He had to tell me about it because he's a Catholic and Catholics think that confession takes care of everything, that I'll forgive him and he can pretend it never happened. He didn't even have an affair with her. He didn't even tell her. He just fell in love. But he'll never leave me, not unless I leave him, because the nuns brought him up too well for that. He'll never sleep with her, he'll just see her every day at work with her hair relaxed and her neck perfumed. She wears gold earrings. He'll see her in her pretty Italian shoes and he'll come home to me, to the white girl from the South who never graduated college, the girl who's twenty-four and looks forty dragging in from Riverside Park. With the sand toys and the faded overalls. He just sees the walls of the one-bedroom apartment closing in on him and knows he'll never get out. He can be the best computer programmer in all of New York City, and he'll still never be able to afford a two-bedroom apartment. He can try all he wants to love me and be faithful, and I'll always come from a town he's too scared to visit. I'll always be a little girl he got pregnant when he was a Marine. He *had* to take care of me."

Finally she stopped. Her voice had whirled into a spin so fast that there was no chance of her stopping long enough for tears or even anger.

"So don't lose your heart to Stephen," she said. "Men go crazy for you, they want to see your belly big with a child, and then one morning they wake up and it's all a burden, a terrible burden."

I thought about Michael Jagger, seventeen years old and never even knowing what burden he'd brought on himself. I remembered his saying he'd wanted to marry me before he took me to bed, and suddenly I could see him ten years from now, working at the post office with his father, trying to take his children fishing and wanting to stay home and read Russian novels instead. I could see his mother coming over to drive him crazy, and then I could see Stephen with his wife drunk in the living room, his beautiful stupid wife with the suntan lotion and the little girl, the little girl he wouldn't leave because he was a Catholic and the nuns had brought him up too well for that. I could see my father running out the back door when the Jaggers offered to take me, my father falling asleep on the couch with the TV on so that he wouldn't have to look at the charge accounts. A terrible burden. My baby was all scrunched up on one side, and my belly was tightening with an early contraction, and I knew that I wouldn't ever feel the burden the way a man would feel it. I had the baby tightening inside me. I would take care of it somehow. I would address envelopes.

"The worst part is," Ruthie went on, "that I'm in love with him. Crazy in love with my husband."

I didn't know what to say. She was just talking into the mirror.

"I hope you didn't love that boy too much," she said.

Then I knew I had to leave. I imagined she'd been sitting all morning, telling herself the things she was now telling me, telling herself she was a burden, that her husband didn't love her. There was the same look on her face that I'd seen on Stephen's face, the look of *nothing to be done, no way out,* and now I had remembered it, I could see it on Michael Jagger's face too. I had to get away from them all. I had to have my baby in another six weeks.

I pedaled the bike right down River Street before I knew what route I'd taken, but thinking of Ruthie, sitting alone on her brother's couch, I didn't care anymore about people's stares. There was hardly anyone out in the heat of the day anyway, and since I hadn't been on River Street for three weeks, it was like seeing Due East for the first time. The shops looked shabbier than I remembered them: there were big new plastic signs on top of Today's Jewelers and the Rite-Aid Drug Store, and they gave downtown the look of a Marine town instead of the quaint little historical place my mother had always brought me up to believe it was. I remembered seeing Michael Jagger walking back and forth down this street, on his way to the library or coming back, always carrying a fat book and his folder of fliers. He and Ruthie, even Stephen, were people as lonely as the street looked.

When I turned onto Oysterbed Road, I saw Buddy Miles in his little blue Chevrolet. He tooted, and before I knew it, he was turning his car around and following me down O'Connor Street, going twenty miles an hour. When I stopped at our house and he followed me into the driveway, I thought how much nicer it was to be lonely than to be with Mr. Miles.

"Daddy's not home," I said. I couldn't figure out what Mr. Miles would be doing driving around town in the middle of the day, but then I caught a sniff of whiskey on his breath.

He followed me in through the back door. "I didn't think he'd be home," he said, and from the way he slurred the words I figured he'd been at it for a while. "I just saw you on the bike, and I came over to apologize. I think I hurt your feelings the last time I was here. I think I hurt your daddy's feelings too."

I didn't want him to sit down, but he made his way over to the kitchen table and slouched into a chair, looking for all the world like a man who planned to stay the day. I didn't offer him anything, and I didn't answer him, either. Buddy Miles was like Due East, getting shabbier and fatter by the year. He wasn't in the same class of men as my father and Stephen Dugan and Michael Jagger. He wasn't the kind of man who brooded or felt burdened. He just opened himself up a bottle of whiskey and came over to people's houses to bother them.

"So what you think, Mary Faith?" he said. "You forgive me?"

"Yes sir," I said.

"I told your daddy there's nothing prettier than a pregnant woman. I didn't mean to offend either one of you bringing it up."

"Yes sir," I said.

Mr. Miles could see he wasn't getting anywhere, and he asked me for a drink of water. I gave it to him, right out of the tap, no ice cubes. He drank it down, and then he kept right on up. "You finally tell your daddy who got you in trouble?" I could tell he thought he was being real friendly. I thought of Michael sitting at that table, not knowing a single thing to say. Stephen, sitting there holding his tongue.

"None of your business, sir," I said.

He hee-hawed and slapped the table and said, "That's what I like, a little girl with a lot of spunk. That's what I like."

I said I had to go upstairs to get some housework done, and he said, "You mean to tell me after all these years you couldn't spare five minutes for one of your daddy's oldest friends? Mary Faith, me and him were in Due East Elementary together."

I sat down, trapped, but I tried not to look at him. I could see him wanting to stay until my father got home, which could have been six o'clock, or seven, or eight, or midnight. His face looked puffy, as if the drinking had been going on for weeks, or months. It reminded me of a watermelon, pitted and slick with sweetness. Suddenly I wished the phone would ring. I wished it would be Ruthie, or Stephen, or even Moira Jagger. Anyone who was not Mr. Miles.

"Mary Faith, you have always been a shy little girl," Mr. Miles said, and when I didn't answer that, he said, "Hadn't you? Hadn't you always been shy?"

I thought I'd throw up on the spot, but it was easier to just say, "Yes, sir."

"You know, I wadn't kidding when I told your daddy how pretty you look. Some folks tell me it's a kind of perversion on my part, but I find you pregnant ladies very sexy. Very sexy."

I wanted to take the water glass and drain it on his head, but he had already emptied it. I thought I would just go upstairs, just leave him there, but suddenly I was afraid to turn my back on him. I might come back to find him passed out. Or he might follow me. Still, I couldn't sit with him drooling over the table and taking up what was left of my sixteenth birthday. Let him go buy a dirty magazine to stare at, instead of me.

So I told him very politely that I had to excuse myself, and I left the room. But as soon as I reached the foot of the stairs I felt his pudgy hand on my shoulder. He must have crept up behind me.

"What is it?" I said, without turning around. Michael had

followed me up these steps. Stephen had followed me. I wanted to turn around and knee him, but something held me back, some worry about how much Mr. Miles might be able to forget himself when he was drinking.

"Mary Faith, I think you owe me an apology now," he said softly. His voice was pitched somewhere between a whine and an appeal.

"All right," I said, knowing full well it wouldn't be enough to make him leave me alone. It was the only way I could think of getting rid of him. "I'm sorry," I said, and started up the stairs again.

I heard his footstep behind me. "Mary Faith," he wheedled, "a man has *needs.*"

Any fear or worry I had left with that word *needs.* I whirled around on my father's friend, the friend who'd probably talked my father into Nell Dugan in the first place, and screamed: "Get out of here! Get out of my mother's house!"

I could feel the purple of my face. I screamed so loud I thought I'd popped a rib, and wondered if the neighbors would think to call the police. Buddy Miles held his hands up, as if to shield his face, as if to say he hadn't meant anything by all of this, and then shuffled away, like a child in a schoolyard stunned by a baseball. I stood just where I was, clutching the banister, until I heard him slam the kitchen door shut, and then I ran and locked it, and looked out the window to make sure he was backing the blue car out of our driveway. He was, his head turned over his shoulder, as if he knew I watched from the kitchen.

My father. Michael Jagger. Buddy Miles. Even Stephen Dugan. A man has needs. There wouldn't be a damn one of them there when my baby was born.

The phone rang as I watched Mr. Miles drive off. A second ago, I'd been praying for it to ring, and now I didn't want to answer it. It echoed in the house, though, and I picked it up. It was my Uncle Zack; I knew as soon as I heard him say *"Mary Faith?"* with that same insistence they'd all been turning on me. I didn't want to hear a man's voice. I screeched into the receiver: "Oh, go to hell, Uncle Zack," and then hung up hard. It wasn't until I was sitting at the kitchen table that I realized he might have been calling because they'd remembered my birthday after all.

18

Faithful to Faith

It wasn't until the Fourth of July had passed that Jesse Rapple realized he'd missed some other big holiday, and when it came to him that it was his daughter's birthday it was too late to make amends. He bought her the most expensive bottle of cologne he could find in Samson's drugstore, and had them wrap it up, but when he presented it to her, awkwardly, over supper, he realized that she'd never worn scent—that had been her mother—and he couldn't blame her for the coolness she turned on him. He'd let sixteen slide by. She told him she wasn't going to the Jaggers, but he imagined it more likely that they had rescinded the offer than that she had chosen to stay with him. Faith came back at night, silently berating him, and he wished the two of them, Mary Faith and Faith, would let go at him right out in the open so that he could at least feel the hot relief of chastisement. But Mary Faith just retreated to her bedroom, and Faith came to him stealthily, in dreams. He never answered either one of them back.

Besides, he'd been sick. Summer had ripped him open in a way he never remembered it doing. In the mornings he felt nauseous and quivery, and through the day he was short of breath. From time to time there was a twinge in his chest, sometimes sharp enough to make him think he should at least go to Dr. Black and get reassurance that it was nothing but heartburn, nothing but gas. The twinges always passed, though, before he had time even to think of driving over to the doctor's office on the John C. Calhoun Road.

Nell had been sick, too. He knew she was pregnant, and she knew she was pregnant, but neither one of them talked about it. Instead their time together dwindled and was spent in comparing ailments. "You feel dizzy now? Me? Just a little. A little shaky." Ruthie's children still stayed at Pinetowne, and Ruthie was still camped out at her brother's house, and everybody but Jesse seemed to like the arrangement fine. He told himself it was good to see Nell so attentive to the kids, that that was a good sign, but the more attention she paid to them the less she paid to him, and it was getting late for them to make wedding arrangements.

It was two weeks after Mary Faith's birthday, a week after he'd remembered it, when he called Nell and asked her for a date. He told her on the phone that they were getting like an old married couple (he wished!) and that he wanted to take her out on the town. He told her to get Ruthie to bring Stephen and Kate over to the uncle's house. He said, "I want that bedroom cleared out for the two of us."

He liked what his authority did to Nell. She said, "Yes sir, Mr. Rapple," in a coy voice, and then she told him she would buy a new nightgown, a nightgown with purple irises, she thought, that would cling to her breasts. She called them titties, and much as he hated himself for imagining her standing by the kitchen phone with her hand on those titties, he was sure that was what she was doing.

He got them reservations at the River House and didn't even *ask* what it would cost, and didn't let himself worry about the seersucker suit looking too ratty. Every lawyer in Due East wore a blue seersucker suit in the summertime, which was why Faith had had him buy it, and when the lawyers' suits got ratty it was just supposed to be part of their carelessness. So his frayed cuffs would have to pass for carelessness, too.

That afternoon he drove Mary Faith to her doctor's appointment—she had to go once a week now, and he thanked God he'd gotten her under a doctor's care when he did. Dr. Black had put up a real fuss over how far gone she was when he first

saw her. He waited for her in the truck, but when she reap-
peared looking white and shaken, he felt guilty for not going
inside so he drove her to the shopping center for an ice cream.
The little smiles she gave him when he did something like that
drove him to distraction; they were shy, and slow-breaking,
and when she finally gave in to the smile she covered her teeth,
just the way her mother had. He couldn't bear knowing how
much an ice cream cone meant to her, couldn't stand to see
that she was still a girl, and when they sat at the little café tables
they averted their eyes, just as if they were eating at home.

He picked Nell up at six, and they were the first ones in the
dining room at the River House. The restaurant was on the
first floor of an old River Street house, and he'd expected it to
be filled with boaters docked at the marina. He could tell as
soon as she sat down that Nell had never eaten there, either;
she picked at the hem of the red linen tablecloth, and ogled the
flowers, and looked at him aghast when she read the menu
prices. Seven-fifty for an appetizer of crab legs. He added up
his cash again—he had no credit cards to cover this—and
thought he could just make it if he ordered broiled flounder,
the cheapest thing on the menu, and didn't have a drink or
dessert. It wasn't that he begrudged a penny of this meal: he'd
decided against coming with a diamond ring in his pocket,
since he *really* couldn't afford that, and could hardly give
Faith's ring away. Since the doctor bills for Mary Faith, and
since he'd realized that they'd have to start buying a few baby
things anyway, at least a crib and some diapers and some little
shirts to put on the kid, his finances were so out of whack that a
fifty-dollar meal couldn't have much impact.

Nell ordered a martini, though, and then another, and a
shrimp cocktail, and veal cordon bleu, and thought they
should have a bottle of wine with the meal, so that by the time
the check came—and by then the restaurant had begun to fill
with people, with Reeve Downs and his secretary, with Dr.
Lupke the dentist and his wife and mother-in-law—by the time
the check came, Jesse was short for a tip and had to whisper to
Nell that he needed to borrow five bucks. She said, "What?"
and "Speak up," drunk and uncaring, and it reminded him of

some situation comedy he'd seen on TV. He tried to tell himself that it was funny to be short for a dinner check, that it happened to people all the time. But Nell seemed annoyed. It didn't bode well for the proposal, the big proposal, the last time he was going to ask her, which was going to be tonight.

They left the restaurant subdued, but as they pulled into Pinetowne, Nell said she had something important to say to him, something she wanted to save up for the bedroom, and Jesse grinned. This was going to be it. The families could start consolidating. But Nell saw his smile and said, "Now don't you get so excited. Isn't it just like a man?"

She led him through the apartment by the hand, into the bedroom, and when he sat at the side of the bed, she unbuttoned his shirt. Everything was slowing down for Jesse. Her air-conditioning felt good, like cold baptism water on his back. He forgot about his shortness of cash and shortness of breath, and drew Nell over to sit beside him. He wanted to tell her that he'd been lonely for her, that sooner than they knew it they'd be getting old. He wanted to hold her like a cat in his lap and stroke her. She was wearing the same pants suit she'd worn to the movies, and he rubbed his hand against the nubbiness of her sleeve. They'd been without sex so long that he wasn't moved to kiss her: he found their sitting together, this stroking, more soothing.

Nell wiggled loose from him, pulled off her jacket, and rose to hang it in the closet. She'd never before bothered to hang up her clothes, and Jesse held his breath for a second. Neatness could so easily mean bad news, an evasion: every time he and Buddy got in from hunting, Faith began hanging things up, putting things away. He had hated that silent, accusing precision of hers, and he wasn't used to seeing any precision at all with Nell.

Nell stood in front of him and pulled her shirt out of her pants, rolling back and forth on the balls of her feet. "I guess you've figured out what's ailing me?" she said.

Jesse shrugged his shoulders, not sure whether to nod or not, not sure whether to smile or not. It was a miracle, Nell being pregnant. Practically like barren Elizabeth.

"I got every doctor at Calhoun Square going," she said. "Change-of-life baby at fifty! Gave *them* all a good laugh."

She sounded bitter, and Jesse didn't budge.

"I said to the doctor, I said well how could this *hap*pen, after I'd already dried up? And he said I musn't have dried up, that my body must have just been taking a short vacation. Ha, ha, I said."

"You ought to be proud as a rooster," Jesse said.

She gave him a strange smirk. "Roosters are male," she said. "You're the one proud as a rooster."

"I am proud," he said.

"Well, you've got five more days to be proud in," Nell said, and let out a long sigh. "They're going to do the abortion next Monday."

He didn't think she meant it. "Nell," he said, and reached out for her brown hand. "Nell, you don't have to have an abortion. What'd you think I was, some teenage boy who wasn't going to do right by you? Didn't you know I'd guessed it when I asked you to marry me? You can move into the house and we can raise the baby there."

He thought then that she might move closer to him, and wrap her arms around his neck, and tell him she'd marry him. But instead she pulled her hand back, a quick jerk, and stared at him unblinkingly. She parted her lips to speak, then turned her back on him. "You *are* cuckoo, Jesse," she said, but there was no lightness in her tone. "You honestly think I'm going to go through having a *baby*? I've gotten way past all that. I put in my time twenty-five years ago. The *thought* of a stinky diaper sends shivers up my spine."

Jesse thought she was just depressed, overwhelmed with the news. "We could—"

"We could forget about the whole thing," Nell said. "Honey, I've got a *good* life here. I'm not about to give up my pension. I live on my own now. I gave up my house because I don't want to clean house. You really think I want to move into an old house on the Point and play stepmother to your daughter? Jesse, we've got a good thing going in bed, we don't need to mess it up with some crazy talk about getting married. That's for kids."

Jesse didn't answer. He lay back on the bed and stared at the white squares in the ceiling. He heard Faith clucking her lips together. Faith had never complained about money. Faith had centered her whole life on keeping a baby, not flushing it down the toilet. All the phone calls he'd put in from the station to see how the latest pregnancy test had come out. All the times he'd rushed home when she'd called to say she was bleeding. The wait for Mary Faith: he'd never believed Mary Faith would grow, would stay anchored inside his wife for a full nine months. He had been so shocked when she was born—a fat, white, mottled *girl*—that he and Buddy had gone on a beer-drinking spree that made him miss the first night of visiting hours. He realized he'd been planning on a boy this time around, he'd been planning on Nell giving birth to a boy. A child who wouldn't have the faintest idea how to sew or cook or clean or balance the checkbook, one who would never berate him with silence.

He said, "Nell, you can't mean this."

"Can't I just?"

There was no elasticity in her voice. He said, "Don't go killing what's inside of you. That could be my son in there."

Nell whirled around and started tucking her shirt back into her pants, as if she were preparing for a quick getaway. "You give me a good laugh," she said, and didn't laugh. "When it was your daughter, all you could talk about was how to get her to have an abortion. Now you think it's a part of you—Mr. Macho all of a sudden—and you start talking about killing. Go on. That's no more a baby than a seed in the ground is crape myrtle. It's nothing yet."

Jesse closed his eyes on the bed. Nell's voice was rough, a raspy transmission he was hearing from far across the room. No baby. No son. No company for Mary Faith. The empty house. He wanted to cry out: *You know what it's like to go into that house of gloom every evening? You think I want to spend the rest of my life having the ghost of my wife and my daughter berate me?* He wanted to say: *I thought we could drink beer every night, every night for the rest of my life, until I fell into my grave with a little buzz on, feeling sleepy from being well fucked. Well I've been fucked all right.* He never used the word *fucked;* it was a word that had repulsed Faith, that she had banned from the house. Nell had brought him to this, to the degradation of all his thoughts, and now even his language. Titties. He wanted to say: *You old bitch, you selfish bitch in Pinetowne, putting down my old house on the Point.* He wanted to say: *You better have that baby. You better have my son.*

Nell said, "Listen, Jesse, there's one thing we have to talk about. I think it'd be the—gentlemanly—thing for you to do, to pay for half the abortion."

Jesse jerked himself up from the bed and tried to speak. He meant to say, *I've been planning to spend my every last cent on this baby, but I don't mean to spend it on killing my son,* but as he opened his mouth bubbles of air came out instead of words. He could feel a tire iron in his left arm, a heavy piece of lead going round and round his nerves until it had twisted them all. Then the tire iron was working its way into his shoulder and battering him on his chest. He couldn't breathe. He couldn't call out to Nell to help him, to call the doctor. He couldn't let her know that he'd been feeling this for weeks, that this wasn't his first heart attack. He couldn't speak, he didn't think—he wasn't sure, because though he couldn't say those things to Nell, he could hear himself calling to Faith. *I wasn't going to marry her, Faith,* he was saying. *I was never going to marry her. I had to be struck down to see how bad she is. I can see it now, Faith. I can see she's wicked. I can see I should have been faithful to you, Faith, and from now on I am. Faithful to Faith.* What he didn't understand was why he didn't pass out, why—if he felt he was crying—there were no tears running down his cheeks, why the terror came over him in waves, and then washed back, leaving him to talk to Faith. What he didn't understand was why he was lying on the bed gurgling and gasping and clutching his arm, seeing out of the corner of his eye Nell, her little mouth twisted in horror. Helpless. He decided he was dying.

19

Deserted Again

Stephen called in sick three weeks in a row, and I took over the tutoring myself, walking all the way there and back because my father wasn't around to give me a ride and never remembered about things like tutoring anyway. It was two miles home. The shortest way was straight down River Street, over to Division, to O'Connor, and by ten o'clock, when I got out of class, my feet were so swollen that I didn't care if the shortest way was the way where I'd see the most people. Carloads of Marines would slow down when they saw me from the back, but when they were close enough to take in the size of me they'd belly-laugh and screech off again down the road. On those walks home I had a sort of perverse desire to see Aunt Lizann, to give her a big wave and a big grin, but she never passed by. Since I'd hung up on Uncle Zack, I hadn't heard from them. There went the baby shower.

On the other weeknights I'd taken to sitting in my momma's sewing room, trying to learn to sew from a book. I'd never taken home ec in school—that was for girls who *wanted* to marry Marines and live in trailers—and when my mother tried to teach me, she got too frustrated, because I am not good with my hands. I am a good housekeeper, but I'm not any good at those womanly things, sewing and knitting and batting my eyelashes and lying to men. Once I cut off my aunt and my uncle, though, I couldn't think of any good way to get enough baby clothes in the house, so I figured I'd better learn something useful, for the first few months anyway, until I could get a job. I wasn't coming along too quickly with it: it took me two nights and three bleeding fingers just to cut out the pattern for a baptism gown—I wasn't going to use it for a baptism gown, but it was plain and simple and white. I had ripped so many stitches out of the white cotton that I would have done better just going down to the K-Mart and buying one of their cheap Made in Taiwan baptism gowns.

I kept at it, though, and I was finishing up one Wednesday night (I was just going to forget about the lace around the neck and the sleeves. I couldn't see spending *that* much money) when I heard a car putter into the driveway and a soft rapping on the kitchen door. I folded up the material neatly, the way I'd always seen my mother do, and went downstairs. Raps on the door frightened me now, because I was waiting for Moira Jagger or Buddy Miles to show up. Moira Jagger had said on the phone that she understood why I wanted to stay with my father, and instead of calling me, she'd taken to sending me pamphlets and mass cards and other propaganda. She gave me the willies. And the last time I'd seen Buddy Miles when my father and I were driving out to the beach on the weekend, he'd waved just as happy as you please.

So when I saw it was Stephen Dugan, it was all I could do to keep from running to him. After Ruthie said he cared for me, I'd waited and waited for word from him—a call, a letter—but when he stopped coming to his tutoring job, I'd given up hope. I figured Ruthie had been right about Catholics.

I didn't run to Stephen. I held the door back, and he stepped in. He looked as if he really had been sick. His face was pasty, and his hair so dirty it stuck down on top of his head. He took his glasses off and put them in his pocket, so that I saw his eyes for the first time. They were pale blue, sunken in his face, surrounded by blond lashes so thin and light that they looked like an aura. His face was naked.

I knew better than to say anything, and let him sit at the kitchen table without speaking. I knew this time, too, not to get him a beer or a glass of wine, and seeing him so nervous, and feeling myself so nervous, I wished there was something I could do with my hands, one of those womanly things.

He sat drumming his fingers on the table, trying to think of what he was going to say. I couldn't tell if he was serious, or grim. Finally, he said, "I've got three things to tell you. Are you listening?" He asked me if I was listening the same way he asked the GED students if they understood what a past participle was. I said I was listening.

"Well," he said, "the first thing is a message from Ruthie." He stopped, and I waited. Between him and me, across my mother's dinette table, the air was thick with beads of wet. Wet, and waiting. July, and pregnant.

"Kate and Stephen and Ruthie are leaving in the morning," he said.

"Going back to New York?"

"Yup." Stephen eased himself a little in the chair. "Ralph Jordan came to fetch them today."

He sat, stiff, waiting for me to say something. When I didn't, he went on: "Ralph Jordan is her husband. I never did get straight what was going on between those two, but from the yelling that went on today it sounded like he'd been having himself an affair."

"No!" I said. "He just fell in love."

Stephen finally smiled and asked me how I knew a thing like that. When I told him Ruthie had told me, he smiled again.

"Well," he said, "that fits in, anyway. I had to take the day off today, there was so much hollering going on in my house. Ralph Jordan walked in the door this morning, fresh off the Greyhound bus, and said to Ruthie, 'I want you and my children back in New York. Today.' " Stephen imitated a deep, firm voice. "And Ruthie wouldn't say a thing. Quiet, clever Ruthie. First she got her husband yelling that he's never loved another woman, can't she see that, and then she got her husband yelling that men are human beings and do the wrong things sometimes, and then—by which time the whole neighborhood was tuned in to this scene—she got her husband yelling that he's found them another apartment in Brooklyn where she can keep the stroller underneath the stairs. The stroller underneath the stairs! That was when Ruthie finally put her arms around him and acknowledged that he was in the room. The stroller underneath the stairs. My poor sister."

Stephen tried to smile and shifted his weight and leaned back in his chair. "Which brings me to Ruthie's message, which was good-bye. I didn't know why she wanted to say good-bye to you, unless she can see more than I thought she could see."

I didn't rush him.

"Which brings me to the second thing I have to tell you," he said. "Which is preceded by a question."

Still I waited. He didn't look grim anymore, but his smile was gone.

"If I should yell as much as Ralph Jordan yelled this morning to get his family back," Stephen said, "would you promise not to keep your silence as long as Ruthie kept hers?"

I thought I knew what this was coming to. I nodded.

"Good," said Stephen. "This is the plan. I can't marry you now without your father's consent and my wife's consent, which we can be pretty sure will not be forthcoming from either party. So I am going to wait two years, two years from July the first, when you will be eighteen years old." He looked away from me, and put his glasses back on. "In the meantime," he said, "I am not going to sleep with my wife, and she will be glad for a divorce by the time it comes around. I am not going to sleep with you, either, but that is a matter of honor with myself. I am going to force Marygail to share custody of Maureen with me. I will not let on that I am going to marry you, so I may not be able to see you and the baby very much. But enough, I think, enough to let us get to know one another." He was reciting the same way his sister had recited, the facts of his life, what would be done. His voice was as cold as a January breeze off the river.

When he stopped, I didn't know what to say. I hadn't been asked a question, so I couldn't offer an answer. "What about divorce?" I said. "Doesn't that go against your religion?"

He looked at me sharply. "I thought I told you I didn't practice my faith anymore." He was annoyed. He hadn't really

asked me to marry him. He hadn't said anything about loving
me. That first day in the p.a. room, there had been some
struggle going on. That first night, when he pulled at my
breast until he hurt me, there had been some passion. At least
in his hands, at least in his arms holding back. Now that he had
worked things out, he was mechanical. He seemed to forget
that I would be part of the deal. He looked weary, like my
father.

"Are you sure you don't just feel sorry for me, because of
Michael?" I said. My voice was pitching higher and higher, a
child's voice.

"Yes, I'm sure," he said, but he was snappy, and he didn't
look at me. We didn't look like a pair of lovers. I felt the silence
weigh down on me the way it did when my father ate in this
room, and when I didn't say anything else, he said: "Mary
Faith, you have to have someone take care of you, and I will
take care of you. What would you do if your father were sick?"

I remembered Ruthie saying of her husband: He *had* to take
care of me. "When did you decide all this?" I said.

"Does it matter?" Now he closed his eyes as he leaned back,
and his sigh was a long tremble. He would wake up in the
morning with two burdens, with four burdens if you counted
the children.

"What made you say that about my father being sick?" I
asked suddenly. A dry taste had come into my mouth when I
heard him ask if it mattered. When my mother was dying, my
mouth would go dry, then my throat. Then I would feel dizzy
and the room would tilt on me.

Stephen opened his eyes and leaned forward. "That is the
third thing I came to tell you," he said, and I could barely hear
the rest. "I wanted you to know the other two things first. I
wanted you to know that Ruthie is taken care of, and I wanted
you to know that you'll be taken care of, too. Your father had a
heart attack at my mother's apartment tonight. She called me
to come get you."

When Aunt Lizann told me my mother was dead, I had been
waiting for it. It was a relief. Now, looking at Stephen, I
couldn't even think about my father lying somewhere, struck

down. But I asked it anyway: "Is he dead?" I could hear that my voice was steady.

"No," said Stephen, "I don't think so. He wasn't dead when she called, but it doesn't look too good. I came to drive you to the hospital. You might have to say good-bye to him."

I thought then that he was already dead, that this was the way Stephen was going to let me know the news gently. Why else had he sat at the kitchen table with his story and his proposal, eating up the time? I rose and cut off the kitchen light, hardly noticing that I was left standing in the dark. I could barely see Stephen's face, but his glasses bobbed up and down. I had nothing to pick up, no keys I needed, no comb to take with me, so I stood at the door until Stephen understood that I was ready to go, ready to have him drive me to the hospital. I wasn't thinking about my father having a heart attack. I was thinking about Stephen getting the news on the phone, and deciding on the way out his front door that since my father was dying, he'd have to marry me. I was thinking about Ruthie, sitting so still in her chair that she looked like one of the mental patients you see on TV documentaries, so still because she thought her husband didn't love her. Now I understood how she made herself so still. My body slowed down. My breath was slow and deep. Stephen felt a responsibility. My father was dying. Stephen wanted to marry me, to take on the burden. There was no passion left in him: it had flickered when he was drunk, and now he wanted to make amends. I would be a burden. I remembered Ruthie saying that word, without rancor. Flat, the way I used to say *Yes, sir* to my father. A burden. I wondered if my father was cold and slow in the hospital. I was sure he was dead. Too many burdens. Stephen opened the door for me and looked at me with pity.

We drove to the emergency room, where they sent us over to Intensive Care. The sign outside the door said: No Admission. Visiting Hours 10 A.M.–2 P.M., Ten Minutes per Hour, with Doctor's Consent Only. There was no clue how to get a doctor's consent, and no way to see in through the curtained window. Stephen and I stood in front of the sign until it was awkward to stand any longer. Then he walked off down the hall, saying he would find a nurse.

I tried to calculate the time. Midnight, I thought. No one walked in the corridor, and Stephen didn't come back. I remembered the candy machines, from when my mother was dying, remembered how I stood in front of them and ate one candy bar after the other until I'd eaten five or six. I thought that if I could only get to that candy machine, I wouldn't feel so dizzy.

Then the door to Intensive Care opened a crack, and Stephen's mother slipped through it. I didn't recognize her at first, because she looked like an old crone, eighty-five years old if she was a day. She couldn't have been the woman my father had spent his *nights* with. She was wearing polyester pants with the shirt pulled out of the waist, and when she saw me she knew she was supposed to know me from somewhere. Finally she said, "Mary Faith?" and when I nodded she said, "It doesn't look too good." She had a pot belly that the shirt didn't cover up.

Mrs. Dugan didn't seem particularly moved by my father's dying. She looked haggard, and she looked put out. She leaned her head against the door of Intensive Care and struggled in her pocketbook until she'd found a cigarette. "They don't let you smoke in there," she said.

My father had meant to *marry* this woman. I said, "Will they let me go in?" and she answered, "It won't do much good. He's out."

I told her I'd like to see him, trying to hold my voice steady. I thought about my father standing outside my mother's hospital room, holding himself straight up against the wall while they bathed her or brought her her bedpan.

"Wait'll the doctor comes out," Mrs. Dugan said, raspy from the cigarette. I wished the door would open up behind her and fling her to the floor, and while I was wishing it, the door *did* open, but she stepped aside with her cigarette and missed being flattened.

It was Dr. Black coming out, and he motioned me aside. "Mary Faith," he said.

Dr. Black had cared for my mother and he'd cared for me, but I couldn't recall a single time before that he'd had to care for my father. He was getting old, and in the hospital at night he looked older. He was a short man, the kind of man with a barky voice who calls you *sweetheart* and doesn't offend you by it. His head was perfectly bald all the way around, a ripe tomato, and he scratched the sunburn that rested there.

"Look here, sweetheart," he said, "your daddy's got a fifty-fifty chance of making it. He's stable now, but his vital signs don't look all that good. I'm going to let you go in there for five minutes to stand by his bedside, but I don't want you to say a word. If he opens his eyes, you motion for the nurse. I'm going to the doctors' lounge to get me some sleep. You understand?"

He and Mrs. Dugan watched me carefully while I nodded. Then he stood aside, as if I would know just what to do, going into an intensive care unit all by myself. Stephen's mother held the door open for me, and I had no choice but to go in by myself. No candy bar first. No time to remember it wasn't my mother's bed I was going to visit. When the door opened, my ears filled up with a swell. Dr. Black was talking about a fifty-fifty chance. That made it better, and that made it worse. My father was alive. My father would die.

The room was filled with white light, and I stood at the door waiting for it to dim. There were five beds in the room, but when I could see again, I realized that only one had a patient. As I walked closer to the bed, the long swinging rows of fluorescent light flickered off the plastic of an oxygen tent. When Mrs. Dugan had said that my father was *out*, I'd thought she meant peaceful, lying still. What I saw when I was next to him was that his mouth was twisted with the effort of trying to breathe. The machine monitoring his heart blipped as his chest heaved and flopped, heaved and flopped, a fish trying to escape its line and running out of strength.

Across the room from his bed a single nurse sat behind a low desk. She gave me a grim smile and a little wave, and then she pushed her red curly hair back under her cap. I stood by the oxygen tent and watched my father's chest struggle. They had changed him into a hospital gown, gray-green, and it matched the color of his skin under the lights. At least his arm, where they'd poked in the IV, was whole: my mother's arms, by the end, had been so bloodied and twisted that my father had to leave the room when they took the tubes in or out.

I was ashamed that all I could feel, or think of, was how hard it was to stand by my father's bed with the weight of the baby bearing down on me. My legs were two hams I had to drag when I moved, and my feet stung with the strain of standing. There was a chair by the wall, but I only had five minutes, and I thought I should spend it by my father's bedside, memorizing his face, in case I wouldn't see it again until the funeral parlor had gotten hold of it and painted it. They had done my mother's lips a bright red, the way my father asked them to, but I knew what they'd do to his. They'd paint them gray, the color of clay, the gray that seeped into his tent now along with the oxygen.

I didn't know his face. As the minutes passed, I traced the stubble on his chin and saw for the first time that it was gray, that the hair around his temples was lightening. My father had sharp features and a small-boned face, and as he lay struggling, it looked like a boy's face, narrower than Michael Jagger's, smaller than Stephen's.

I tried to remember what his eyes looked like when they were open, whether the brown was a deep one or just a regular brown, and I tried to count up how long I had stood by him. I thought five minutes had passed, and passed again, and finally, when I felt I would sink to my feet if I stood another minute, I turned to go. His right fist was clenched at his side, as if he'd had the heart attack wanting to punch someone. Probably me. He'd probably been telling Nell Dugan the burden I'd been.

As I walked away, I returned the nurse's grim smile and wave without whispering a word. She mouthed one, I thought, though I couldn't say for sure. I thought she was signaling to me the word *pray,* and I wasn't a bit surprised. These Christian nuts were everywhere. Didn't it occur to her that I'd prayed when my mother died? Didn't it occur to her that every relative who stepped through these intensive care doors prayed? If they all prayed, and most of the bodies shriveled up anyway, what did it matter? The only prayer my mother ever had answered was the one she made on the last day, to let her go quickly.

When I opened the door into the hallway, a sea of people seemed to part. There were only four there, but they were clustered around the door: Stephen had come back, and was standing by his mother, smoking, and Aunt Lizann and Uncle Zack had shown up, Aunt Lizann in a muumuu and flip-flops and Uncle Zack with his shirt coming out of his pants.

"Dr. Black called us, sugar," Aunt Lizann said. She put her arms around my neck and squeezed me until I thought I'd pass out from the stench of her cologne. "We have to pray, darling," she said. "All we can do now is just pray."

I looked up at my uncle, whose eyes wouldn't meet mine. He'd never cared much for my father, one way or the other. I always had the feeling he thought my father was a little slow. He looked shaken, unkempt: shaken by the thought of his own heart, not my father's.

"Now, I've already talked to Dr. Black," said Aunt Lizann. "He's going to call us if anything goes wrong, if there's any little turn for the worse. But meanwhile he wants you to get home and get some sleep. There's not a thing in the world you can do for your daddy standing here. Not a thing that you couldn't do at home, and that one thing is prayer."

I could see my father lifting his clenched hand while the nurse was turned away, staring at her fingernails. I could hear him calling out in a voice that gurgled, while I lay upstairs in my cousin's bed. I looked to Stephen for help, but he was grinding his cigarette into the floor. It didn't seem that he and his mother had exchanged a single word with my aunt and uncle. I saw what was supposed to happen: Uncle Zack and Aunt Lizann were supposed to take me home with them, and then my father was supposed to die, and then I would have to stay with my aunt and uncle until I had the baby and until I turned eighteen. I supposed they were my legal guardians once my father died. They wouldn't let Stephen past the front door. They would give me Betsiann's old room and take me with them to church every Sunday, once I'd apologized to Dr. Beady.

"Aunt Lizann," I said, "let me go say good-bye to Daddy." I didn't know what I was planning to do—I sort of doubted there was a back window in intensive care that I could just climb out of—but I had an idea that if I stood by his bed for five more minutes, feeling the pinpricks in my legs, remembering what it was like when we stood together by my mother's bed, that I would think of a plan.

No one made a move to hold me back or discourage me, so I pushed open the door of intensive care again, and flapped the little wave the red-haired nurse expected, now that we were such intimate friends, and made my way to my father's bedside. I touched the plastic encasing him, knowing that if the plastic were not there I could never reach over for his arm, or his hand. My father and I didn't touch.

I decided to look as if I were praying, to move my lips a little so that the nurse would stay her distance. And just as I had found myself reaching out to touch the plastic that protected my father, I found myself whispering to him. It was something I had done to my mother: when she was unconscious with pain I would stand by her side and tell her about my day and which stains came out in the wash. I was twelve years old. I pretended that I was dying, too, that when I bled I was bleeding for her and would soon go into a coma. She hardly turned her face to me in the last week.

At first I whispered *Daddy*, once and then twice and then three times. The nurse was not watching me, so I went on. Daddy, I said. That was it. I could think of nothing else to tell him, dying. I had known my mother would care about whether the wash came clean, but I didn't know what my father would care about.

Daddy, I said, the Sears charge is probably insured or something. It probably gets paid off automatically when you die. And I won't get a penny in debt to Uncle Zack. I swear it. I hushed my own whisper, stopped its echoing off the white walls of the room. I would have to think these things. I reached out and touched the plastic, hoping that he would feel the touch and know what I was thinking. I had whispered the wrong things about the charge account; I had whispered that he was dying. Now I thought, *Daddy,* I can take over for a while if you have to stay in bed. Lee Mac can run the station. I can pay the bills. I can go on welfare and see about money for the baby, anyway. I know you won't take a cent. But I could take some money. I could make sure we get by.

There was no change in his troubled breathing, no difference in the blip on the screen, no unclenching of his fist. He wasn't hearing me. Daddy, I thought, Daddy, I wasn't going to *go* with those people. I thought you didn't want me around. Don't you remember how it used to be when you came back from hunting, how momma would put on that big fuss and you would take me out back and swing me in the hammock until she cooled off? That was all I wanted, just for you to swing me in the hammock, just to take notice of me, just know I was around. You thought I was so close to her—everybody in the whole world thought I was so close to her because I was the only daughter—but by the time my momma got sick I had started to not like her. I had started to hate her sometimes. I had started to hate how she had to pray for everything. If she wanted the azaleas to come up early, she'd pray for it. If she wanted her lemon cake to rise right, she'd pray for it. I had started to hate how she got when you walked in the door, so cold and self-righteous. Before she got sick, we had stopped going to the beach together or going out for ice cream together or doing anything as a family anymore. She just had to show you. She just had to show you you stayed out too much fishing and hunting. She just had to show you you stayed too long at the Plaid King. And she just had to show me how I had to cook and clean and be boring. She wanted me to learn how to press my lips close together, like hers. And I just wanted to be with you. I just wanted you to ask me to go fishing sometimes. I didn't want to stay home with her breathing down my neck while I did my homework, checking every *t* I crossed. I had started to hate her so much that sometimes I wished she would die, and you would marry somebody young with loose hair and a messy kitchen. Then she got sick. How do you think I felt, Daddy? I had wished her dead. So then I wished her alive, then I prayed every morning and every night that she wouldn't die, that she wouldn't leave me. I baked about five hundred lemon cakes so she would live. I cleaned cleaner than she ever cleaned. I waited up for you. But she just gave up. She could have fought it sooner, she could have gone to the doctor when she knew she was sick. But no, she just gave it all up to her damn Jesus and what did he do for her? What did he do for me? How do you think it felt to be left all alone when I was twelve, not knowing whether I hated her or loved her? How do you think it felt to be left all alone, with you not even noticing I was in the house? I remember when I realized that you loved her, that you were going to miss her. It was a big surprise to me. I thought you stayed away because you hated her, too. I remember when you emptied out the drawers and gave her underwear to Aunt Lizann. I remember you holding up one of her big white bras, not knowing I was in the hallway watching you. I remember you holding that bra against your chest, and I remember hearing you choke. I thought you were going to die then, Daddy. I remember the sound of the elastic tearing when you twisted the bra apart.

And once she was gone, it was like I wasn't there. It was like she had drained all that hammock-swinging out of us. Well damn it, you can't run out on me now. I'm not getting married, I'm not going off with some thirty-year-old man who doesn't even love me. I'm going back to live on O'Connor Street with my baby. You want to know something about that baby? Half the time I don't even want it, half the time I think that baby is going to ruin my life. And I don't care. I'm not going to puzzle out anymore whether I hate people or love them. That baby is coming and I'm just going to care for it. And you're just going to care for me. If you mean to make anything of your life, you're not going to desert me now. You hear, Daddy? You turned your back on me when she died and you turned your back on me when I got pregnant but you're not going to turn your back on me and die. She died, and Michael Jagger died, and I'm sick of you all dying just when I need you. So don't you die, hear? Don't you die.

The nurse had slipped over to the other side of my father's bed. She watched me watching my father and finally whispered: "Time to go," in that cheerful way nurses have. I found myself saying, "What do you think?" as if it mattered what this lackbrain red-haired nurse thought of my father's chances. She pressed her lips together and smiled without a word, as if to say, I *don't* think, and then she mouthed that other word again. Pray. Damn them. Damn my mother and damn Aunt Lizann and Uncle Zack and damn Stephen. I would not pray.

"You live, Daddy," I said on my way out, and this time I didn't whisper or try to transfer my thoughts by telepathy. "You live," I said again, louder, so that by the time I opened the door to face everyone in the hallway, they could hear me. "You live," I said for the third time, and was suddenly filled with a swelling confidence that maybe Dr. Black was right. That maybe he had a fifty-fifty chance. That maybe he wouldn't walk out on me the way my mother did.

20

A Chaste
Recuperation

It felt like having the flu, which he'd had only twice since he
was married. He was exhausted. He could barely turn over in
bed. He could feel the same twinges he'd been feeling for
weeks in his chest, but now, lost in his tiredness, woozy on the
hospital bed, they didn't bother him. Dr. Black told him that he
was a fighter, that things had looked bad the first night and
couldn't look rosier now, but he knew he hadn't fought it.
Someone, something, had lifted him out of his heart attack and
let him live. He was too tired, too dreamy to have fought
anything.

On his third day he'd asked the doctor when he could get
back to work, and when Dr. Black said, "Oh, maybe a month,
you're lucky," the fatigue had doubled, and with it came a wave
of nausea. He asked for a phone in his room, so he could call
the station and get *something* worked out, so that there'd be
something coming in, but Dr. Black told him he wasn't to have
a phone. He wasn't to have a phone, and he wasn't to have a
roommate.

"Dr. Black, the insurance doesn't pay but a piddling fraction
of a *semi*private room," he moaned, and Dr. Black said they
would just have to worry about that later. Easy enough for a
doctor to say. Easy enough for the doctor to say he should let

Mary Faith take over the arrangements for the station, that she could relay the messages. Jesse said, "But you're her doctor. You know she's due in three weeks. And she's sixteen years old. She can't handle that." Dr. Black said it would take her mind off things, and Jesse had no choice but to do what he was told, and lie flat.

Nell came visiting the first day he was out of intensive care and Jesse, terrified that she would see the catheter hooked up, pulled the sheet up next to his stubbled chin. Dr. Black said he could have one visitor at a time, for ten minutes, and he'd been expecting Mary Faith to walk through the door. When he saw it was Nell, in a sleeveless shirt and a little pair of white shorts, he almost groaned. He couldn't remember much of their last night together, but he remembered the abortion. She still had a little belly through the shorts. She hadn't done it yet.

"Hey, Jesse," she said. "You sure put a scare in all of us."

Jesse turned his head away on the pillow. He had the luxurious sense that he didn't have to speak to anyone.

"How you feeling?" she asked him.

Still he didn't answer. The night came floating back toward him, on wispy clouds: the first hard pain, calling out to Faith, telling Faith that Nell was wicked. She *did* look wicked now, a wicked witch. He'd put the right word to it. She looked too old to be wearing shorts, for one thing, and she was wearing some bright blue eyeshadow that made her a harridan. He wished she would let him sleep. He thought the heart attack was God's way of letting him act like he was five years old again, and he wanted a nurse to come in and take his temperature.

"Don't scare me anymore, now," Nell went on. "You let me know you can talk at least."

"I can *talk,* " Jesse said.

"You still mad at me?" she said, and stretched out one of her hands to cover one of his. He drew his fist tighter around the bedsheet.

"Go away," he said and, closing his eyes, wished he could see the look on her face. He liked the power of his illness. He liked telling Nell Dugan to go to hell. He liked his body feeling so filled with sleepiness that there was not an inch left for guilt.

He waited thirty seconds, and when he opened his eyes and turned to the spot where she'd stood, she was gone. Good. She could stay gone. Twinges followed the thought, but they were minor. They were nothing. The weight was off his chest.

When Mary Faith walked in two minutes later, he was more energetic. He had her crank up the top of his bed and listened to her reel off what she'd done in one morning: she'd hired one of Lee Mack's friends to work mornings, she'd gotten Zack to go down to the station to look over the ledgers and fill out a W-4 for the new guy, she'd called up every single customer who had a car waiting to be fixed and told them about her father being sick and the new mechanic's doing the jobs with only a slight delay. That was how she reported it: a slight delay. She had found all the Blue Cross claim forms and with them the overdue bill; she'd had Zack write out a check before the insurance was canceled, and she'd had Dr. Black arrange with the hospital staff for Jesse to be billed at the semiprivate rate.

What he couldn't get over was how much she sounded like her mother, toting up what she'd done. She was just as efficient, just as slow to smile, just as driven about taking care of the details. Faith had paid the bills the same way, and that was why he had never been able to face them: just writing out a check was for him a process that took twenty minutes once he found the pen and the checkbook register and the bill and an envelope and a stamp and then a place to file away the paid stub. For Faith and her daughter, it was second nature. They'd been born with the kind of brains that organized, that made lists and crossed items off the lists, that got things done.

"How'd you get here?" he asked Mary Faith. Her cheeks were flushed, a flush that came with her recitation.

"I rode the bike," she said, and then—for some reason he didn't understand, and he was pretty sure she didn't understand—they grinned at each other. He *thought* he was grinning at the idea of her looking so big on that old white bicycle, but he wasn't sure. He could have been grinning at the idea of her mother saying: "Mary Faith, don't you ride through town on that bike. In your condition." He could have been grinning at the idea of a little girl riding a bike and running a gas station.

"How you feeling?" he said, and she grimaced. Everything hurt, she said. Her ribs hurt.

"It'll be soon," he said, and had her crank the bed back down again. His ribs ached when she said hers did. His jaw felt heavy, corroded.

After she left, he closed his eyes and listened to the hospital clatter in the halls. Soon he could see Faith, wearing white shorts and a white bra. She seemed to be vacuuming his house. She seemed to be sucking all the insurance forms into the vacuum cleaner, clogging it up with a *whoosh*. Mary Faith was crying in the cradle, and when he went to pick her up she stretched—first her arms and then her legs and then her belly, a balloon—until she had grown into Nell Dugan. The sight of her belly stretching like that, like rubber, shook him awake, and as he opened his eyes, he realized first that there was no pain in his chest. The dream was not giving him a heart attack. He rolled over on his side and went back to sleep.

Dr. Black let him go home after a week, on the stipulation that he lie flat on his back for ten more days. If Mary Faith went into labor, the doctor said, he was slapping them *both* in the hospital.

In the hospital he had slept sixteen or eighteen hours, fitful hours, but sleeping ones. At home he was awake sixteen or eighteen hours, and Mary Faith brought him stacks of cheap magazines she'd slipped out of the hospital waiting room: *People* and *Time* and *Reader's Digest*. The very act of reading bored him, the stretching to find a comfortable spot to lie in, the sameness of the pages. What he really had an urge to do was grab *The Joy of Sex* out from behind the headboard, but he was sure that the sight of a bare nipple or curved back would excite him into another heart attack.

Mary Faith looked pale and tired when she brought him his meals, and he could hear her tossing and turning in the night when he tossed and turned. She kept the air-conditioning running for him until a breeze came through at ten or so, and he began to worry that she was the one who should have the air conditioner. He was too tired to do anything about it.

One night Nell called, past ten, and when he picked the phone off the hook he could hear her drunkenness. "When you getting out of that bed?" she said to him. "When's that doctor going to let you squeeze my ass again?" She said that Ruthie had gone, and he knew the baby was gone, too. He hung up on her.

As the ten days dwindled, his angina lessened. He still popped the nitroglycerin, but he felt above concern for the pain. What was such a small pain? He knew it would have frightened any other man who'd just had a string of heart attacks—the doctor said probably three, four mild ones before the big one at Nell's—but he was more interested on concentrating on the rest of what the doctor said: that he was only forty, that this looked like the classic case of the heart attack brought on by stress, that there was no reason once he got up again that he couldn't live to be eighty. As long as he kept up with the new diet and started exercising. Those damn joggers.

He didn't even know where Mary Faith was getting the food money for the new diet—all that chicken—but he let her work it out. She was running everything. From time to time she came in with a check for him to sign, and she seemed to have balanced the checkbook, and made a deposit from somewhere. Zack probably, but he'd worry about that later. Where in God's name had she learned to balance a checkbook?

When the doctor stopped by the house to listen to his heart, he said Mary Faith looked as if she had another couple of weeks to go, at least. He knew why Dr. Black thought to tell him: the doctor could imagine him lying in bed, wondering what he'd do if she started contractions when he couldn't get up to drive her to the hospital. He knew they could call Zack, but that only made it worse. He wanted to be taking care of her now, and here she was taking care of him. Just the way it had always been with her mother. Up to the end, Faith had repeated, "Now you promise me, you won't let the health insurance go if I die. You promise me." She must have seen the heart attack coming.

The doctor finally said he could get up for a couple of hours a day and putter around the house. Jesse wondered what *putter* meant to a doctor. He just had his room, the den, the kitchen. Years ago, before Faith's sickness, he had fiddled with carpentry, but he hadn't hammered two pieces of wood together in four years. When Faith got sick, the sight of wood made him think of a coffin.

It came to him, though, that he could make a cradle for Mary Faith's baby, that that would fall under the category of puttering. His tools were still boxed in the basement, alongside the worktable, and when he went to plug in the drill and the saw and the sander they all seemed to be working. He drew a cradle swinging from chains on an inverted *y* frame and made a list of the hardware he'd need. He couldn't bring himself to ask Mary Faith where the checkbook was, and how much money was in it, so he called Donny Sanderson at the lumberyard and told him about the heart attack, and asked him if he could send the lumber over and take a check next month. The words *next month*, spoken about money, choked him.

He was clumsy at first with the wood, cutting off the mark, and he could only stand for a half-hour or so before he felt too dizzy to work. He thought it was all the lying in bed that made him feel so weak, not the heart attack at all. After two mornings on his own in the basement, Mary Faith came downstairs with corn bread and stayed, watching him work and not asking him what he was making. After an hour they walked back upstairs together, and watched television for five hours.

The next day, when he sat at the breakfast table, she asked if she could help with the carpentry.

"You know what I'm making?"

She shook her head. "As long as it's not a coffin." She was grinning.

"Not for another forty years," he said. "I'm making a cradle for that baby of yours."

She turned her head away.

"What's the matter?"

She shrugged and tried to bring back the grin. "I don't know," she said. "Just don't wear yourself out."

"I'm not about to," he said, and told her to come down with him so he could teach her a thing or two.

He had already glued the frame together and told her she could work on planing and sanding the wood, but he wasn't prepared for how clumsy she was with her hands. She gouged out the wood so badly that he wasn't sure she'd be able to sand it down, but she was persistent and kept up with the planing until the cradle's frame looked nicked and beaten. "Like that, Daddy?" she said, and he almost laughed at the mess she'd made. He sent her upstairs to make lunch and tried to undo the damage. When she came back, she didn't seem to notice that he'd been over her work.

They ate sandwiches at the worktable—bland chicken sandwiches that made him long for a salt shaker—and it brought back the times he'd brought her down in the cool when she was little. Some of her old toys were still stacked up in a corner, a Betsy Wetsy doll on top, and the sight of them made him breathe deeply, evenly. He felt home for the first time in years. This was what home had been like.

The next morning she was ready to go again, and he told her she could sand the frame now, holding his breath at the thought of how she could mess that up. It was amazing that she could be so efficient around the house, and such an eager incompetent downstairs. He was hoping hard that she'd have a boy, a boy who would take the place of the one Nell did away with, all the ones Faith had lost. The next-to-last miscarriage had gone to four and a half months, and they had both seen the fetus Faith wrapped in a bathroom towel: a perfect little old man, curled up in death. Jesse could see Mary Faith clucking around upstairs and sending her little boy downstairs to the basement to work with his grandfather. He could see swing sets being made down there, and toy chests, and when he could see himself cutting out shelves for a boy's models, he told himself to quit, and he showed Mary Faith how to sand with the grain of the wood, and put her off in the corner where the sawdust wouldn't choke him up as badly. He watched his daughter biting her lower lip while she worked, and realized after five minutes that she was weary, trying to stand and then squat and then crouch. He dragged over a low chair for her to sit on while she worked, and rubbed his hand over the surface she had finished. She looked at him anxiously for approval, and he was almost moved to stroke the top of her head, or put his arm around her shoulder, or do something she would know was fatherly. He didn't know what the right gesture was, and the moment passed.

They worked too long, until he felt unsteady and sick to his stomach, but he sent her upstairs first. Along with feeling ill, he was feeling horny, and he didn't want his daughter in the same room with him. Images of women were lounging on his worktable, beckoning him, and the women he was seeing were all Mary Faith's age, not women really, but girls. They were stretched out on long sofas, black leather couches, stroking their own breasts and each other's breasts, taunting him. The sicker he felt, the more inclined he was to pursue them.

Nell came by while he was sleeping. Mary Faith tiptoed into his room to tell him Mrs. Dugan was there, waiting in the den. His daughter's face was a challenge to send Nell Dugan away, but he ignored her, and punished them both by taking five minutes to roll over and stand up and get slippers on. Then he went downstairs to face her.

Nell barely looked in his face when he came into the room, but reached behind him and closed the den's door, a door that probably hadn't been closed, hadn't been moved, in ten years. When the door clicked shut, she rested against it, both hands behind her back, holding the knob, and said, "Jesse, I've got one thing to say to you."

Jesse sank into his recliner and stared at the glass face of the television set. "What's that," he said finally, in a flat voice.

"You look at me."

He looked at Nell. He knew Mary Faith was in the kitchen, or back in her own room, but he could almost see her standing behind the door, her head pressed forward to listen. He was on top of Faith, his body rigid, his head twisted behind him to see if their little girl was awake. If she had slipped in behind them and opened the bedroom door.

"I want to say this." Nell was unbuttoning her blouse, a plain little sleeveless white blouse. Underneath, her skin was as brown as dried blood, and her boy's breasts were bare, the kind that grow on thirteen-year-olds who eat too much and don't play sports. Her shoulders were a boy's, too, too broad for the rest of her frame. He watched her take the blouse off and slip it onto the doorknob. Then she came toward him.

"Stop," said Jesse.

Nell stopped halfway between the door and his chair. "Did the doctor say?"

The doctor hadn't said a word about sex. He hadn't asked. "No," he said to Nell, "the doctor didn't say."

"Then what's the matter, cupcake?" she said. She touched her nipples with a long index finger as she spoke, and then she cupped her right breast in her right hand and held it, an offering to him.

"Stop it," he said. He was hard. He was ready to explode in her. He had always wanted to spank Faith, to pat her fat bottom, and he had never moved an inch in that direction. Now he wanted to hit Nell. More than hit. He wanted to beat her. He wanted to hurt her, her and the line of young girls reclining on that long couch. He wanted to shake them all, and hit them hard on the face, and take off his belt to slash at them until they bled.

"Get out of here," he said.

Nell's eyes flickered, but she kept walking toward him. "You know you want it," she said.

He kept his mouth shut until she was by his chair, offering him the breast again, and then he drew in a long, deep, racking breath and spat at her feet. He held onto the arms of his chair so that he wouldn't leap up and throttle her. The spitting was no release; it fed his fury.

"Get out of here," he said again, and this time she backed off, and then turned and grabbed her blouse off the doorknob. "You're a fool, Jesse," she said, but still he kept his silence from the chair.

He hadn't known such a surge of violence since Faith had died and he had wanted to pick up the corpse and shake it until

her teeth rattled in her dead mouth. He sat in the chair while
Nell buttoned her blouse, and while she turned the doorknob,
and while she waited for him to call her back. He sat, and
waited for his passion to abate. Nothing eased. He feared
another attack would overtake him, and he prayed Mary Faith
would not walk into the room to gloat over Nell's departure,
because he felt he would jump up and slap her, too, his own
daughter, shake her, hurt her. No one walked into the room
after Nell left. He heard her leave by the front door, and he
heard her car start in the driveway.

The heat of the den closed in on him as he heard her car
grow faint in the distance, and it wasn't until he was no longer
sure whether he heard a car sound, a buzzing, that he discovered he was sobbing into his open palm. He shuddered once, a
long, reverberating shudder, and he missed his wife.

21

Birth

By August 15, I was two weeks late. For two weeks I had been feeling little spasms and cramps that mostly turned out to be gas. They'd come in the middle of the night, and I'd stay awake to time them, so that by the time dawn broke I'd be too tired to take care of my father. I took care of him anyway. We watched a *lot* of television. My father's favorite show was Merv Griffin, and I learned to sit in front of it without hooting or throwing up.

On the morning of August 15, I got out of bed at eight. My father had started back at the Plaid King—he went in three hours a day, from nine to twelve, only allowed to sit at his desk—and I'd have to hurry to get his breakfast on the table. If he got downstairs first, he forgot and put salt in the eggs, when he wasn't supposed to be having salt *or* eggs. But as soon as I stood up from the side of my bed, sweating already from the gray air that pushed in at the window, a great gush broke, and I felt a warm spray go sliding down my legs. There on the floor seeped a pool, the baby's waters a clear puddle spreading over my bedroom floor.

Maybe other women get anxious about being two weeks late, and want their babies to come soon, but not me. I wanted the baby to be three weeks late, four weeks late. I didn't want to face any pain, and I didn't want to face any drugs, not the kind of drugs that made my mother forget my face and my father's name. I had been reading every book on natural childbirth that

I could get hold of, but that didn't mean I was ready. All those books talked about how your husband could help you out, except for the enlightened modern books, which talked about your *mate*. I could just see Michael Jagger thinking of himself as my mate. All the books described how women might get panicked toward the end, how they might throw up or start shuddering or cry out that they'd never let a man near them again. I couldn't wait.

I lay back down on the side of the bed until my father came and rapped on the door. He'd been cheerful since he got back to work, feeling pretty proud of himself for living and telling Mrs. Dugan off (he didn't know it, but I'd heard him kick her out. I'd listened at the door), feeling pretty proud of himself for making a cradle for my baby and sitting down to meals with me, even if he was forced by circumstances into the company.

"Mary Faith," he said through the door. "You stay in bed. I'm heading off now. You call me if you feel anything."

"What you going to do for breakfast?" I called back. He said he'd pick something up at the 7-Eleven, and I yelled not to get coffee, coffee wasn't on the list. "And get a roll or something," I said, "not a doughnut."

He laughed. "Yes, ma'am." He said he'd be back by twelve-thirty, and he said again to call if I felt anything. I heard him clump downstairs and leave.

As soon as he was gone, I pulled my nightgown off and mopped up the floor with it, so he'd never find traces of my water breaking. I went into his room naked, the only pain I felt the ache in my feet. Why should my feet ache in labor? They felt as if I'd walked fifty miles, when for two weeks I'd been lounging around.

I dialed Dr. Black's home number, hoping he'd already left, but he answered the phone himself, and told me—couldn't I have guessed it?—to get myself straight down to Admitting. "I'll stop in and see how you're getting along, sweetheart," he said, and I felt like climbing back into bed and going to sleep. I'd been a fool to call the doctor. I didn't even have a decent contraction, and I'd be locked up in the hospital.

Dr. Black said I wasn't even to have breakfast, nothing but

water, and I could have fainted at the thought of going without food. I hadn't had but a tiny sliver of flounder for my dinner the night before. Daddy was supposed to have fish three times a week, the new diet said, and the only way we could afford fish three times a week was to cut off tiny portions from a frozen block and spread them out on the plate so they didn't look too pitiful.

I went back into my room for my bag, packed for a month. All I had to do was get dressed and start the walk, but I couldn't bring myself to open up my closet and get out my clothes. I didn't want to go to the hospital. I couldn't see the need. There was no pain. I couldn't imagine that in a few hours there would be a *baby*. It made me excited enough to giggle, or to cry. Not knowing which to do, I finally pulled out clothes, and sat down to ease them onto me. The baby kicked the way it had been kicking for four and a half months, the same sharp stab at my side. It hadn't even dropped the way it was supposed to do. I wondered if the waters breaking had all been a big mistake. Maybe I just hadn't been able to hold my bladder back. Then I remembered the warmth of the gush, and the quickness of its flow, and I strapped my sandals on.

It was two and a half miles to the hospital, and if I took the bike I wouldn't be able to take the suitcase, so I was going to walk. For a minute I wished that I'd told my father; I could have used somebody to drive me there, and to steer me by the elbow to Admitting, and to squeeze my hand before they did all those horrible things they do to women about to have babies. But I knew I couldn't make him walk through those corridors again. I had to go to Due East Memorial myself, so I buttoned up the coolest, biggest sleeveless shirt I had, and I grabbed up the old red Samsonite suitcase, and I figured by the weight of it that if a two-and-a-half-mile walk in the mid-August heat carrying that clumsy bag didn't start contractions, nothing would.

The house was picked up from the night before, nothing out of order. My father had left the cradle in the kitchen, by the basement door, saying he was thinking about putting another coat of varnish on it but really, I think, just wanting to look at it. The last thing I saw as I shut up the house was the wall phone in the kitchen, and it made me wonder if I should call my father, or if I should call Stephen Dugan—*someone* should know, some man should be helping me—but I passed out the door without lifting the receiver. This was my walk. They would be my pains. I would pass the Breeze Theatre, and the marina, and anyone driving through Due East at nine o'clock in the morning.

My Blue Cross card was sitting in my pocket, and I breezed through Admitting in fifteen minutes. Swell. They put me in a wheelchair to roll me down to the labor rooms, and I kept willing my body to at least start with the contractions, so that I would have something but dread to deal with. There was not a pain in my body, except for my feet, my aching arches. My belly was in movement—the baby's flutter, a little squeeze—but there wasn't anything I could call a pain. Just my own short breath and the urge to faint dead away.

I had to look cheerful with the nurses. I had to be on my toes. I knew that in a matter of hours they'd be wanting to put pills on my tongue and stick needles in my arm, and they weren't going to do it. I tried the relaxing exercises the books told you to do, letting my shoulders ease down, but the minute we turned a corner I was all tensed up again. It wasn't as if I were going in to have a baby. I'd forgotten all about the baby, and labor hadn't even started. It was more that I was going in for a test—a test to see if I could make it through this pain business—and I didn't think it was any too fair that I had to go through it all by myself. I was getting sick of going through things all by myself. Well, it would have been too hard for Stephen Dugan to explain to his wife that he'd spent the day helping me go through the labor. Besides, I didn't want him to see me that exposed. They were going to *shave* me. I eased my shoulders down again.

I had a practical nurse wheeling me down the corridor, one who didn't say a word to me. The minute we went through the swinging doors into the obstetrics ward, though, one of the pert little RNs was waiting, and she couldn't hush up for a minute. How are we doing, she wanted to know. Are we feeling any pain, she wanted to know. Weren't we glad this was all going to be over soon. She gave me a green gown and a paper bag for my clothes, and in the narrow labor room she hoisted me up onto a narrow bed and told me all about the indignities they were planning: first they were going to give me an enema, and then they were going to shave me, and meantime the whole staff would get a chance to peek up inside me to see how we were getting along. I lay sideways on the bed watching her get the bedpan out. She was about five feet two, with curly blond hair and a suntan she'd been working on since April Fool's Day. Her legs were brown spindles in white rubber shoes, and she thought of herself as a little beam of light on the ward. A little Tinker Bell bobbing up and down between labor rooms, offering hope and sustenance to the women lying terrorized and hopeless in front of her.

"We are *crowded* today," she said. "We just don't understand it. It *never* gets crowded at ten o'clock in the morning, but here we are. You never can tell in the baby business. No sir, goodness gracious, you never can tell. We might have to put somebody else in here with you. We wouldn't mind that, would we?" She motioned toward the empty labor bed.

I still couldn't feel any contractions, but once they started the enema I started thinking about dying. Twice a year in Due East a bad stomach virus gets passed around, and we all lie in our beds leaning over the edges or run to the bathroom and grab hold of the base of the toilet as if it will save us, and we think of all the things we could have done better in our lives. That was what it was like having the enema done, and hearing outside the gossip of the nurses and the moans of a woman a few doors down who was shouting, "Jesus. Jesus. Jesus. Jesus. Oh. Oh. Oh. Oh. Jesus. Jesus. Jesus. Jesus." I could have beat a drum to her cries. I began to wonder how long I had been there, and how long I would stay. I knew the contractions might not start for eight hours, or twelve, or twenty. I began to realize that when my father got home he would know where I'd gone and that he would come down to the hospital anyway.

Finally they sent in the same practical nurse to mop me up. I was shamed by her cleaning up my mess, but she would not so much as meet my eyes to let me be shamed.

Then I waited. The perky nurse came in and asked if we weren't feeling anything yet, and when we said no, she said, "Okey-dokey," and bounded down the corridor again. Five minutes later she came back and said, "How are we *doing*?" and when we said still nothing yet, she frowned a big pouty frown and said, "We want that little baby to just hurry up, don't we?"

Dr. Black came through on the end of his morning rounds to see how I was doing, and when he examined me he said my cervix was greener than an unripe peach. "You might be here awhile, sweetheart," he said.

I was hungry. I was thirsty. For two hours I lay on my side with my body rigid, thinking of a cheeseburger or a swig of wine from under the sink, feeling nothing but the baby swimming inside me. The little nurse had given up hope that I'd *ever* have a contraction, and so had I. Finally she poked her head in to say "Howdy-do!" and rolled in another patient. She could have been rolling in a baby grand. I knew the body on the bed right away as the girl who'd given me a cigarette in the bathroom at Due East High School, but I didn't think she knew me.

She was massive, flat on her back, two and a half months bigger than when I'd seen her last.

"You two are in the same boat," said the nurse, "so I expect you'll have *plenty* to talk about." She scooted out with a little wave behind her. "What boat you in?" the girl asked me. She didn't change her position or look at me. "The rowboat or the motorboat? Damn it. My waters busted two weeks early and I ain't got nothing ready for that baby."

I told her my waters had broken two weeks late, and then we seemed to have run out of conversation. We both sighed three or four times, until she said there was no pain yet, but she felt like a turtle on its back, with a mess of eight-year-old boys poking at her with sticks. I rolled over on my back to see what she meant. The helplessness of the position was almost satisfying. My mother, once she was in and out of consciousness, always curled up into a fetal ball, and rolled back and forth with her head tucked in. I wondered if she'd struck up conversations with her hospital roommates. I wondered if she'd waited for the pain the way I waited.

Suddenly the girl wanted to talk. "My momma carried ten of us," she said. "And with all the little ones she had the same dream."

"From the medicine," I said. I rolled back onto my side to watch her stare at the ceiling.

"It wasn't no medicine dream," she said. "My momma dreamed God came down and said wouldn't she please take over for him. God said he was so tired, he couldn't take being God no more. And my momma in the dream said no, God, I don't know nothing about being God. That's too scary for me. And God said please, you got to take over for me. You got to." She rolled her eyes toward me. "That dream didn't come from no *medicine*," she said. "I think God was speaking to her direct. Can't wait to see what I'm going to dream."

"My mother used to dream, too," I said. When she was dying, she dreamed that Jesus wouldn't let her die, that she would step to the edge of the grave and Jesus would push her back and say, "Not yet, now. We're not ready for you yet." I had heard my Aunt Lizann telling Uncle Zack about that dream while we all drank coffee after the funeral.

"And what you going to dream?" the girl said.

"I'm not going to dream," I said. "I'm not going to sleep, and I don't believe in Jesus."

"You believe in Jesus quick enough you start feeling those labor pains. You be calling out *Help me Jesus! Help me Jesus!* You wait. I'll listen for you."

I smiled and then we lay in silence together again. But after a minute I said: "Why should I call out to Jesus? He wouldn't even let my mother *die.*" First he wouldn't let her live, and then he wouldn't let her die. He wouldn't even let her step into the grave, he just let her throw up and then moan through the dry heaves and then forget the name of her child. Of me. "I don't believe in Jesus," I told the girl. "My mother died of cancer. I believe in cancer cells."

Now the girl rolled over to stare at me. She gave no sign of recognizing me from the girl's bathroom, but she watched me steadily, daring me not to look away. "That suffering was a *gift,*" she said deliberately, and when I turned my face away she said it again, softer: "That suffering was a *gift* from God. What you raised as?"

"Baptist."

"All right," she said. "All right. I know you went to Sunday school. What did they teach you about Jesus suffering on the cross? What did they teach you about re*demp*tion?"

"My mother's puking for three months didn't redeem a damn thing," I said.

The girl laughed and then rolled back to look at her ceiling again. "You might be puking yourself before you know it," she said, and then she closed her eyes, as if she were going to sleep for a long, long time. I closed my eyes, too, without the hope of sleep. I could see my mother choking at the side of the bed, a long thick thread of yellow spittle and phlegm dangling from her lips. She never called out *Help,* but her whole body said it. Help me. Help me. Stop this. Stop this, Jesus.

A low moan woke me. It was impossible to tell how long I had slept, but the curtain between the two labor beds had been drawn, and I could see my friend's shadow traced there, her arms massaging her belly. "Ohhhhhh," she said. "Ahhhhhh."

The little nurse's voice chirped out from the foot of the bed. "Oh now," she said. "We don't have anything to cry about yet. We're only *three* centimeters dilated. We have *seven* more to go."

There was silence until she had swished the curtain back. Then, as she was leaving, the girl called out behind her: "I'm not crying for no pain. I'm crying because that little baby's going to be born with something wrong. He's going to be retarded."

The nurse swirled around and laughed a tinkly laugh. "Oh, no," she said. "All the mothers think that. They all think that their children are going to be born with some big problem. And do you know what we tell those mothers? We say, 'Just you concentrate on saying a good long prayer asking Jesus not to make your baby deformed.' Can you try that?''

The girl looked at her impassively and went back to massaging her stomach, sure that her baby would be born with some swollen head or twisted back. I saw all the mothers who had lain in beds like that, praying that their children not be born monsters. Some of them got monsters. My mother lay in beds like these, three months, four months, five months earlier than she should have been put there. I saw her praying that she be allowed to keep this baby, or that, or the next one. I could just see Jesus yucking it up on the other end of the prayer line. Oh sure, Jesus was saying. We'll spare this one. And then zoop—my mother'd lost another one. Another miscarriage, another blob of flesh to be wrapped in a clean white cloth and disposed of in the incinerator. Well at least it wasn't a monster, Jesus said. We get these prayer lines a little crossed.

"Ooooh," said the girl next to me. Great tears were rolling down her cheeks. My own baby was quiet, but I was beginning to feel nauseous without food. I thought I would be too weak to go through the pain. This girl was only three centimeters, and I wanted to ask her what she'd had to eat for breakfast. I wondered if she'd had thick grits and sausages, and I had to roll over almost onto my stomach at the thought of food. There was a queer pressing in my abdomen, but it wasn't pain. It was just a sensation, something mixed with the hunger. My back ached, too, as if I'd been working in the garden too long. The girl's moaning swelled. I couldn't wait.

They cleared my roommate out half an hour later. The nurse said she was only five centimeters, but she was screaming, "You bitches! You bitch!" meaning, I guess, the nurses or her mother or me or all of us, and they gave her a bed that had opened up down the hall. I could still hear her, dimly. She sounded full of energy. "Jesus cocksucker!" she yelled. "You bitches!" It was like being on the mental ward.

They had stopped examining me. Every twenty minutes or so they came in and asked if I was feeling any contractions and when I said no, they backed out of the room, shaking their heads. I was a big disappointment. I *was* feeling something, but it wasn't anything I'd put the name *contraction* to. It was a rumbling in my stomach, the pushing and shoving of indigestion. Contractions were supposed to be like waves, backaches or stomachaches that began to form a pattern. What I was feeling was the after-Sunday-dinner-don't-you-want-to-die feeling that came after one of my mother's heavy gravies. I wanted a magazine. I wanted television. I would have watched Merv Griffin. I would have read *The Idiot. The Brothers Karamazov.*

Dr. Black came in smelling of grilled cheese and bacon and looking like it, a grease stain on his lapel. He told me that it was three-thirty and that my father was out in the waiting room. "You didn't tell me you walked down here, Mary Faith," he said, and pulled the curtain around us, though there was no one else in the room. He clucked his tongue and rolled his eyes and waited for me to answer, and when I didn't, he said, "It is ninety-five degrees outside, honey. You shouldn't ought to walk to the hospital when it is ninety-five degrees outside. Your mother had a history of dif-fi-culties."

But by then he had pulled on his rubber glove and had me hoisting up my gown, and he wasn't waiting for an answer. He grimaced when he was way up inside me, and when he was done—shaking off his rubber glove into the trash can—he said, "I thought those nurses said you weren't feeling anything."

I told him I didn't feel anything.

He chortled and grinned. "That's a good one, sweetheart. You're halfway there." Then he opened up the door to the corridor and yelled, "Let's get us the monitor going in here."

So my own blond nurse came jogging in and wheeled over a fetal monitor on a stand, its scope gray-green and empty, like the television set turned off. She spread gooey jelly over my abdomen and strapped a big black belt around what was left of my middle, and then she and the doctor hooted some more when they saw the screen. "And you weren't feeling contractions!" she chided. A wave was breaking every few minutes on the screen, and below it blips raced continuously. My contractions, my indigestion, and my baby's heartbeat, rapid enough to blast her out of me. My father's heart. The baby's heart. It was beating too fast; no baby could survive that speed, that pressure building in its rib cage. But the doctor and the nurse were oblivious. "I never," the nurse said. "I never did. You must have some threshold of pain, young lady."

"You've been having contractions for *hours*, Mary Faith," Dr. Black said. "At least you had the good sense not to spoil my lunch. Well, you've still got a few hours to go. Lie back and rest."

This was pain? This was labor? This was nothing. If the doctor and the nurse were so unconcerned about the blipblpbp of the baby's heart across the screen, I would be unconcerned too. This was nothing. I remembered my first-stage breathing: a deep cleansing breath. I didn't even need it. Dr. Black said he would come check on me every little while, and they both said to push the call button if I felt any sudden changes. The nurse brought in a capsule of Demerol, and I said I didn't want it, and she and the doctor exchanged knowing glances while she took it away. Then they both left me, and I smiled a good-bye through my deep cleansing breath, the one I didn't need, and I laughed all by myself when they had left me alone. I was a master of pain. I had seen my parents suffer so much that I practically didn't feel pain. What was supposed to be labor was a little stomach discomfort for me. I let my head sink deep into the pillow, and massaged my black rubber belt, and felt in powerful control. I would just ease this baby out. She would just slither her way into the world. I was able to fall into a light sleep.

A twisting push woke me, and I was the turtle on my back again, the sticks still poking at me. A new nurse was adjusting my belt and watching the monitor. The doctor was slipping on a rubber glove.

"Everything's fine, honey," Dr. Black said. "Everything's just fine."

But after he had examined me, he shook his head and deliberated. "What time you call me this morning, Mary Faith?"

I told him I'd called at eight-thirty.

"This is going too slow, honey," he said. "You been at this all day long, and you're not moving. Still at five. Stuck. What you feeling?"

I still felt my indigestion, the baby's kicking, a little fist poking me. My backache. I shrugged.

"Well, I've got no intention of staying here all night," Dr. Black said, and he told the nurse to set up an IV.

"What for?" I asked. I peeped.

"We're going to get you going here," the doctor said.

"With what?"

"With just a little shot of hormone that's going to start your contractions going harder, Miss Nosey," he said.

"Pitocin," I said.

"You read too much, Mary Faith," he said. "You have to put some faith in the doctor. Remember, sweetheart, I brought *you* into the world. Now, listen, Mary Faith, the pit is going to make your contractions start coming hard and heavy, so I'm giving you a shot of Demerol."

"I said I wanted natural." I tried not to sound petulant. I had talked to him in the office for the past four weeks. He hadn't paid much attention.

"That's what I'm *doing*, Mary Faith." He wouldn't look at me. "Do you see me giving you a spinal? Do you see me putting you to sleep? No, ma'am. You want natural, you can have natural. I'm not too old to change. But you wait to take the Demerol, it's not going to have any effect. The nurse is going to give you a shot now, and I'm going to check on another patient, and I want no arguing, hear?"

So by the time my blondie came back to give me the shot, I had set my face as nasty as I could. "I don't want that shot," I said. "The doctor said I didn't have to have that shot. I'm having natural."

She looked confused. "It's not *anything*," she said, and pulled my sheet down.

I grabbed the sheet back up. "You can't make me take it," I said. "It's the law. I could sue the hospital."

She seemed to have heard the line before. She flashed a big, toothy smile, and said: "This is a little old painkiller. Like aspirin, only stronger."

"Ha," I said. "It removes you from the pain, but it doesn't remove the pain from you."

"That's just silly talk," she said. "That doesn't even make any sense. So you just pull up your nightgown and let's follow Dr. Black's orders. The pit is going to make those contractions come on really heavy, now. You don't want to go under with that pain and make us give you the gas, do you?"

"I don't want it," I said.

"Now, don't be a little scaredy-cat," she said.

"I don't want it."

"Now, look, Mrs."—she looked at the chart—"Rapple. Mrs. Rapple, we don't want any trouble. But I have many other patients in Delivery today. Let's not be so selfish and take all the nurse's time. I've got to set up that IV before the doctor gets back and I don't want him annoyed with me. It's not like I'm giving you anything strong anyway. So let's just cooperate, shall we?"

"I'll sue you personally," I said. "Not the hospital. You."

Now my skinny little nurse jumped back from the bed as if I'd brandished a pistol. "You have some nerve," she muttered, and flounced out of the room to find the doctor.

I watched the door slam and fretted directly. I couldn't stand lying on my back, flat, much longer. Maybe now that I'd given her trouble she wouldn't crank my bed up. I was beginning to feel short of breath, and nauseous again. Maybe Dr. Black would come back with the hypodermic. I tried to start the first-phase breathing again, a deep in, a deep out, but all I could think of was how I needed somebody to fight my battles for me, somebody to fetch me a glass of cool water. My lips were dry now. The bad pains were going to come on all at once. But there was no pain yet, nothing but this slow-breaking storm in my belly, pushing against my back, nothing but this anxiety, this apprehension. I couldn't wait.

I let them push the IV needle into my arm three times, trying to find the vein, my blondie nurse calling for another to help her. There were only so many battles I could fight by myself. I decided, anyway, that hurrying the pain was not against my principles. It terrified me, but it wasn't against my principles.

Dr. Black came in to check the insertion, and then settled himself in the straight-back chair in the corner of the room, by the sink, and I realized with horror that he meant to stay there and be with me. I was getting adjusted to feeling all this alone. I wanted to be alone.

But still nothing much seemed to happen. Five minutes passed, and then ten, I suppose, and maybe fifteen or twenty. With nothing to do but lie flat on my back and watch the drip and feel the elastic belt across me, time was hard to follow. I was beginning to think I could tell what a contraction was: a real pain that started low in the back and moved around me like a girdle, pressing me flatter into the bed. But I could stay on top of it. Perfectly manageable. This pain business was just a matter of discipline, of attention. I did my breathing, and Dr. Black stretched his legs and walked over to the window.

Almost as soon as I began to think I knew what a contraction was, I began to doubt that I knew. The rest between the pains shortened and then disappeared, and suddenly there was only one pain, and it was hot and sharp and spiky and it dug into my groin. I was being ripped open, not stretched, and I didn't need the doctor to pull on his rubber glove and check me and call out, "Eight centimeters! He-he, we're getting there," to know that I had reached the real pain, and I was supposed to be doing something, some kind of fancier breathing, and I had practiced it for eight weeks and couldn't remember exactly what it was and didn't need to, because I was panting, out of need. And out of control.

"That's right," Dr. Black said. "That's right, you've got that breathing right. You're a tough cookie, Mary Faith."

I didn't smile or look up at him. I had forgotten before to have them crank me up, and now—when I needed most to be up, to be in control—I could not imagine summoning up the energy to speak or stop the breathing. I wanted to rip the belt off so that I could swing to my side and curl up in my own fetal ball. But I was stuck flat. Prostrate. All I could manage was

swinging my head as close to the side of the bed as I could. My
mouth was dry and phlegmy. I needed to spit. That long dangling thread of my mother's.

Jesus Christ, I thought, this must be what it feels like when
they torture political prisoners in Central America, all those
electric prods violating the genitals. Electric prods. Electric
blps. My heart, too fast. The baby's heart bleepblepblpbpb,
too fast. My father's heart, too slow. I couldn't come up for air.
I could breathe and count. Breathe and count. Breathe and
count. Two minutes. Five minutes. Ten minutes. The doctor
was standing up. No. To measure me again. No. I would have
to swing my legs up. No. If only I could stay in this little ball I
imagined, a little fetus, if only I could never move from this
breath, this count, this drowning, this spiky pain, this ripping
open, I knew it. Suddenly the pain was pure and long and as
dissociated from the rest of the world as my grief had been the
night I remembered my mother and tried to make Stephen
Dugan love me. The pain was a cloud, the pain was around me,
the pain was my whole body lifted up. Climbing up. Breathe.
Pantpantpantpant. Count. Pantpantpantpantpant. Breathe.
Pant. Cloud. Count. Climb. Pant. Lift.

"Ten centimeters!" the doctor said. "Mary Faith, we're going to start you pushing. You remember how to push? You got
to hold onto the side rails now, darling. Hold on. You got to
pull your legs up there. Hold on. Angie, give her a hand there.
We're going to try a few practice ones now. Are you ready?"

I wasn't ready. I was clouded, I was so far beyond Dr. Black
and so high up in my mother's territory, pain, that I wasn't
ready. They didn't know. They didn't see me. The new nurse
who had come in to help said how *good* I was, not a single cry.
And they went on as if my paincloud were not in front of them,
as if I were ordinary: they took my arms, two deadweights, and
made them grasp the side rails, when all I wanted to do was
stay back in my mother's pure, silky cloud, muttering "Jesus.
Jesus. Jesus. Jesus."

I was pushing for an hour. I was pushing until my voice was
dry and I began to tremble. Pushing was not part of the old

paincloud; it was a slicing pain. I knew not to throw up in front of those nurses. I knew not to cry. But every five or ten minutes I would whimper, "It hurts so bad. It hurts so bad," and they'd make me start in again, drawing a deep breath in and pushing out until the veins in my neck and forehead bulged, until I felt more ripped, more shredded, more exhausted, more alone.

"Harder, Mary Faith, harder!" Dr. Black said, and when my push didn't move the baby any farther down he was still cheerful: "You're just a little girl, you can't push any harder, can you, sugar?"

But he checked his watch every five minutes, and said we'd have to get in the delivery room soon, and maybe this next push, no maybe this *next* push, no maybe this one would do it. There was no strength left behind any of my pushes, not an ounce of will, but I was still Miss Obedient Student, and when the nurse said push, I did it. The new nurse was fat and old, but I hadn't been able to see her face, her eyes. She hovered over me, and once in a while put her hand to my cheek or my forehead. I thought of Aunt Lizann putting me to bed after the funeral. After the coffee. After the dream. Putting me to sleep. Taking me away. The nurse's hand was cold and wrinkled. She didn't speak. I didn't care if they had to do a cesarean. I didn't care if they had to stick a needle in my arm and knock me out. I couldn't stand the ripping. I couldn't bear it. I couldn't push one more time.

"Come on, let's wheel her in," Dr. Black said.

I took a deep swallow and breathed the word: "Forceps?"

"No, no, sugar, don't worry about that," he said. As if I'd worry about forceps. As if I'd worry about anything he'd do to get me out of this. If only I hadn't shoved that needle away. If only that nurse, that blonde Angie, would offer me her gas, her pills, her needle. I would take anything. I would take a blow to the head as they slid me from the labor bed to the stretcher. They were mad, mad nurses saying, "Breathe! Don't forget to breathe!" As if I could do anything but lie and pantpantpantpantpantpantdie.

Time was gone again. I didn't know how long the corridor from the labor room to the delivery room was. I didn't know how long it would take to slide me from the stretcher to the delivery table. I felt like a corpse laid out. I had stopped functioning. I didn't know how many hours they would make me push.

It was cruel to call this bright hall a delivery room. It was an operating room: big silver lights above, narrow bed, white tile, IV bottles, sink. Medicine. There was a mirror above, beside the light, for me to watch the birth. They were all mad. Why in God's name would I want to watch?

Still they were at it, their *push!*es and their *breathe!*s slapping against me as they moved me from table to table. Dr. Black had gone on ahead to scrub, and then stood before me, at my feet, his white mask a grin all by itself. They hoisted my legs into horrible stirrups. Mother, my poor mother. They must have strapped her wrists. I wanted the paincloud back. I wanted my father. I wanted the jabs to stop. I wanted to.

"Push," the doctor said. "Wait now! This next one's going to do it," and I saw him slide forceps into place. Did he think I wouldn't notice? Did he think I'd try to stop him, lying like this in his horrible stirrups?

"Push!" the doctor said, and I felt a pop. My eyes blinked open against their will, and in the mirror I caught a glimpse of furry head, black-edged and violet underneath. I had forgotten that there was going to be a baby at the end of this.

"Push!" the doctor said. "Once more now. Let's get him out here."

I pushed. I guess I pushed. It still hurt. I knew the baby was out. It still hurt. It still hurt.

"A boy!" said the fat nurse.

"A boy!" said the blond nurse.

"It's a good-looking boy, Mary Faith," Dr. Black said. "And he's a size. I bet you've got a nine-pounder here. No *wonder* you had such a time."

He held up a cheesy blue baby turning red by degrees, head wet with goo, while the nurses wrapped a white cloth around him. He didn't look like anything, not like a person. A rat.

They would clean him, and then they would probably want me to hold him. A boy. I hadn't wanted a boy. I hadn't wanted a baby. I didn't want to hold him. I didn't want to look at him. I didn't want him. I wanted to die.

22

Firstborn Son

They let Jesse Rapple in to see his daughter after she was cleaned up and settled in on the maternity ward. Dr. Black said she was wide awake, undrugged, but her eyes opened only halfway when he approached her bedside. Her face was bloodless, her lips white and chapped. He had been expecting the look Faith had acquired after her first healthy child: an exhausted dreamy just-wakened glazed ecstatic rosy look. But instead Mary Faith wore the look her mother had taken on with the stillbirths, the miscarriages.

"How you doing, baby?" He knew he was awkward. He knew he shifted from foot to foot. No other words came to him.

"Okay." Mary Faith spoke tonelessly, and he knew he'd make the visit short.

"What you naming the little guy?" he said after a minute.

"Jesse," she said, and he'd never heard his own name spoken so flatly. So lifelessly.

"That makes me proud," he said, but she closed her eyes on him. He could see a bloodstain on the sheet, a neat round one the size of a dime, and he told her he would be back in the morning.

Stephen Dugan came to see me during *father's* visiting hour. I felt like throwing up anyway, and all I cared about was getting ten minutes' sleep to blank out the soreness, and on top of that I didn't need to see him carrying on this joke about marrying me. He'd let his beard grow too long, and his hair was greasy, the way my father's got when he was trying to show me how much *pressure* he was under. I'd given birth one hour and forty-five minutes before. I felt like the turtle did after the eight-year-old boys finished poking at her and left her on the river-bank shell-down.

"How you doing?" Anyone could tell he'd visited his share of maternity wards.

"Okay," I said, and closed my eyes.

"I saw your father in the hall. He says you named the baby Jesse. That was good of you."

I kept my eyes closed. There was a bloodstain on the sheet I was hoping he wouldn't notice.

"Do you know what today is?" I could sense him moving closer to the bed, closer to the pillow.

I said it was August the fifteenth.

"In the Catholic church," he said, "that's the Feast of the Assumption. Holy day of obligation. Mary conceived without sin. Assumed into heaven, body and all."

"Go away," I said.

The morning visiting hours were scheduled from ten to twelve, but Jesse didn't leave the station until eleven twenty-five, so he didn't have time to stop for flowers or call Lizann and Zack, or buy Mary Faith the latest copy of *People*. He had to leave the truck in a doctor's space once he got to the hospital: a space marked R. Szysmanski, a doctor he'd never heard of.

It was ten to twelve by the time he reached her door, and he saw Mary Faith, robed, still looking pregnant, standing and holding on to the side of her bed for support. She grimaced as she shuffled forward.

"I'm just going to the nursery window," she said.

"Mary Faith!" They had kept Faith in bed for two or three days afterward. Mary Faith had given birth the afternoon before. His daughter would bleed to death. Faint. Something.

"It's all right," she said. "They woke me up at 6 o'clock in the morning to feed him. And they woke me up at 10 A.M. to

feed him again, and then they made me get up and walk down
the hall. It's a regular boot camp here."

"I think you ought to be in bed, baby. I can go see him on the
way out. You get your rest. They'll be bringing him back soon
enough."

She ignored him, sidling down past the edge of the bed and
heading out the door. He gave her his arm, and she hung on to
his elbow. They shuffled down the hall together, wordlessly.

At the nursery window she let go of his arm and craned her
neck to see. The nurses were changing diapers and powdering,
and the babies' name cards shifted and blurred.

"Joseph," he said. "No, Josephs. Washington. *That's* not
him. He must be in this little blue gang in the corner."

They moved to see a cluster of five bassinets, and he felt his
daughter stiffen.

"What color's his hair?"

"I don't know," Mary Faith said. "Brown or something."

"That one?" Jesse pointed out a long, fat baby with mottled
red skin and black, wet-looking hair. In sleep, his eyes were
slanted, and his head came to a point.

"I don't know," said Mary Faith. She sounded desperate,
and turned her back to the nursery window. "I don't know."

When they brought the baby to me for the two o'clock
feeding, I had two resolutions. The first was to take a good
look at him and make sure I knew what color his hair and his
eyes were. The second was to get him to eat something. I had
tried sticking a nipple into his mouth two times before, and
neither one of us knew what was going on. He'd starve to death
by the time I figured it out.

My roommate was the girl who'd shared the labor room with
me. The nurses called her Washington. She fed her baby dirty,
thick-looking milk from a half-size bottle the nurses kept in the
bottom of the bassinet, but at least her baby was getting something into her belly. She'd had a girl, a little five-pound baby
with almost as much hair as I had on the top of my head. She
couldn't understand why I'd want to nurse my baby, especially
after having a boy. Especially after a nine-pound boy. She said

boys ate too much. She said he'd wear me out, that I'd run out of milk, and when I opened up my nightgown and undid my nursing bra, she didn't exactly look at me with longing.

The nurses wheeled the babies in and drew our curtains. I couldn't make myself comfortable, sitting—not as sore as I was —and when the nurse handed him over to me without so much as a glance, I wished I'd bought a book on how to nurse your baby. The nurses weren't interested. When they said the word *breast-feeding,* their mouths puckered.

Jesse settled in my arm and let out a yowl. Washington's baby wasn't crying. I got my breast out as fast as I could, and tried holding my nipple between two fingers. I managed to jam it into his mouth. He held it there, uninterested, and tugged a little. Stephen Dugan, sucking at my breast. At least he wasn't crying. I couldn't see his eyes, but his hair was sparse and brown, a dark oily brown like my father's. Jesse. The forceps marks on the sides of his face were lightening, and his head didn't look so pointed anymore. His face was red, as if he'd taken a scrub cure for acne, and his cheeks bulged out plump.

There was no feeling in my breasts, no feeling of the nipple being tugged or milk spilling out. My arm grew sore from being held crooked, and I wanted to lie down. The babies would be left with us for half an hour. I wanted to sleep.

I could hear Washington burping her baby already, calling her Stinky, and finally I decided to switch Jesse to my other breast. He got a good hold on the nipple, and sucked hard. I couldn't feel anything squirting into his mouth, but he ate away. At something. Or nothing. Once he blinked open his eye. Dark brown, almost black. It was lies about all babies being born with blue eyes.

I closed my eyes, holding him, and didn't hear the nurses sneaking up on their rubber soles to reclaim the babies. An old woman stood at my bedside, stretching out her fleshy arms to take Jesse back. He was still sucking away, and she said, "You stick your finger in there. It breaks the suction." I looked down at him sucking, his eyes closed now, and asked her to come back in fifteen minutes.

"Oh, no, hon, we have to get them all back together." She

laughed, and stuck one of her own fingers into my baby's mouth. One nipple, one finger, one mouth. The nipple slid out, and she took the baby away.

Washington was humming, and then switched on her TV set with the remote control. I couldn't sleep.

Jesse was late picking his daughter up, and she was dressed in her maternity clothes, sitting on her suitcase in the corner of the room, when he finally got there. Her roommate had already cleared out.

"Where's Jesse?" he said. He didn't know how to apologize. He'd just taken his sweet time, shuffled around the station, refused to look at his watch.

"Jesse's in the nursery," Mary Faith said, "if they haven't closed it down yet."

It took them an hour to pick up the baby, to sign all the forms and have him weighed: he weighed less than he had at birth, and Jesse knew he'd have to talk to Mary Faith about switching to the bottle. Her mother had been that determined about nursing too—and she'd never been good at it. She'd had to give it up after three months, and he couldn't see Mary Faith going through all the doubts only to end up buying formula in the drugstore anyway. The nurse said she'd have to carry the baby down the hall, and Mary Faith looked at him with her lips pressed together. She had her mother's expression down exactly now, and he hadn't even voiced his idea about the bottle.

He carried the baby to the truck, getting ahead of Mary Faith, forgetting how slowly she still walked. He was more interested in watching Jesse, sleeping inside a cotton blanket, his cheeks flushed by the sudden heat. It would be hard for Mary Faith, after three days of air-conditioning, to get used to the clammy weather again. He drove slowly through town, and every time he braked he reached his right arm over to stop the baby from slipping forward. He thought Mary Faith smiled at him.

It was baking inside the house. The kitchen was bright and dirty—my father'd left his coffee cup leaking onto the counter —and baking. It made my head reel to see it after three days.

My father had stuck the cradle next to the kitchen table, and folded a big white sheet over the little mattress he'd bought for it. There was something pathetic about the sheet: he must have dug it out of the back of the linen closet, where it had been growing dingy in the years since my mother died. When I laid Jesse down on it he started howling, so I picked him back up again. I wanted to lie down in my own white room, with the door shut, with no baby screeching. I hadn't slept in three nights, not for more than an hour at a time. I was whipped. For a minute I stood holding Jesse, but then he began the yowl again, and I knew I had to walk him around the kitchen. I thought I might faint from dizziness. It was two o'clock, time to feed the baby if I followed the hospital schedule, but I couldn't feed him until I had something in my own belly. There couldn't be any milk for him in my hungry breasts. There couldn't be enough energy in my aching arms to lift him up to my breasts. My father sat at the kitchen table as if he expected me to put lunch on it. I could feel my cheeks turning red, turning scarlet. I wanted to faint. If only my father had been on time to pick me up. I circled the kitchen again, and Jesse seemed to doze off. If only my father would get up off his seat and wipe away his dumb grin. If only he would stop looking at my baby. His namesake. I lowered the baby into the cradle again, and his cry shimmered out with the heat. If only there were someone there to help me.

He heard the baby waking in the dark, two or maybe three times: it was hard, in the damp night, to tell what was bringing him so close to the surface of sleep. At three o'clock the little howl grew so desperate that he went to Mary Faith's room, where she was pacing quickly, walking the baby back and forth in front of the open window. Tears streamed lightly down her cheeks, and when he asked if he could hold the baby for her, she hugged Jesse tighter to her chest. "No," she said, toneless again, "I'll walk this baby." And then, almost as an afterthought and with a little choke: "He's not getting any milk. I know there's no milk coming out." Just then, the baby spat up, what looked to Jesse like a quart of watery milk that spewed out over Mary Faith's shoulder and landed at her feet. "See," he said, "and you thought he wasn't getting enough!"

He was glad, actually, that she hadn't wanted him to walk the baby. He wasn't comfortable holding a baby, and he thought it best if Mary Faith understood from the start that this was her job now. He would make the money, but she would have to take care of the little boy. Boy. He could hardly believe it.

The next morning she was still aloof, and turned a scowl on him from the kitchen sink. He was dressed for work but she was still robed, still pale, still pregnant-looking, and he realized suddenly that she'd expected him to take the day off. The first full day home. He hadn't even been able to do that when *she* was born, and now it was out of the question. The sweet Lord Jesus himself knew that he couldn't leave the station closed down one more hour. The hospital had charged for the *telephone.* The mattress for the cradle had cost almost thirty dollars. They didn't even have a real crib set up yet, and the ones he'd priced were in the hundreds. And Mary Faith was dressing the baby in undershirts and Pampers until they had time to go shopping for some real clothes. No baby showers for this Jesse Rapple.

Besides, he wanted to get out of the house. He wanted to call someone with the news that his grandson was home, but he couldn't bring himself to make it Lizann or Zack, and there was no line open now between him and Nell, or even between him and Buddy. Why should Mary Faith begrudge him his chance to get out, his chance to tell some old high school friend, some acquaintance, that he was a grandpa now? He was past caring what they thought of the circumstances; he just wanted *some*-one in the outside world to know there'd been a birth. Mary Faith would get her chance to get out. Looking at her lank hair, unwashed for weeks, at her old pink plastic slippers, he *knew* he'd have to get her out of the house. He would have to drive her out to the beach, or for ice cream. The things he'd done with Faith when she was a new mother, inside her dark house all day. The only difference was that Faith had craved the darkness of the house, the solitude of it, the order she had brought to it, and Mary Faith—who had only been back half a day since her baby was born—already looked ready to climb the walls. She was holding the baby with one arm and trying to wash a coffee cup with her other hand. Both the cup and the baby wobbled.

"You've got to support that neck," he said.

"I *know*," she snapped. "But the coffee in the bottom of this cup has moss growing in it."

He swallowed back the list of things he'd done, preparing the house for his grandson. Faith had always bitched about coffee cups left around the house, too.

"You aren't even supposed to be drinking coffee," Mary Faith went on, and he could hear the weariness in her voice, he just knew she was thinking, Here I am with a new baby to take care of, and now I've got my *father* on my hands, too, him and his heart attacks and his messy ways. A spasm tugged at Jesse's chest. Just like her mother, just ever so ready to moan and groan and pretend the weight of the world was on their shoulders. When he was the one paying the bills. When he was the one leaving the dark house for the glaring ride to the station.

There was a rap at the back door, and he almost ran to answer it. It was Lizann standing in the doorway, her hair newly permed and a new shade of copper, her long maroon nails tapping idly against his door frame. A deep sigh of relief rose up in Jesse until he almost shuddered, and he held the door open wide for his sister-in-law to pass into their kitchen. He heard himself saying, "Welcome, Lizann." He must have said it more than once.

After my aunt left me alone in my mother's house, the baby woke up. He had slept for three hours while my aunt fussed and visited and scolded and drank coffee and tidied up. She had told me to sleep, too, but I knew she didn't mean it, and I couldn't let her in my mother's kitchen alone anyway. So I kept her company and felt better, even if it was Lizann and she was saying obnoxious things like "You better get you a supplementary bottle or you're going to drop dead from a heart attack yourself." My mother and my aunt had always believed that being a mother was like being one of Napoleon's soldiers marching through the Russian winter.

But then Jesse woke not five minutes after she'd left, and I wished I had just shut my eyes for a few minutes when I'd had the chance. I stroked Jesse's hot cheek and nursed him, and then I changed his diaper and turned on "Days of Our Lives" and then he cried and then I walked him and then I was hungry and had to go to the bathroom but didn't know what to do with him. I wasn't getting the knack of any of this baby business. I had seen other mothers, even ones young as I was, cooing and gooing to their little ones. But I'd be damned. I wouldn't talk babytalk to my baby, not even if we were dead alone in the house in the daytime.

I couldn't make him sleep for beans. I went to the bathroom while he was in the cradle, and he howled, and I made myself a cheese sandwich and stuffed it down and he howled, and by then he'd been up for two hours and I'd run out of things to do with him. I tried nursing again, but he cried at the sight of my nipple. I tried more television, but he screeched. There had been a few minutes in the last few mornings when the feel of him, so small, so compact in my arms, had been warm, but now he weighed me down. I couldn't walk anymore, I just couldn't. The bleeding was too heavy and my head was too light. When I set him down in his cradle, though, he cried for fifteen minutes, not only without stopping but with a choking sound that grew wild and high-pitched. He was desperate, and so was I. I went to pick him up and my whole body rebelled: at picking him up, at caring for him, at sacrificing another minute's sleep, at the sight of his wide cheeks. One second I was reaching down to pick him up, and then next second I was grabbing him by the shoulders to shake him. As if he were a second-grade brat back-talking me. I shook him up and down against the mattress without a word, until his cries shuddered through my own body. My face was wet with heat and sweat, my mouth rigid. I understood now. I understood for a minute the women who throw their babies out the window or burn them with cigarettes or leave them in a closet. I almost understood my own mother, all her cold order. Oh, Jesse, I said out loud, but I was still shaking him. Oh, Jesus, I said, and picked him up.

He was five days old. I had shaken him into crazy fear. He would grow up a madman. I would be his mad mother. Oh, Jesse, I said. Oh Jesse, God forgive me.

Jesse walked in at five-thirty to find her sitting in her night-gown still, watching Merv Griffin and holding the baby as if she hadn't moved all day. He stood in the doorway of the den waiting for her to look up, and whispered her name three times before she did. She stared at him blankly and put her finger to her lips. The baby was asleep.

There were no vegetables on the stove, no chicken defrosting on the counter. Nothing sliced or cooking for supper. Jesse pulled the last beer out of the refrigerator—hadn't there been two or three?—and saw that there were no eggs, no bread. No supper. He pulled a chair up to the kitchen table, hungry. Now that he was home, she'd come in to cook. He sipped slowly, imagining a box of cheese crackers, a bag of pretzels. There was no sound in the still house. No Mary Faith coming to cook his supper. He was still waiting for her when he chugged the last of the beer.

"Damn," he said, and rose wearily. They could *not* afford to call up for pizza. If there was no food in the house for supper, couldn't she have called him and asked him to stop by the Piggly Wiggly? How long did it take to call? Had she sat in that chair all day? He hadn't sat once: disobeying Dr. Black's orders, he had been on his feet for eight hours, trying to get repairs caught up. He had opened up hood after gaping hood, on a hot August day, and now he was rummaging through the cabinets, pulling out a can of *tuna* fish. The last can of tuna fish. Now he was making his daughter a tuna fish salad for dinner, after working all day so that she could lean back in the recliner and watch Merv Griffin and hold his grandson.

His grandson, who should be sitting on his lap now, while Mary Faith made *him* supper and he drank a second beer, the beer which had been sitting there—he was sure now—when he left the house this morning. He slammed the tuna fish on the counter, but the thud of the can did not summon her, and he made his way through mayonnaise and celery and onion and was warming up some leftover new potatoes and peas by the time she stole up behind him.

When he spun around, he thought her face was pouting *Should-I-tell-him-now-what-he's-done-wrong*, but all she voiced was, "You don't have to do that, Daddy. I was going to fix supper." He started to open his mouth in protest—she had just had a baby, she *did* look pale—but handed over the cooking spoons instead and sat at the table, drumming his fingers. She started to cook one-armed, and he almost rose, offering to take the baby, but her stiffness held him back. Finally she brought Jesse to him herself, wordlessly, and plunked the baby into his arms. Then she fetched a cloth diaper from somewhere and put it over his shoulder—where had she learned *that?*—and said, "I just nursed him. He might spit up." She looked so much like her mother—gray eyes, set lips, weary shoulders—that the word *Faith* almost slipped from his lips. Almost. He hoisted the baby to his shoulder and stroked his grandson's back in smaller and smaller circles.

"So what's the matter with that salad?" he said, watching her eye it mistrustfully.

"Nothing," she said. "You didn't have to do that."

"Too much mayonnaise?" he said. "I put too much mayonnaise in it?"

"It looks like mayonnaise *soup*," she said, and grinned in such a quick flash he thought he'd imagined it. "You got Jesse quiet."

"He's no trouble," Jesse said, and knew it was the beer that made him say it. If he'd had another beer he might have said *I wish she could have seen him just once*, but he hadn't had another beer, so he watched his daughter set out glasses for tea and spoon the vegetables into a serving dish. He thought that maybe her shoulders were lifting as she moved around. Maybe he imagined it, the way he'd imagined the fleeting smile.

"Maybe this little boy will be quiet while we eat," Jesse said.

"Oh, sure," Mary Faith said. "If you can eat in thirty seconds. That's his record."

But she almost smiled when she sat down and started to serve, still looking like her mother, all her mother's tight, precise gestures. The kitchen filled up with a deep silence. Jesse shifted the baby's weight to pick up his fork: he had forgotten how to eat and hold a baby at the same time. Green peas rolled off his plate onto the table's shiny surface, and for one confusing second *he* felt like the child, waiting to be berated for spilling his food. Mary Faith hadn't noticed the mess, though—she was watching her son settle into Jesse's chest. She was breathing in the silence. She was luxuriating in her moment of peace, resting in it the way her mother had rested in the darkness of this house. He didn't say a word, but scooped up his peas again, and the baby was quiet for a few minutes, while they ate.